A GENTLEMAN OF THE OLD SCHOOL

A SANTORE SECURITY NOVEL

KATIE PRESSA

Three Fires
PRESS

SANTORE SECURITY SERIES

Copyright © 2018 by Three Fires Press, Inc.
Published by Three Fires Press
Cover and internal design by Three Fires Press
Cover art by Les3photo8/Dreamstime
ISBN-13: 978-1983401930
ISBN-10: 1983401935

A GENTLEMAN OF THE OLD SCHOOL

February, 2015

*I*ronic, that's what it was, and not in the way of that stupid little Alanis Morissette song. Edie Bayette parked her car a block away from the clinic, not because she needed to. In theory, she didn't care if anyone saw her five-year-old Audi down here. She'd parked it near the clinic a dozen times before, and no one said a word.

But today—today, it bothered her.

She slung her purse over her shoulder, got out, slammed the door, and locked the car, chiding herself as she did so. If she parked in the clinic's parking lot, the new security guards could keep an eye on it. But here, she was stuck in a transitional neighborhood, where she—and the car—stood out like a sore thumb.

Not that she was scared. She wasn't. She was the most capable woman she knew.

Most of the time.

She took a deep breath and glanced at the car. It wasn't its usual shiny self. Covered in road sand and ice goop, it looked like its owner didn't care about it. Her mother, the therapist, always said that the way a person took care of her car reflected on the way she took care of herself.

Screw you, Mom, Edie thought, then put a hand to her forehead. Chastising her dead mother in her mind for some casually made comment that just happened to return at the wrong time just showed what a state Edie was in.

She shouldn't have come to work today, and she certainly shouldn't have answered this call. She'd been off balance all afternoon, handling pretrial motions and one recalcitrant client who just didn't listen.

Now she was coming here to acquire yet another client who probably wasn't going to listen.

She took a deep breath. The air was frigid and her coat really wasn't up to the walk. Neither were her legs, peeping out from underneath the skirt that had seemed so sensible this morning, nor the shoes, which had never seemed sensible.

But she always wore high heels on court days, even if she had to carry them in her briefcase and change in the ladies room. It hadn't been snowing today, so she hadn't done that, and this morning— sensibly again—she had parked in the courthouse's parking garage so that she wouldn't have to traverse ice.

Which she was doing now.

Picking her way over ice was probably more accurate.

All right. She was wrong. She really didn't want anyone to see the car and jump to conclusions, which was just stupid because what conclusion could they jump to?

She was acting counsel for the Margaret Sanger House, a volunteer position that she had thought would be real easy and would count as her pro-bono work. And it would have been easy, too, if it hadn't been for the nutballs who somehow thought being pro-life meant you could bomb the shit out of a place where women went for their reproductive health.

She exhaled and saw her breath float away from her. She wasn't wearing a hat because warm hats were one of the few things that could muss her black hair, cut in a wedge because wedges were easy to maintain. She had left her leather gloves in the car, because she always took them off to drive. And her feet already felt like blocks of ice.

Yeah, yeah. Going to the Sanger House today of all days didn't bother her at all.

Pregnancy tests had evolved since she last used one, in college fifteen years ago. Now they had easy-to-read red lines with great graphics, instead of color coding that seemed easy until you peed on one of the strips and realized that your interpretation of a color might not be the manufacturer's interpretation of a color.

Still, after she took the test on Sunday, she had gone out and bought two more tests from different manufacturers. She used one yesterday, decided to dismiss it (two positives couldn't mean anything, right?), and then used one this morning.

Bleary-eyed and hoping against hope that the other manufacturer's test and her urine did not get along.

Nope. This new test had an even more emphatic feature than the old test did. This test didn't show little color bands in the window. This test actually said *pregnant* or *not pregnant*. There was no mistaking that little word in the window of the test. That little *single* word.

Pregnant.

Heaven help her.

She picked her way across the ice, her pointed heels sinking in. At least she wasn't sliding. She crossed the street like an elderly woman searching for balance, arms out.

So much for not calling attention to herself. She was the only stupid person on the sidewalk. She should probably mentally rephrase that. She was the only person on the sidewalk, which automatically made her stupid.

And that irony thing: it really was ironic that the day she found out (okay, the day she actually *believed*) she was pregnant was the day she had to make an emergency trip to the Sanger House. She felt awkward and icky and worried that everyone would 1) know she was pregnant and 2) think she was going in for an abortion.

It was like she couldn't control her brain or her emotions. Neither of those items should have bothered her—visiting the clinic, which she had done dozens of times, not just for work, but for herself—and having an abortion. She'd defended the clinic for its right to provide the service, defended women who wanted an abortion, and given money to every pro-choice group she could give money to.

So why the hell was she so bothered about the perception?

Her right foot slipped, arms pinwheeling, but her left foot—heel caught in the ice—grounded her. Pregnant woman, falling on ice.

Not that it mattered at this early stage. She wasn't even showing yet. She had some symptoms, but jeez, she'd had worse PMS.

She managed to make it across the street and over one thin sheet of ice before she got to the part of the sidewalk that had both salt and sand, and had also been recently shoveled. Her heels clacked on the concrete, and for a moment, she felt like she had found nirvana.

The clinic loomed before her, a red brick building that had seen better days. All of the money the clinic got in the form of grants, donations, and charitable gifts went toward improving the interior. Five years ago, the clinic had received one large charitable gift upon the death of one of their benefactors, which allowed the clinic to provide more services.

Some on the board were talking about moving to a new location, one with better protections and an easier path inside. Right now, there were five entrances. Two were staff entrances and one was for medical emergencies (usually departing to the nearest hospital, for things the clinic couldn't handle in-house), but two were on the front and side of the building, both leading into the waiting area.

She hated the two entrances, and tried to talk the board into closing one. But there was a long history of patients who didn't want to go in through the front door, for precisely the reason she had used, almost subconsciously, to park two blocks away.

Perception.

She let out another breath, watching the fog move past her. The air felt barbed, as if some moisture she couldn't see was already turning into ice crystals.

She was thinking about perception because she was thinking about her mother. Of course, she was thinking about her mother.

The first time she had gotten pregnant, she had been at home.

You've ruined your life now, her mother had said. *All that work to get you to a good college, wasted, and for what? One good fuck?*

Leave it to her mother to say the worst possible thing. Edie had flushed.

It wasn't good, she had said and walked away. Even though it had been. She had loved Kyle, her high school boyfriend. They had talked marriage, although his mother had talked her out of it, for both of their sakes.

And his mother had gotten Edie into her gynecologist, who talked options. Edie and Kyle were weighing all of the options—without the help of Edie's mother—when the miscarriage happened.

That had been more devastating than she expected. Even though her mother told her that God took care of these things. As if her mother had ever believed in God.

Edie just believed that there should always be retributions for crimes. Which was why Edie, much as she loved the law, never went into criminal law.

Too dangerous. Too Old Testament.

Just like her mother.

Edie squared her shoulders and walked the remaining distance to the clinic. She wasn't going in as a patient. She was going in as a lawyer.

She had to remember that.

And then maybe, just maybe, talk to a therapist about all the other crap. Because she clearly couldn't handle this on her own.

2

The weird entry into the clinic was cold. Mack Santore wanted to sit on the stool near the metal detector with his hands in the pockets of his official uniform jacket. The jacket was too big, because he refused to get one that fit. He usually didn't wear a security uniform; he didn't have to. He ran the company.

But the company was small, and short-handed, at least for this job. Damn employment rules, and damn his bleeding heart. Half his staff didn't want security duty at a women's health clinic, particularly at one that had been the target of one attempted shooting and several bomb threats.

One of the doctors had been murdered a year ago at her home by an unidentified sniper, in a case the police believed was related to her work at Sanger House. Mack wasn't sure he agreed. He had investigated on his own when he was initially approached to provide security here, and that doc had a messy personal life.

The shooting could have been tied to her work here, but it might not have been. It didn't help that one of those rightwing hate groups had claimed credit, even though they had no one in the area and police (and Mack) could find nothing to connect them to the shooting.

His staff usually didn't care about the politics of a situation, but when you mixed babies, pregnant women, abortion, politics, and bombs, six of his toughest guards bowed out. He understood why three of them left. They had served tours in Iraq and had gone into the security business to guard empty buildings and occasionally bust up a fight, not watch innocents get threatened all over again.

But the other three—they had said some things to him that he wished they hadn't. Technically, he couldn't fire people for their political opinions—free speech and all that, not to mention how firm employment law was on this matter—but if he could, he would have fired them instantly.

Especially when one of them told him that women who went to "that place" deserved whatever they got.

He couldn't fire those three employees for what they said, but he could certainly scrutinize them more carefully. Any and all infractions, no matter how minor, had crept into their files. Zero tolerance, not that he would tell anyone that's what he was doing. Those three would simply be judged more harshly now that he knew what they were made of.

And it sure as hell wasn't the Right Stuff.

He didn't need to keep employees on staff who believed that some jobs just weren't worth doing—particularly jobs that left families vulnerable.

That was the thing he hadn't realized until he had gotten here. This was a *clinic*, not a place where zealots murdered fetuses. In the waiting room right now, behind a glass wall (that he wanted them to replace with something bullet-proof), were six children under the age of five, two fathers holding babies, three heterosexual couples with the women in various stages of pregnancy, and one lesbian couple with one of the women about to pop. (Although the woman who ran the clinic, Ruth Talbot, told him he should never use that phrase. Apparently women found it offensive.

Or some women did.

He didn't know. He couldn't quite keep track. Much as he hated the way his people had discussed the patients of this clinic, he knew that some civilians hated the way men like him talked about women.

He had to clean up his language, primarily because he was around kids more than he expected to be.

He hadn't been around kids in years.

Mostly he saw them as they came through the weird entry. Ruth called it an anteroom, but that made it into a *room*, which it wasn't. Back in the 1980s, when the people who opposed abortion decided to embrace the crazy whackadoo camp in pursuit of the goal of "saving lives," someone had taken the waiting room and walled it off from the actual entry.

Which would've been all good and fine if the walls had been made of sheetrock or concrete or, God forbid, wood. But they weren't. They were made of glass, so, apparently the docs or the staff or someone could see the Bad Guys coming a mile away.

He had no idea why glass, not really. For all he knew, one of the donors who supported the clinic ran a glass contracting business. It was expensive, thick, and double-paned, which was good, kinda.

It was also good that there were no windows around this anteroom, just the two entrances on either side of the building. Someone (that same glass company?) had bricked over the windows.

So there were only two entry points where someone with a gun could shoot through the glass. It would take a sharpshooter or a sniper of tremendous skill to shoot through the tiny glass in the side door and the even tinier glass in the front door, and actually hit someone.

He comforted himself with that idea.

But that wouldn't stop someone who managed to get through the door with a rifle or a pistol or a semi-automatic of some kind or another causing all kinds of carnage in less than thirty seconds.

He'd been making a list as he sat here of all the things that needed redesigning in this entry. The two doors needed to be rethought. The glass. The placement of the metal detector, which was in the very center of the room, so that everyone got to enter and walk several feet (from either door) before ever having to go through any kind of screening.

Yeah, the building was old, and yeah it was on the register of historic places because it had been one of the first banks in the city, but that didn't make the building sacred. If he had his way, this clinic would take some of the inheritance it had received recently, and build its own facility with some state-of-the-art security as well as state-of-the-art medical practices.

Not that he had any control over what the clinic did with its funds. The clinic hadn't even been his problem until four rival firms had passed on providing security for the place, saying it was simply impossible.

It wasn't impossible, but it was a challenge. He usually had a security officer at every door, at least during business hours. One of his people monitored the metal detector. Someone continually walked the property. He had at least one person in a car—sometimes in the parking lot, sometimes on the street—and one person in the waiting room, just in case all the other measure failed.

The clinic paid part of his fee, and some donors paid another part. The city—through a discretionary fund for police services—also contributed, because the presence of Santore Security meant that they didn't have to provide round-the-clock protection.

Santore Security had met all of the state's requirements for a security firm and more. Everyone that Mack hired had gone through rigorous background checks, firearms training at a training facility he knew and trusted, combat training, and a battery of psychological exams.

His people were licensed and bonded. They carried the right cards and had the proper identification at all times. And, for a job like this, half of them wore uniforms. The woman currently sitting in the waiting room, pretending to read her iPad, wasn't in uniform, nor were the two women who had car duty.

But the man walking the property was, and so, to his everlasting irritation, was Mack.

At some point, he would really have to be realistic and realize that there were a handful of days in this business, particularly on tough jobs, where he'd have to go in just like one of the staff.

But he hadn't expected such a pushback from his operatives, not on a job like this. Nor had he expected the exponential growth in business that Santore Security had seen in the past year. Doing good work truly paid off. Everyone wanted to hire his company, particularly after the news coverage from the thwarted kidnapping last year.

But he was one of those business owners who grew his company when he had the money in the bank, not when the demand increased. He hoped the demand would remain high when he had the funds to meet it. But he wasn't going to go into massive debt, chasing an ever-increasing list of clients, only to have the bottom drop out of the security market.

He'd seen that too many times.

Besides, keeping close rein on his finances meant that he had the luxury to take jobs like this one that had no real financial upside. His usual clientele—rich, entitled, paranoid—tended toward the politically conservative side of the spectrum, and guarding a building like Sanger House was a black mark on the résumé.

But it was places like this that needed Santore Security more than some media-hungry celebutante who took risks every night by going out drinking with so-called friends.

Mack glanced at the waiting room. It was still pretty full, considering the clinic was supposed to close in fifteen minutes. He'd seen this every day for the past week: the clinic's hours ran until 6:00, but the clinic staff sometimes didn't leave until 7:30 or later.

Just last week, he'd revised his active schedule to reflect that change, but it wasn't soon enough to switch employees. The Reluctant Six, as he was privately calling them, could handle celebutante duty. He would take some of his better operatives off the latest scandal monger and put them here, where they might actually prevent a death that would horrify the entire country.

Right now, though, some of the celebutantes were complaining about getting new operatives. So he had to accommodate that and make the changes slowly.

He let out a small breath. He was taking a gamble this afternoon. He was understaffed, and he knew it. He simply had no one to pull to fill out the schedule today. If he made it to tomorrow with no mishaps, he would be able to put more staff on this job.

Not enough still, but more than today. Today was the thin day.

He hoped that the deep cold would keep the crazy whackadoos away. Betting on hope was a bad thing, but he had no real choice at the moment.

He also knew that four guards was better than no guards at all.

The front door opened, letting in some of that frigid air. At least he stayed warm. He had a bulletproof vest on underneath the jacket, and the vest fit. It also kept him comfortable in this cold lobby.

But he stopped thinking about his comfort as a woman he never would have expected in a place like this walked inside. She had perfectly cut glossy black hair on her uncovered head, heels so high that they looked deadly, and shapely bare legs that disappeared into a wool coat that probably cost three times his weekly payroll.

Her cheeks were a bright red, which wasn't a makeup failure because the tip of her small nose was the exact same color. Her lips were a glossy rose, covering a wide and generous mouth. Her intelligent black eyes assessed him with a single glance, and he had the sense he had come up lacking.

He wanted to tug on that oversized security jacket to show he wasn't as large as he seemed.

Instead, he said, "Over here, ma'am," and indicated the metal detector.

"Yeah," she said brusquely. Her voice was pitched low, that alto—almost contralto—way of speaking that made a shiver run down his spine.

He didn't care about her tone: her voice was liquid sex. Just one single word left him breathless.

But he kept his expression neutral, trying to focus on his job.

Apparently she knew the procedure, or she was smart enough to figure it out. Hell, he would have thought everyone was smart enough to figure it out until he'd spent the day here, and watched patient after patient enter, look around, and then walk slowly—hesitantly—toward him. Some even asked if they had to go through the detector.

He had always said yes, but he had never explained why, which the receptionist later thanked him for. Apparently one of his people had explained why, which unnerved the patients. He would have to have a meeting with the employees at some point, reminding them that explanations weren't their business; guarding people was.

This woman set her purse on the conveyer belt, removed a smart phone and keys from her pockets, and peeled off her coat, all without instruction. This system wasn't as complicated as the ones the TSA ran in the local airport, but it was more sophisticated. At least someone had spent a goodly amount of money on the right kind of equipment.

Underneath that coat, this woman was a marvel. She wore an understated black-and-white dress that seemed both professional and too upscale for this part of town. The skirt had black and white panels, the top squared her shoulders and accented her breasts—which really didn't need accenting.

He forced himself to look away from her figure, which was damn near perfect. Breathtakingly perfect, in fact.

A woman like this, dressed like this, didn't need to come to a place like Sanger House. She probably had some expensive gynecologist near the hospital, with a reception area that doubled as a coffee bar or something.

If she was here, she was either here to harass the people inside, or she was here because she didn't want something on her record.

"Problem?" she asked him.

He had been staring at her, and she had caught him. His cheeks started to grow warm, and he willed the flush away. Not that it would have mattered. His skin was dark enough that only his close friends realized when he was blushing.

"No, ma'am," he said.

"Ma'am, Jesus." She shook her head, those generous lips thinning. Clearly the word bothered her.

But she wasn't a "miss." She wasn't a girl, either, or a honey, or anything else he could possibly call her without knowing her name. She was a full adult, who automatically commanded respect.

"Please stay behind the line for a moment," he said.

When he had taken this job two weeks ago, he had put tape near the front of the machine so that people wouldn't just rush past. He wanted to staff this part of the security area with only one person, and that meant that patients had to wait until he was ready to scan them with the wand. Most people wanted to get this over with quickly and would blow on by. He needed a way to control them.

He had found that lines worked.

She gave him a withering look but didn't move. He turned on the conveyer belt, and it moved her purse forward. The purse was as expensive as her clothing, shiny black leather with a gold designer clasp that looked like it might have an actual diamond on it.

He didn't scan for that, but he did watch her out of the corner of his eye. She adjusted her coat so that it wouldn't get caught in the mechanism, then she crossed her arms beneath those magnificent breasts.

When she thought he wasn't looking at her, her face relaxed ever so slightly. Her lips weren't as thin, and her eyes were cast downward. She had thick shadows beneath them.

In repose, most people's faces looked tense or anxious or happy, but hers had slid into a gentle sadness. He wanted to reach out and put a hand on her shoulder, telling her that everything would be all right.

But it wouldn't. He had no idea what made her sad, and it was none of his business.

He made himself focus on the images in front of him.

Unlike most women's purses, hers was relatively clutter free. He saw a wallet with a wide variety of credit cards and bills, some makeup, a notepad, several pens, and women stuff, as one of his old colleagues called it. The coat had nothing in the pockets at all.

He took the little case with the phone, clicked it on, and saw that it was locked, which surprised him, since so few people did that.

Then he set the case beside her purse, came around the detector, and grabbed the wand. He had it set on paranoid (as he called it) simply because he was so short-staffed.

"Okay," he said. "Please step forward."

She stepped across the line, her heels rapping firmly on the marble floor. She then assumed the pose, arms out. She had clearly done this before.

He got close to her, as the wand required. She smelled faintly of lilacs, an old-fashioned scent that he wouldn't have expected. He would have thought a woman like her would smell a little too strongly of super-expensive perfume, but she didn't.

The lilac scent was delicate, and he had a sense—he did not know why—that she was too.

This close, he could see her jewelry. Black-and-white art deco to match her dress, but not clunky. Delicate again, including two thin chains on her left wrist that were intertwined as if they couldn't get enough of each other.

No rings at all on those hands. Which weren't manicured like he expected, but had short, stubby nails and chewed cuticles.

A woman with problems. A sad woman with problems.

He stepped back, because if he didn't, he'd ask what was wrong, and she wasn't the kind of woman a stranger asked that question of.

"You can go through now," he said.

She didn't thank him, which was the Midwestern way. Inappropriate thank-yous that seemed polite but were really passive-aggressive ways of saying everything from *fuck-off* to *I'm glad we're finally done here*. Oh, and sometimes, thank you actually meant *thank you*.

She stuffed her phone into her purse, then slung it over her shoulder. She didn't put the coat on, and she didn't say anything to him as she walked through the waiting room door, head held high.

The receptionist smiled and said, "Hey…" in a familiar tone, just as the door eased closed.

He watched her for a moment. He couldn't see her face, but her posture changed, became a bit more relaxed, a little broader, and he knew she was smiling.

One of the little boys, playing on the floor, watched her as if he'd never seen anything like her.

Neither had Mack. And he didn't dare watch her anymore. He was supposed to be monitoring the lobby and the outside, as best he could.

He set the wand down, then walked toward the other door.

The lobby was just as cold as it had been earlier. But it smelled better.

It still held a trace of her lovely lilac perfume.

3

_____

_W_ow. When they talked about pregnancy hormones in the first trimester making a woman horny, they weren't kidding.

Edie hadn't been hit with a wave of lust that strong maybe ever in her entire life. When she walked through that door into the ugly lobby of Sanger House and her gaze met that security guard's, her legs wobbled, and her mouth went completely dry.

She wanted to jump him, right there on that conveyer belt. She wouldn't even peel off his official trousers. Just unzip them, then remove her panties, and—

She wiped that image from her mind, and tried to concentrate on what Darcy, the receptionist, was telling her. Something about Ruth being behind schedule, which was completely normal at this time of day.

The waiting room smelled of bubble gum and little kid sweat. A woman who looked a little too buff sat on one of the couches, watching Edie over the lip of an iPad. Probably another one of the security people.

Edie gave her a hesitant smile, walked past the three children playing with toy cars and blocks, and sat on the only available chair while she waited.

She most decidedly did *not* look back into that lobby.

But she was still feeling the effects of that man's gaze.

He wasn't even normally her type. The open collar on his extra-large security guard shirt revealed a bit of dark hair over muscles that didn't look like they were the product of hours at the gym. His face was lean, his eyes warm, his cheekbones and jaw creating some kind of square that looked like it had come out of a Perfect Man model kit.

His eyes were a warm brown, and his skin even darker—that kind of chocolate color that would only deepen with hours in the sun. Not that there was much sun around here in January.

His voice was deep and rich, the flat vowels of an Illinois native. Not Chicago, but somewhere close.

He spoke with authority, telling her what to do, which irritated her. Or maybe the way that her entire body suddenly felt alive—alive in a way that made her want to rub herself against him—maybe that irritated her.

She hadn't even felt that way about any of the men she'd slept with in the past year. They had simply been around for release. They weren't even fuck-buddies, because they weren't buddies.

They were hook-ups, and the last one, the one whose sperm had somehow managed to hook up with her egg, she hadn't even known how to reach him.

Because she'd tried to find him, and all she got was a message on the Tinder image that she'd saved, which said he was no longer in town. Then when she'd tried again, it had said the Tinder account was no longer active. It took a lot of work to find him, and when she did, he had thought she was shaking him down.

She closed her eyes and leaned her head back. A headache was building. She couldn't tell if it came from the other aches, still active in her system. The idea that the security guard was right outside that glass was driving her crazy. She wanted to touch him, just once.

Standing still while he waved that wand over her—too slowly, at least for her tastes—had simply ratcheted up the sexual tension. She had been scared to look down, to see if her hard nipples showed through the lace slip and the heavy material of the dress. As powerful as her arousal had been, she was pretty sure her entire body had pointed itself at him like a needle on a compass.

The minute he told her she could leave, she had turned away from him, picked up her purse, and struggled with her phone. If she had grabbed her coat and held it over her body, she felt like she would have been telegraphing the degree of her desire, just by the urge to cover it up.

Instead, she had spoken to him as if he were beneath her. He hadn't been (or she would have enjoyed it), and the aside made her smile reluctantly.

Who hired sexy security guards, anyway? Especially at a women's clinic? Half the women here had crazy out-of-control hormones. That man was lucky he wasn't jumped every hour of the day.

"Edie?"

The sound of her name made her sit up and open her eyes. Most of the people in the waiting room were gone. Only the lesbian couple remained, as well as the woman with the iPad. The other security guard.

Someone had picked up the toys.

Clearly, Edie had dozed. Although she wasn't certain how she had dozed while she was thinking about that man in the lobby. Maybe she had been so focused—

"Edie, you okay?"

She looked up. Ruth was standing beside the receptionist's desk, looking frazzled. But Ruth always looked frazzled. She wore a lab coat over a pair of white pants and white shoes. The lab coat looked like it had come fresh out of the wash, which it probably had. By this point in the day, Ruth had usually gone through two different coverings—usually because of baby spittle, but sometimes because of other things.

Dealing with spittle and fluids and peeking into other women's private parts would have been a deal-breaker for Edie for any job, which was why she never considered medicine. The law was messy all the time, but it wasn't *physically* messy.

Physically messy was in her future, though, particularly if she kept this baby.

"Seriously, Edie, are you—"

"Yeah." Edie wiped her face. She hadn't realized how tired she had been. In spite of herself, she glanced through that giant glass panel.

He was walking around the lobby, checking everything. He moved with an athlete's ease. And that lust, which she had sort of tamped down, came roaring back.

She made herself look away.

"Sorry," she said. "Tired. Long day."

Long week. But she didn't say that.

She stood, felt an exhaustion in her bones that was unfamiliar, but which all kinds of websites told her was perfectly natural for a woman newly pregnant. In fact, everything she read about pregnancy made her wonder why in the hell women ever went through the experience twice.

Except for the hormonally charged lust. She understood how that might be enjoyable, particularly if she were going to have a child with a man she actually loved.

She sighed, and Ruth eyed her speculatively.

"Something is going on," Ruth said softly. They had been friends since college—roommates their very first year. Sometimes dorm assignments worked.

"Yeah," Edie said. "We'll get to that. But you need to tell me why you called, first."

Ruth nodded, then turned to Darcy. "I suspect I'll be with Edie for longer than usual. Let me know when you're ready to leave. We'll figure out what to do about the—"

Darcy made a face, stopping her from saying any more. But Ruth's gaze had given it all away anyhow. She had looked directly at the woman with the iPad.

"I'll come get you," Darcy said, pointedly.

Ruth nodded, then opened the door to the back. It always seemed quieter near the exam rooms, although Edie wasn't sure why. Maybe the thick blue carpet absorbed more sound, or maybe it was the layout of the nurses' station, almost hexagonal, with a privacy barrier that went up to Edie's chest.

Or the fact that the exam rooms themselves had been soundproofed, which was a good thing, considering.

Ruth led her past the rooms. One had a door standing slightly open as a nurse pulled a blue hospital gown out of a drawer beneath the exam table. Another had a red metal flag sticking out above eye level, indicating that one of the doctors was with a patient. A third had a yellow flag sticking out, indicating that some poor woman was waiting for a doctor to show.

Ruth had been clear with Edie, though. Their appointment was Ruth's last of the day, and it wasn't going to take place in an exam room —at least as far as Ruth knew. Edie was going to consult with her, though. Edie felt like she had no other choice.

She sighed quietly, hoping Ruth didn't hear that. Ruth was far enough ahead of her so that she probably couldn't hear anything.

She opened the thick wood door that led into her office, and Edie followed her inside.

Ruth's office would have been extremely comfortable if she had kept it organized. But she kept it the way she had kept her dorm room in college—files piled everywhere, a computer on the edge of one desk, and a laptop on a table beside the door.

The files covered both available chairs on the patient side of the desk.

"Oh, sorry," Ruth said as she gathered the files off the chair farthest from the door and set them on the edge of her desk. "I forgot we were going to meet in here. I was sorting, like I always do at the end of the day."

Edie usually did that too—made sure any paper documents she had removed in the course of a day got into the proper pile for her assistant to file. She thought of her own office longingly, knowing she probably wouldn't return to it for another hour or more.

She sank into the newly cleared chair. "So, what is it today? Another threat?"

Ruth shook her head as she walked around the desk to the large custom-made chair that dominated the back part of the room. As she sat down, she said, "The threats come every day now. We're in someone's sights. That's why the stepped-up security."

"I didn't see stepped-up security," Edie said. "One more person does not equal stepped-up."

"There's an entire team," Ruth said. "We try to keep them as invisible as possible. We want our patients to feel safe."

Edie had helped secure the funding for the new security measures. She had been arguing for the past year to move the facility from this location to a brand-new one, an easily defendable one, but Ruth was holding out.

There wasn't a good location in this part of town, and this was where most of the patients came from. Most were so poor they couldn't afford a car, and public transportation in the city was spotty. Ruth worried that moving the clinic would effectively deny the poorer clients of much-needed care.

She was probably right.

"I brought you here to sound you out on something else," Ruth said.

That was what Edie's job was, primarily. She was the sounding board for the clinic. They did have a bevy of lawyers that they could use, but lawyers—even those who donated half their fees—were expensive, and the clinic preferred to avoid using them whenever possible.

Edie's consults usually resulted in suggestions for legal solutions that didn't require lawyers, at least in the early stages. Every now and then, she would write a letter on the clinic's stationary, signing it as general counsel, and that too resolved a lot of matters.

But this didn't sound like one of those issues. Usually she and Ruth handled those on Friday afternoon, then accompanied each other to a bar near Edie's office that had great happy hour snacks and nice out-of-town pickings who would drop in from some of the nearby hotels. Ruth had picked more when her divorce was being finalized, but she indulged every once in a while even now.

"This isn't for us, per se," Ruth said. "It's for a patient."

Edie leaned forward in her chair. She consulted sometimes on patient cases, simply advising who they needed to hire or getting their insurance companies involved or letting them know they didn't really need a lawyer.

"Indigent?" Edie asked. Because right now, the pickings at the various charitable law services were slim. Idealistic young lawyers usually lasted six to eight months at the various charitable law offices and then fled into the private sector. It wasn't so much the lack of money as the never-ending hopelessness that drove them away.

"No," Ruth said. "That's the difficulty."

Edie raised her eyebrows. Usually poverty was the difficulty. Some cases just cost too much to pursue in court because no one had the funds to litigate a long case.

"We have a patient who has been coming to us for more than a year." Ruth folded her hands together. "She's being horribly abused. I've been trying to get her to one of the shelters, but she won't go. She has other options, but she's not willing to take them."

Edie waited. It wasn't uncommon for women to stay in an abusive relationship, afraid that the world outside of the relationship would be harsher than the relationship itself.

"But she just found out she's pregnant." Ruth lowered her voice, as if the woman could hear them discussing her. "And she doesn't want to raise the child in that relationship."

Edie nodded. That too was common. It was easier to save someone else than save yourself, at least for some women.

"She wants an abortion," Ruth said, as if that were the important detail.

"Well, then, what's to stop her?" Edie asked.

"Her husband, very active in the right-to-life movement," Ruth said. "He successfully sued when his first wife tried to get an abortion, claiming that his parental rights were being violated."

Edie immediately shuffled through cases in her mind, trying to remember that one. It must have been before her time.

"Not in this state," Ruth said, "and not recently."

"What happened to the first wife?" Edie asked, thinking that the husband had to be one of those people who tried to control the so-called sins of everyone around him, but kept sinning on his own.

"Died," Ruth said. "In childbirth."

"Great," Edie said, sarcastically.

Ruth nodded. "He's made it very clear that his second wife will not try the same thing. He believes the first wife died because she had offended God."

"Better and better," Edie said.

"So he monitors his wife," Ruth said.

"He knows she's pregnant?" Edie asked.

"Not yet," Ruth said. "But he will. He checks every two months or so. Fortunately for her, he doesn't keep a calendar."

The way that women did. Edie frowned.

"Sounds like you need to perform the abortion now," Edie said.

"It's not that easy," Ruth said. "He's one of those influential right-wing types who believes that women who get abortions should be prosecuted for murder. If he finds out—"

"You can't prevent lawsuits," Edie said. "The best thing to do is keep him from finding out entirely. Take action now."

"You know that and I know that," Ruth said. "But this woman is terrorized. She's worried that he will sue to stop an abortion. She's worried that he'll be able to track her down if she leaves—and she's probably right about that—and she's worried that he will have the police charge her with a crime if she goes through with the abortion."

"They can't do that in this state," Edie said. "And they won't."

"I know," Ruth said. "But she doesn't believe me."

Edie let out a small breath, finally understanding. "You want me to talk to her. To inform her about the law."

"I do," Ruth said. "She can't come to your office. She comes here by a circuitous route that she's worried about. But I think it's best to meet here, so that once you've talked to her, she can't change her mind. We go through with the procedure immediately."

Edie nodded. She hadn't done anything like this before, but she had counseled women on the legal aspects of abortion before. The media had them scared. She usually just had to calm them down.

"When's her next appointment?" Edie asked.

"Tomorrow morning," Ruth said. "Eight a.m. We can make it earlier if you're due in court."

Ruth was smart. She'd been thwarted by Edie's court cases before.

"I have no reason to go to court tomorrow," Edie said. "I can be here."

That stupid Alanis Morissette song—that incorrect damn Alanis Morissette song—played in her mind again. Just the chorus, though. The part about it being ironic.

She tamped it down.

"Can you give me information on this before we meet?" Edie asked.

Ruth shook her head. "I have to keep it confidential until she meets with you."

Edie had guessed that, but she had to ask.

She adjusted the skirt over her knees, thinking about the cold, which then led her to that man in the lobby, with his panther-like grace and his amazingly magnetic eyes. That lust remained, a steady thrum beneath everything.

"Is that all?" she asked.

"Isn't that enough?" Ruth asked.

Edie smiled just a little and then nodded. "I meant, enough on that topic. Because there's something I want to discuss with you."

"Fire," Ruth said.

Edie took a deep breath, then folded her hands over her skirt. She knew what she was about to say would shock her friend down to her core.

So best to get it over with quickly.

"You see," Edie said quietly. "I'm pregnant."

4

*M*ack tried hard not to watch the woman, but his gaze kept going to the inside of the clinic rather than the lobby where he was stationed. After talking to the receptionist for a moment, the woman sat on a chair near the door, tilted her head back, and closed her eyes.

Even her neck was beautiful—graceful, revealing a lovely hollow underneath her chin that he wanted to touch, ever so lightly, just before he kissed her.

And at that thought, he turned away. He would fire one of his crew for obsessing like that. He paced the lobby, peering out the doors into the growing dusk. The days were getting longer, but sometimes it was hard to tell in the perpetual grayness that had been this Michigan winter.

Through the side door's small glass window, he thought he saw some movement near the grove of trees at the edge of the sidewalk. He squinted, unable to see anything clearly.

He didn't dare open the door and look outside, so he tapped his earwig, turning it on.

"Hey, Corinne," he said to one of the women operatives in the car, "you see something over near that copse of trees?"

"No," she said. "We're too far away. Want us to pull up?"

"I got it," Lashon said. He was the one patrolling outside. "I thought I saw something a moment ago, and I'm heading that way."

"You need backup?" Corinne asked.

"Don't get that close," Mack said. "Just report what you see."

His stomach clenched. Of course, something would happen today, when he was shorthanded.

One of the couples left the reception area, laughing and holding hands. A woman trailed them, pulling two small children with her. She looked exhausted.

The patients were leaving.

Mack held the front door for them. He didn't want anyone going out the side. He wanted to step out with them but knew he didn't dare.

As they all headed down the sidewalk, he said to Corinne, "Got an eye on the civilians?"

"Yeah. They're heading in the opposite direction."

He glanced into the reception area. The beautiful woman had disappeared. Only Jade and the lesbian couple remained. As he looked, the pregnant woman in the couple smiled and stood. The other woman rose a little more slowly, hand on her partner's back as if supporting her as she got out of the chair.

They slipped into the back. Jade turned slightly, her gaze meeting Mack's. "You need me out there?" she asked.

He didn't know. That was the thing: he had no idea what he needed.

"Just give it a moment," he said. "You have anything, Lashon?"

"Yeah." Lashon's voice sounded strangled. "Really suspicious package right beside the gas tank of a rust bucket car. The car has even more suspect stuff inside. We have to call it in, Mack."

He knew that. Call it in and evacuate, but which direction?

"Where's the car?" he asked.

"Close enough to the side of the building to take out the exam rooms," Lashon said quietly.

"I'm calling it in now," Jade said. The receptionist looked up, clearly alarmed as she heard that.

"Want us to drive around the block, see if we see anyone?" Corinne asked.

"Not our job." Mack's heart was pounding.

He hoped to hell the suspicious package was innocent, and they were worrying for nothing. But its location answered at least one of his questions. He knew where to evacuate.

"Get out of the blast radius, Lashon," Mack said.

"Already done," he said. "Keeping an eye on those trees, but not seeing anything."

"We're evacuating out the front door," Mack said. "I'll need you there. Corinne, make sure no one's nearby with a sniper rifle."

She made some kind of snorting sound. They both knew his request was damn near impossible. There was an apartment building across the street, and they wouldn't be able to clear it in time.

Still, she said, "On it."

He headed into the reception area. Time was now of the essence.

"Jade," he said. "I need you to go back."

She had already set her iPad down and grabbed her jacket with its built-in vest. It was bulletproof, but she didn't put it on. Smart thinking. But she was tiny. Muscular and small. He could help more.

He peeled off his jacket and took his own vest off. The receptionist watched him, her mouth an oval.

"How many pregnant women do we have back there?" he asked.

"Um," she said, blinking, clearly not expecting the question.

"How many?" he asked.

"Um," she said, "um…"

"Three," Jade said. "Unless they left through another exit."

The receptionist shook her head. "They have to make another appointment. Or pay me."

"All right," Mack said. He handed his vest to Jade. "The most pregnant woman gets this one. The next, yours. After that, we have to flank them."

He grabbed a coat and a purse, hoping it all belonged to the receptionist. "We have to get you out of here."

"I can help get them out," she said, clearly gathering herself.

"No," he said, not even having to weigh the offer. He needed to get as many people out as possible. He tapped his comm. "Lashon, I'm sending the first person out."

"I'm nearly to the front of the building," he said.

That was all Mack could hope for. Lashon would shield her with his body.

He hoped to hell that Jade convinced the police that this was an urgent matter. Because sometimes it took the cops over an hour to get to this part of town.

He couldn't ask, though. Jade and the bulletproof vests had already disappeared into the back. The receptionist was putting on her coat as if it was quitting time. He hurried to her side and wrapped her in it, half carrying her through reception. She caught on quickly, and assisted.

He got her through the doors and into the lobby, hoping no one had come in while he was in there. But he didn't see anyone at all—the good thing about that weird setup. He could see people.

"Coming to you, Lashon," he said, pulling the receptionist forward. She had bent over, like she had been instructed days ago, and he was able to get her through the main door.

The cold air hit him like a fist. Lashon was beside the door. Mack saw him only as a blur of gray coat and hands. Lashon bundled the receptionist in his arms, protecting her with his body, covering the tree-side of the sidewalk, and as much as he could of what was in front of them.

Mack couldn't see Corinne's car, but he knew it had to be around somewhere.

Then he went back inside, hoping to God that their actions wouldn't incite whatever nutball had left that package to remotely blow it up.

5

The office wasn't as sound-proofed as Edie thought. Voices echoed in the hallway outside, shouting, sounding urgent. Ruth folded her hands on her desk and smiled at Edie's obvious surprise.

"Sometimes babies come early," Ruth said, "and dramatically."

Edie nodded, but something about those voices didn't strike her as baby voices. "Shouldn't we—"

"I still have two highly competent doctors in the building," Ruth said. "Everything will be all right."

Edie knew she should trust Ruth. But Edie had been jumpy all day—something about that third pregnancy test, probably, and she couldn't sit any longer. Or maybe she just didn't want to continue this conversation. Ruth, asking if she meant to keep the baby. Ruth, offering medical services. Ruth, trying to find out Edie's state of mind.

Edie's state of mind was distressed. She stood, and walked to the door, pulling it open. The voices got much louder—a man's and two women's—

"*Now*," the man was saying. "We have no idea what the hell that thing is. We're not risking your lives because you might have some quibbles."

"They're not quibbles." The woman's voice, responding, sounded

28

much calmer, but with an undertone of anger. "You're distressing my patient—"

"Good," the man said.

Edie sighed, and stepped into the hallway. Before she came to Sanger House, she'd done some legal work for the women's shelter, and that had always involved wading into some domestic dispute. She had the skills. She knew how to handle domestics, maybe better than she knew how to handle this conversation with Ruth.

"Edie!" Ruth called from behind her.

But Edie didn't stop. The hallway was cooler than Ruth's office, and surprisingly empty. Edie had thought the voices came from here. But she followed them.

"Jade, get them out of here," the man said. "I'll handle this."

"I thought we were going to flank them," said a different woman— probably the aforementioned Jade.

"We were, but we're not risking everyone's lives because someone thinks she knows better than we do."

Edie rounded the corner. The man—Jesus, it was the security guard. His jacket was on, and all he wore was a black t-shirt over his tight pants. His handsome face was set in firm lines.

The woman with the iPad was beside him—without the iPad—and she was smaller than Edie realized. She had another woman beside her, wrapped in a black vest, a man beside her wringing his hands and looking over his shoulder. The woman in the black vest might or might not have been pregnant. If Edie had to vote, she would have voted for pregnant.

They were all standing in front of one of the exam room doors.

The security guard looked up and saw Edie. "Well, there *you* are, at least," he said as if he'd known her forever and had been looking for her.

"What's going on?" she asked.

"I was about to ask the same thing." Ruth came up beside her.

"There's a suspicious package outside, right next to a car that we don't have keys to. If that package blows," the man said, looking at Ruth, "then it'll take out this corner of the building. We have to get everyone out. *Now.*"

"Then let's leave," Ruth said.

"It's not that easy," the man said. "We have to protect you. We're funneling out one door—"

"Oh, Jesus," Edie said, understanding immediately. He was afraid that someone would get shot as they got funneled outside. "Have you checked the exit?"

"I don't have time for anyone to second-guess me," the man said, "and even if I did, I'm not a cop, we can't get into the apartment buildings across the street, and I would really like to avoid casualties, so you all have to listen to me. *Now.*"

Edie understood that. She put a hand on Ruth's back to ease her forward.

"The last thing Anna needs is stress," said a voice from inside the room.

Ruth let out a breath. She clearly recognized that voice. And Edie recognized the look on Ruth's face. It was her arguing face.

Edie didn't recognize the look on the security guard's face, but she understood it as if she had been reading his expressions all of her life. He was getting angry because he believed this was a real emergency. And he might be a rent-a-cop, but Edie had seen the bona fides for the security service. The rent-a-cops that Santore Security hired were the best in the business.

If this guy thought they were in danger, they were in danger.

She shoved her way past the cluster of people into the door. She had a courtroom voice that damn near made judges salute. She used it now.

"Like it or not," she said as she walked into the exam room, "there's stress in this situation, and you're all making it worse. Now get your coats, and get the hell out of here."

The doctor, a heavy-set woman whom Edie had never liked, glared at her. A very pregnant woman was easing off the exam table, her partner reaching for her. The partner grabbed her arm, steadying her, even though the partner herself wasn't much bigger than a twelve-year-old child. The security guard had followed Edie into the room. He was holding a vest.

It took her half a second to realize the vest was Kevlar.

Her gaze met his as her heart rate spiked. And this time, it wasn't because he was so good-looking. He thought the woman needed the vest.

That meant the other woman wrapped in a vest was pregnant too, and that other vest was Kevlar as well.

Edie took this vest from him. It was heavier than she expected, and a little more flexible than she would have thought.

The poor pregnant woman was at least seven months along, maybe farther, and wearing a hospital gown. Her partner was reaching for their coats. Edie wrapped the pregnant woman in the vest and fastened it loosely over her stomach.

"Oh, my God," the woman said. "Really?"

She clearly understood too.

"Really," Edie said. She wrapped her arm around the woman, finding bare flesh in the back. Her partner draped the coat over her shoulders, and the pregnant woman shoved her feet into a slipper shoe.

"This is not what she needs," the doctor was saying to Ruth.

"This isn't what any of us need," Ruth said. "But it's what we have to do."

Edie got the pregnant woman and her partner to the security guard. He gently braced the woman against his arm, then stopped everyone. He had an air of calm, despite his urgency—rather like Ruth did in a medical emergency.

"Here's what we're going to do," he said. "You're going out in a group. The pregnant women will be in the middle of that group. Jade will get you to the door. Once you're all there, Lashon will meet you. He and Jade will make sure you get to your cars. I want the rest of you to surround these two women, just in case."

"In case what?" the doctor asked.

"Just do what he says," the partner of the pregnant woman snapped. "We have to get out of here."

The security guard had not included himself in that scenario. Edie hoped he wasn't going to go all cowboy, head out the back, and try to deal with the suspicious package himself.

"What are you going to do?" she asked.

"I'm going to make sure no one else is in the building," he said.

"I'm sure everyone's gone," Ruth said.

"I'm sure you are," he said dismissively. "Go. *Now*."

They clustered around the women, Jade moving them forward. But Edie stayed behind.

"*Go!*" he said to her.

"You have to clear these rooms in a hurry," she said. "It's easier if two of us do it."

"You're wearing the wrong shoes," he said.

It made her smile. He thought she would hold him up.

"I could run a marathon in these things," she said. "Let's stop arguing. I don't have time for second-guessing either. We need to get moving. I'll go left."

He half-smiled when she quoted his words back to him—a kind of irony smile, as if he got what she was doing. He tilted his head in a resigned way.

Edie didn't wait for him to try to stop her again. She went left, where the rest of the exam rooms were. He moved right.

The others headed toward the reception area, with Jade and Ruth shouting at them like drill sergeants.

Their voices were fading, which was good.

Edie headed down the hall, pushing open doors, shouting, "Anyone there?"

The lights were off in the exam rooms, tables empty, counters cleaned off. Computers were shut down at the nurses' station. It was darker than she liked. She was moving slower than she wanted to.

She could hear the security guard's voice, calling out, "Hello! Anyone?" and doors opening. Like her, he didn't close them. He just moved to the next.

The last exam room still had lights on, and bunched-up tissue paper over the exam table. Rubber gloves littered the floor, along with a tiny pink stuffed dog.

Edie's throat went dry. Who threatened family clinics, for God's sake? What kind of sick mind—

She didn't have time to think about that. She had to search this room and the area particularly well, because of that stuffed dog. She picked it up. It was new, the stuffing intact. She clung to it, looking in the cabinet beneath the sink, in all the small room's storage areas, in the cabinet—

"What the hell are you doing?"

It was the security guard. He was at the door.

She waved the stuffed dog at him. "It was on the floor. I'm making sure there's no kid hiding in here."

"There isn't," he said. "One of the women we just got out of here had gotten that as a gift after her ultrasound. I guess it's a girl."

So he had had the same thought, and had done the same kind of checking.

"We have to get out," he said. "The building's clear."

He extended a hand to her, and she took it. His fingers were callused, strong, and warm. He pulled her forward, and she nearly lost her balance on the shoes, but she was going to be damned if she said anything.

"Where's your coat?" he asked.

"Not close enough to grab," she said. "Let's go."

And so they did.

6

---

*M*ack liked her. She was ballsy and useful, and she cleared her half of the clinic as if she'd been doing recon work her entire life. She hadn't panicked. She had gotten that damned doctor —who had panicked—to set her patient free.

But she was wrong: those stupid shoes were a problem. He felt her legs wobble as he helped her out of that exam room. He wanted to sweep her up in his arms and carry her from the clinic, but she would probably fight him. It would slow them both down—not quite as much as the shoes, but enough.

And she knew her way around better than he did. She took a shortcut behind the nurses' station that opened into reception behind the reception desk. No one in there either, but the door was open, as was the door near the glass panel. He could see into the lobby, and thank heavens, no one was there.

He was still holding her hand. She was clinging tightly. They moved in synch around the reception desk, past some blocks and brightly colored kids' toys he couldn't identify, and had nearly reached the door when he heard it.

A gunshot.

"Shit," he said, and dropped her hand, reaching for his own weapon instead. He pulled it, heading for the door. She followed and didn't ask a single question, which he mentally blessed her for.

Sirens echoed in the distance.

The cavalry. It was probably too late.

He slipped out the main door, past the metal detector, the woman following, her heels clicking on the marble. He wanted to tell her to pull them off, they needed the element of surprise, but he couldn't tell her to go barefoot because it was frigid out there, and he had already sent two half-naked pregnant women into the frosty cold.

He hoped they were still alive.

He hoped their babies were still alive.

He raised a finger at the woman beside him, commanding her to stop as he peered through the door. He didn't see anyone—not Lashon, not Jade, not Corinne or the damn car, not the troop of people he had sent to so-called safety.

The woman was beside him. He pushed her behind him and stepped out the door, weapon first.

There was no wind, and the air was crisp. Usually conditions like this meant that sound traveled. He should have heard yelling. He should have heard *something* besides those sirens getting closer.

He scanned the apartment complex in front of him, the windows dark, shadowy emptiness, except for a handful that already had their interior lights on.

The gunshot. The gunshot. The gunshot bothered him. He shouldn't have heard it, not if it came from inside one of the apartments, from a rifle. Any good shooter would have silenced the weapon, so that no one would be able to identify where the shot came from.

That shot had been close.

Mac glanced over his shoulder. She was right behind him, keeping even with him, not saying a word.

He had to focus on the mission. He had to get her to safety first, then worry about that gunshot.

He hurried them down the sidewalk, which, fortunately, the clinic kept shoveled and sanded. No ice, or she would have been flat on her back in those ridiculous shoes.

He scanned the woods to his left, the open block to his right, the apartments across the street from him, looking for any kind of flash or signal or something that might indicate another shot coming his way.

He also watched for anything suspicious, although he didn't know what that would be. He would know it when he saw it, though.

Corinne's car should be here. The cluster of people he'd gotten out of the building should be somewhere nearby.

His heart was pounding harder than he wanted it to, mostly because of that gunshot. Part of his brain was trying to figure that out.

The sirens were getting closer. He couldn't tell how many vehicles were on the way—more than two, judging by how loud it was getting.

He finally reached the street, the woman beside him. Nothing to his left. To his right, the car, parked down the block. It looked like many people were inside of it.

He let out a small breath, and the woman beside him turned toward him. The cold had made her cheeks bright red, and her nose as well. Her eyes glittered.

The sidewalk that direction wasn't shoveled. He slipped his arm around her waist.

"What—?" she asked.

"Trust me," he said, without telling her why. Instead, he picked her up and carried her against his side down that sidewalk toward the car.

She didn't fight. She didn't lean in either, and she didn't complain.

Sensible. Jesus, he liked sensible people.

He encountered so few of them in his work.

He reached the car, saw it was stuffed with doctors and pregnant women and partners. No Corinne. No Aldis, Corinne's assistant, who should have been near the car.

No Jade. No Lashon.

He set the woman down, and rapped on the window. The fat doctor who had nearly prevented all of them from leaving jumped. The hugely pregnant woman wearing his Kevlar rolled down the window. For a woman who theoretically couldn't handle stress, she was looking incredibly strong.

"Where is everyone?" he asked.

She pointed at the intersection just ahead of them. He looked up, and saw nothing. Then Jade came around the large apartment building, holding her weapon as if she knew someone was after her. Aldis appeared from behind a car, and headed toward this group. He was taller than Mack, and stronger too. He was supposed to switch off with Lashon all day.

Aldis nodded when he saw Mack, then glanced at the woman beside him. Aldis's gaze went past them, to the woods behind them, but he kept coming. He holstered his weapon, but kept his hand on the grip.

The sirens had become deafening. The first police car rounded the corner, slipping on the ice, then recovering.

Mack waved at them, and they pulled over.

He left the woman and headed to the cop car. More sirens behind them, coming closer.

The driver rolled down his window, and Mack leaned in. "We had shots fired a few minutes ago," he said, "and I think we have a bomb behind the building. Two pregnant women, some civilians, and a lot of fear in that blue Dodge at the curb."

"Thanks," the cop said. "We—"

Mack didn't wait to hear the expected platitude, the *we got it from here*. He loped away from the cop car, heading toward the side of the building.

As he did, he saw the woman's face, of all things. She looked worried, as if she thought he was making a mistake.

Maybe he was. But Corinne and Lashon were missing; there was a gunshot and a possible bomb. He couldn't wait and liaise with the police.

He had to act.

And he had to act right now.

7

*E*die watched him hurry to the side of the clinic and then pause, just like people did in the movies. He had a gun in his hand, the hand that had been holding hers.

She wrapped her arms around herself, suddenly cold. She had left her coat inside, and it was damn near zero out here.

One more siren hit the block, then shut down. Out of the corner of her eye, she could see activity in the street. Four police cars and an ambulance, plus some kind of van she didn't recognize.

Jesus, the response was unprecedented. She had known that Sanger House had been threatened a lot lately, but this? Maybe it was the word "bomb."

She swallowed against a dry throat. The security guard slipped around the side of the building, and she couldn't see him anymore.

She started shivering. Her teeth chattered—something that hadn't happened to her in years.

Suddenly she was wrapped in something warm. Her heart rate spiked. A blanket. Someone had wrapped her in a blanket.

"Come with me," said an unfamiliar woman's voice.

Edie turned. A female paramedic stood behind her, a hand on her arm.

The police were fanning out around the property. People had come out of the apartments and were watching, arms crossed, in a few cases wearing coats over sweatpants, slippers on their feet. Some were recording events on their cell phones.

Cell phones. Edie's was inside the clinic, along with her coat.

"We're taking the pregnant women to the ambulance," the paramedic said.

Edie nodded. It was a good idea. Over the woman's head, she could see another paramedic and a police officer helping the clinic staff and patients out of that car.

"So, please," the paramedic said, "come with me."

Edie glanced at the paramedic with surprise. She almost said, *I'm not pregnant*, and then she remembered that she was.

And unlike the two women in the car, she wasn't showing, so the only way the paramedic could have known was Ruth.

Dammit.

"I'm fine," Edie said.

"I'm sure you feel fine," the paramedic said, "but you're going through a stressful event. The adrenaline and endorphins are kicking in right now. We want to make sure that nothing happened that will compromise the baby."

Nothing did, Edie almost snapped, then realized that her very anger itself was unreasonable.

"Shouldn't we be getting everyone out of here?" she asked.

"Yes," the paramedic said in that patient tone taught to everyone in the medical profession. "That's what I'm trying to do."

"Of course," Edie said, and almost apologized. But for what? Bad thoughts?

She let the paramedic guide her toward the ambulance. They walked around two police cars to get there, and that was when Edie realized the cars were parked in a semi-circle.

"Should those people be standing outside?" she asked the paramedic, nodding at the people near the apartments.

"The police will handle them," the paramedic said.

As she spoke, a police officer walked toward the group, hands moving, clearly urging them back inside. Two satellite vans rounded the corner, with TV station logos on the side, and above them all, the chop-chop-chop of helicopter blades caught Edie's attention.

This was a bigger deal than she had thought—even though she knew it, intellectually. She had just been so involved.

That security guard—

She turned, hoping to see the police lead him from the back. Her hand, the one he had held, twitched slightly.

The paramedic took her elbow and guided her to the side of the ambulance. The pregnant woman whose doctor didn't want her stressed was on a gurney. Another paramedic was taking her vitals, while her partner—the small woman—was holding her hand, looking much more ill than the pregnant woman did. The heavyset doctor stood outside the ambulance, speaking to a police officer as if her patients weren't even there.

So much for all that concern that nearly trapped them in the clinic.

The other pregnant woman was standing beside the ambulance. Her husband had his arm around her protectively, and he was watching the scene rather than listening to one of the doctors from the clinic who was speaking to them both. That woman shook her head and spoke.

Edie caught some of the words in the crisp air.

"...can't afford the hospital," she was saying. "We're saving up for the deductibles and the baby. Not right now. Can't we...?"

Edie took a deep breath. The air was ice-cold, stabbing her throat and lungs.

She shook off the paramedic, who still held her elbow.

"I'm the legal counsel for the clinic," she said to the pregnant woman. "We'll make sure that any costs you have because of this incident get charged to us."

Ruth hadn't approved this idea, but she would. This was something Ruth would support without a problem.

Tears filled the pregnant woman's eyes, and her lower lip trembled. She almost collapsed against her husband. He held her up.

"Let's get you in the ambulance," he said. Then looked at Edie. "Thank you."

She nodded.

The paramedic who had been helping her had followed her. Edie looked at her. "Tell you what," she said. "I'll meet you at the hospital—"

Behind them, shouts echoed in the cold air along with some loud bangs. They didn't sound like gunshots.

The husband bundled his wife into the ambulance, and everyone else hit the ground, except Edie, who crouched. The paramedic pulled her down. The ice scraped her knees.

People nearby were yelling, and Edie's heart raced again. That chopper flew over another time. The reporters, who had started coming out of their vans, jumped back inside.

More shouting came from behind the clinic, and more bangs.

"We have to get them out of here," she said to the paramedic. "Close the ambulance doors, get in front, and drive them to the hospital."

"Only if you—"

"I'm not coming. I'm needed here," Edie said. "I *told* you I'd get checked out. But I'm not done yet."

The paramedic's lips thinned. Edie pushed her, and the paramedic half-stood, half-crouched, then made her way to the passenger side of the ambulance. She said something about driving to the hospital now as she climbed inside.

Edie backed away from the ambulance just as it pulled forward. One of the police officers still in the front of the building looked over in surprise.

"Hey!" he shouted. "We might need that."

Edie's heart fell. The security guard—

She made herself think about something else.

That man could clearly take care of himself.

"Call another ambulance," she yelled at the police officer. "That one was full."

And then she let out a frosty breath. The pregnant women were safe. So were some of the doctors.

She looked around, saw Ruth standing behind one of the police cars, arms crossed.

Edie made her way there, feeling vulnerable and exposed, the heels of her shoes falling through the road ice. That security guard had been right: the shoes were impractical.

She wanted to tell him. She hoped she could tell him.

She looked at the clinic, shaking—she hoped—with cold, although she suspected it was something else because the blanket the paramedic had given her was still so very warm.

She reached Ruth's side.

"You were supposed to leave," Ruth said sullenly. "You're one of the pregnant women."

"I'm also your lawyer," Edie said. "You need me."

"Careful," Ruth said, staring at the clinic. "Your ambivalence is showing."

It took a moment for Edie to realize what Ruth meant. Ambivalence about the baby, not ambivalence about the clinic or about being a lawyer.

"Yeah," Edie said. "That too."

She opened the blanket and drew Ruth inside it. They were protected somewhat by the police car. Edie doubted anyone in authority would want them that close, but she wasn't going to let them move her.

Because she cared about the clinic, and she didn't want anything to happen to it.

And she wanted to know what was happening with that security guard.

She hoped that he was all right.

---

8

*M*ack slipped around the corner of the clinic, weapon drawn. He hadn't drawn a gun in a long time, not in an active situation. He was calm, though. That never changed. Once he was in the middle of the action, his heart rate slowed and his body felt more alive than it ever had.

He resisted the urge to glance over his shoulder to make sure that woman was all right. He had gotten her to the car and had felt reluctant to leave her there. Maybe it was the situation, but he had felt a pull he couldn't remember feeling before.

Or maybe it wasn't the situation. Because he'd rescued and worked with dozens of beautiful women, and none had drawn his attention like she had.

There was snow piled up against this side of the building, and a small trail of footprints tamping down one area. The footprints were not filled with ice from the sort-of thaw from a few days ago, so the prints had to be recent. He suspected they came from Lashon on his rounds but didn't know that.

It seemed awkward for Lashon to walk around the building's perimeter by tamping down snow. But he had been instructed to look at all sides of the building, so maybe he had done that.

Lashon had also been instructed to remain with the group from inside the clinic, and he had not done that. Neither had Jade or Corinne. None of Mack's people had followed standard protocol—or maybe they had. Maybe they had disappeared after that single gunshot.

The snow squeaked beneath his boots. He could do nothing about that. It was almost impossible to be stealthy in this extreme cold.

He stepped around the corner to the back parking lot. The car that Lashon had mentioned was parked perilously close to the building. Now, Mack's heart rate increased. Because that car was leaning against the examination wing, where that fat doctor had argued to keep the pregnant woman because of stress.

Sometimes people were impossible. That doctor was one.

He scanned the lot, trying to see clearly. The afternoon light was fading, not that it had been good to begin with. The sky was a grainy gray, the ground was dirty white, and the trees dark spikes against the growing darkness.

He looked for movement and finally saw some: Jade, behind a parked Prius, moving her arm as if she were encouraging someone to come closer to her.

He didn't see anyone, but the edge of the parking lot almost looked like the horizon over Lake Michigan—it was impossible to tell where the sky ended and the ground began. He wanted to rub his eyes, as if that would clear them, but he knew it wouldn't.

The air carried the sounds from the street in front of the clinic—instructions to bystanders to go inside, the last gasp of a siren, and then the rotor wash of a helicopter. He glanced up.

Oh, joy. The media was here.

He didn't move until the helicopter had gone overhead. Then he sprinted across the parking lot, looking in all directions as he ran. He saw no one except Jade, until he got halfway to the car.

Then he saw Lashon crouched near the bumper of a Subaru, gun drawn. Lashon was looking at the trees and didn't even seem to notice Mack running slightly behind him.

Or maybe Lashon had glanced as Mack started running and realized he was no threat.

Mack slid behind the car next to Jade. She had been watching him.

"Who got shot?" he whispered.

She inclined her head toward the woods. Mack peered around the car from her angle, saw a man sprawled a few feet off the parking lot, one hand open, a gun near his fingers.

Mack was missing only Corinne, so he knew that sprawled person wasn't one of his people.

"What was he doing?" Mack whispered.

"Dunno," she whispered back. Her voice was so faint it almost sounded like the wind. "Lashon was there when I got here. I'm pretty sure he thinks there's someone else in the woods."

"Cops are here," Mack said, not caring if his voice carried now, even though he still wasn't speaking very loud. "We need to let them handle this."

"Fine with me," Jade said.

Almost as if he conjured them, a group of police officers in tactical gear came around the building. They split into three parties. One stopped near the car—which Mack thought highly stupid, but to be fair, none of his people had been there to brief the cops on where the dangers might be. Another party headed to the body.

The third came his way.

Mack didn't know the officer who crouched beside him, a man in his mid-thirties, ruddy face, and intense eyes.

"What's going on?"

"Suspected bomb under that car," Mack said, nodding at the car that five officers were near. "Dead suspect near the woods. My people think someone else is still in those woods—and your guys are in trouble if that bomb has a remote detonator."

The officer nodded, then relayed all of that into a tiny microphone near the left side of his mouth. The first group of officers moved away from the car, heading toward Lashon.

"That man behind that Subaru," Mack said, suddenly worried about Lashon. Black man, gun, someone shot, and nervous police. That could go wrong in so many ways. "He's one of mine. You let your people know."

The officer nodded, and then passed that along as well. At least one officer heading toward Lashon shook his head as if he couldn't quite believe it.

"You might want to repeat that," Mack said, "or send that cowboy into the woods to see if he can find the other villain."

"And maybe trigger a detonation?" the officer said. "Not a chance."

Mack let out a breath. He was about to head to Lashon when Lashon set down his weapon, and lifted his hands so the police could see he meant them no harm. Apparently he had had the same thought that Mack had.

The officers crowded behind Lashon. After a moment, he picked his weapon up again, and they all looked at the woods.

"We need to call in the bomb squad," said the officer closest to Mack. "I need you to get your people out of here."

Mack nodded. He tapped Jade on the shoulder, and she nodded. She had heard the instruction.

"Where's Corinne?" he asked.

"I thought she was with the patients," Jade said.

Mack shook his head.

"Shit," Jade said, and stopped, her gaze landing ever so briefly on the cops. She knew where Corinne was if she wasn't with the vehicle as instructed.

Then a man stepped out of the woods. He looked like a lumberjack from an old Disney film—bulky on top, wearing a red plaid jacket and black trooper hat covering his head and ears. Black pants over spindly legs, and shit-kickers that had seen better days. He wasn't wearing gloves, and it took Mack a moment to realize the man was holding something in his right hand.

The man wasn't bulky—he had a bomb vest. He was holding a detonator.

The bomber took sideways steps toward the car with the bomb underneath it.

If he had explosives on his body, and there was a bomb under that car, and the car's gas tank was full, then the blast radius went up exponentially.

46

Mack hoped the cops had gotten the civilians out of the area, because if that car had any kind of shrapnel inside, then who knew how far the damage would travel.

"You people are protecting murderers!" the bomber yelled.

The officer next to Mack glanced at him, and Mack realized in that moment that the officer had no training for situations like this.

Mack did, thanks to the U.S. government. He just didn't like to think about it.

"We need negotiators, now," the officer said quietly into his microphone. "We got a nut with a suicide vest and a detonator."

Mack closed his eyes. Two nuts. This guy had no idea how sound traveled in this cold.

"A nut?" the man with the detonator yelled. He had clearly heard the officer. "A nut? You people are the ones who are crazy, letting those women murder their babies. What is wrong with you?"

Mack put his hand on the officer's arm. "Let me," Mack mouthed.

The officer shook his head. "Can't. You're a—"

Mack didn't wait for him to finish the sentence. He holstered his weapon and stood, all in one movement, and slowly put his hands above his head.

"Hey," he said. "I'm not with the cops."

The bomber tilted his head, as if that didn't quite make sense to him.

"Can I talk to you?" Mack asked.

The bomber didn't move. Mack took that as an assent.

The officer tugged on Mack's pant leg, trying to pull him down. Mack shook him off, somehow managing the movement while keeping his torso stationary.

"Tell me about your cause," Mack said.

"Why?" the bomber asked.

Because, stupid, I'm stalling for time. We need tactical officers here instead of the neighborhood cops who have ready trigger fingers.

"Because," Mack said, "today was my first day here as a security guard, and I have to be honest with you, the place makes no sense to me."

He wondered if the bomber knew that whenever someone said *to be honest with you* it was a sign that person was fudging.

"You work there?" the bomber asked.

"I'm new to the job," Mack said. "They sent me to what they told me was a clinic."

"It's no clinic!" the bomber yelled. "It's a murder factory!"

"I was wondering," Mack said. "Please. Tell me what you know."

The bomber looked at him, then at the cops, who were watching Mack like he had grown a third head.

"They kill babies in there," the bomber said.

"Babies?" Mack managed to sound shocked. "How is that possible?"

"The unborn babies. Didn't you *know* that when you got hired?"

"I work for the security company," Mack said. "I just go where they tell me to go."

"They sent you to *hell*," the bomber said, shaking his arm. "You shouldn't guard this place."

"I'm beginning to understand that," Mack said. "May I step away from the car? I want to find out what you know."

The officer grabbed at Mack's pants again. Mack shook him off again.

"You should just leave," the bomber said. "I'll let you leave."

Crap. Mack had been too sympathetic. He didn't want to leave. He wanted the bomber to stand down. And the officer had been right. This bomber was too wrapped up in his own cause to be reasoned with. The bomber was a nut.

"Thank you," Mack said. "But my girlfriend is here, and I want to get her. May I do that?"

He'd walk over to Jade, maybe. That might get him close enough to distract the bomber.

"Girlfriend?" the bomber asked. Mack didn't like his tone. "Your girlfriend came to the clinic?"

Oh, Mack finally understood where the bomber was going with that. He thought that Mack's "girlfriend" had come for an abortion.

"She works for the security firm too," Mack said.

"She's the bitch in the woods?" the bomber demanded, suddenly furious.

Mack's heart rate, which had been steady, increased slightly. The bomber had seen Corinne. Mack hoped she was all right.

"No," Mack said, sounding confused. "She's behind one of the cars."

The bomber tilted his head again. Apparently he did that when someone said something unexpected.

Then he took a step forward. "Which car?"

Mack wasn't going to point out the exact one. He nodded toward the bomber, hoping it looked like Mack was nodding at one of the cars.

The bomber looked toward the three cars in the lot, then his knees buckled and he nearly fell.

"Davis!" he said. "What did you do to Davis?"

Apparently the bomber hadn't known that his accomplice was down.

Mack swallowed hard. "Who is Davis?"

"*Davis,*" the bomber said, as if repeating the same name was an explanation. "He's *Davis*. He's *bleeding.*"

Mack almost volunteered that he and Jade had medical training, but then the nut would think they were affiliated with the clinic.

"We have to stop the bleeding," Mack said. "Want me to help with that?"

"His eyes are open." The bomber wasn't listening to Mack at all. "He's *dead!* You assholes *murdered* Davis!"

The bomber tossed something toward the body. Mack ducked behind the car as whatever it was banged against the side of another car. The officer beside Mack had his hands over his head, as if he expected to die.

"You *murdered* Davis!"

Apparently, the bomber hadn't tried to blow them up.

"You—"

The bomber's voice cut off in mid-accusation. Then there were grunts and the sound of something hitting the ground, hard, accompanied by the cracking of ice.

Mack stood, weapon out. The officer stood a half second later.

Lashon was sitting on the bomber's back. Corinne had his arm, her own hand wrapped around the detonator. The bomber's arm was twisted into an impossible position. His thumb wouldn't have worked if he wanted it to.

Cops rushed them.

Mack turned to the officer, who started to leave the side of the car. "Your people shouldn't get close. You still need the bomb squad. You have no idea if someone else is in those woods."

The officer looked alarmed, then he nodded.

He started speaking into his microphone as Mack ran around him, heading toward the bomber as well.

"Get him out of here," he said to the gathering group of cops.

"We can't," one of the older cops said. "Your boy is sitting on him."

Mack's eyes narrowed at the word "boy." He wasn't sure if it was meant as a slur or not.

"Lashon," he said, "coming in."

Mack shoved his way past the group of cops, who all stood around. He grabbed the top of the bomber's collar, and looked at Corinne.

"You have the detonator?"

"It's not attached to anything," she said. "I noticed that from the woods."

Meaning she thought it was safe to tackle the man. It probably hadn't been. God knew how many explosives he was wearing. Apparently, nothing that was unstable, though, or half his team would have been blown to high heaven.

He'd yell at them later for playing cowboy.

"You got it?" he repeated.

She nodded.

"Then cuff him and let's move him," Mack said.

"Fucking liar," the bomber said, his mouth against the ice. "You're a cop."

"Nope, I'm not," Mack said.

Lashon cuffed the bomber's arms behind his back. The bomber screamed in pain.

Good, Mack thought. *Couldn't happen to a nicer asshole.*

Lashon's gaze met Mack's. Mack nodded. Lashon acknowledged him with a nod, then stood. Mack dragged the bomber across the ice, away from the car with the bomb beneath it, away from the other cars as well, to the far end of the parking lot.

Lashon followed, as did Corinne. She still held the detonator, in the same position that she had gotten it from the bomber, just in case.

Mack wanted to tell her that wasn't necessary. It looked like a decoy. Which meant someone in the woods—or the hapless Davis—had the real means to detonate the bomb beneath the car—or this guy—or both.

Some of the cops were following.

"Stay back," Mack said. "Stay away from this man, and stay away from that car. Where the hell's your bomb squad?"

"On the way," said the officer who had been hiding with him.

"They've been on the way forever," Mack snapped.

"Less than five minutes," the officer said.

Who the hell failed to send a bomb squad to a reported incident involving a bomb? Apparently this police department. They'd gotten all kinds of anti-tank and -bomb gear after 9/11, and they still didn't know how to use it.

The bomber didn't struggle. He moaned as Mack dragged him.

The cops were watching, clueless, not moving out of the way.

He could envision dozens of casualties if they had the wrong person.

He hoped that woman had gotten away. Her image returned to him, searching the rooms, holding that small stuffed toy, determined to find the child that might have been left behind.

Determined like he had been, until he realized there was no child. Not at that moment.

But there could have been. He resisted the urge to kick the bastard in the ribs. Going after families because he believed the clinic was committing murder.

Didn't these nuts think things through?

But Mack knew the answer to that. These nuts didn't think at all.

The cops were moving away from the cars. In the ice-cold air, the sound of slamming doors reached Mack.

He hoped to hell that was the bomb squad.

Because this situation was barely under control—if it was under control at all.

9

---

*T*hree official looking blue vans showed up. The chopper continued its patrol overhead, and the reporters were starting to stand up, thinking maybe the worst of it was over.

Ruth wouldn't let Edie move away from the police car they were crouching behind. Edie's thighs were getting tired, her knees aching from their encounter with the ice. The blanket wasn't keeping her that warm anymore, but Ruth was. That woman was a small heater.

The van doors slid open and people wrapped in bulky black gear got out. The gear was like something out of a science fiction movie—one of those astronaut suits that let them survive in space. She couldn't even tell the gender of the people emerging because they were wearing helmets.

All except two guys, who lifted down some equipment. She squinted, trying to make sense of the metal pieces. She finally realized she was looking at a robot.

She must have gasped, because Ruth looked at her.

"What?" Ruth asked.

"I guess they really did find a bomb," Edie said.

Ruth's head whipped around as if looking for a big sign that read *Bomb's Right Here!*

"Or they think they did," Edie said, trying to ameliorate what she had just said.

"I thought the security guards would stop this," Ruth said. She wasn't watching Edie; instead, Ruth's gaze was trained on the two men who weren't in protective gear, who were setting up computers and dealing with the robot.

It was smaller than Edie wanted it to be. She wanted it to be some gigantic rescue robot that could sweep people up and cast them aside before it found the bomb and disabled it. (Maybe bring the security guard back. He hadn't reappeared. That worried her.)

The robot was the size of a go-cart, but tall, with one grappling arm, a camera mounted on a pole, and antennae in the back. It had the big tires that she associated with tractors or tanks, and it moved much too awkwardly for her taste.

One of the police officers came over to her and Ruth.

"You need to get out of here," the officer said to them both.

"That's my clinic," Ruth said. "I'm not going anywhere."

"And I'm her lawyer," Edie said. "I'm staying if she is."

Edie would have stayed anyway. She had to see this out. But she wasn't going to say that.

"Then we need to move you out of the blast radius," the officer said. As if they knew what the blast radius was. As if they knew what kind of bomb was back there and what kind of threat it posed.

He helped them up. Edie was surprised to find her legs wobbling. She blamed it on the crouch and the sore knees, not the stupid heels, which were beginning to get really cold and maybe a little damp. She let him guide them to some barricades the police had set up. She hadn't even noticed that.

Reporters stood behind it, cameras filming, others taking notes. A few of the local TV reporters, whom she recognized but couldn't name, were doing some kind of live report beside the apartment building, almost talking over each other.

"Were you inside?" a woman asked Edie, shoving a microphone in her face.

Edie gave her the death stare that she gave to lawyers for the other side when they were being particularly stupid.

"I'm a lawyer," she said. "Get that mic out of my face."

The woman flushed and stepped back, but several of the other reporters eyed Ruth as if making a note that she was someone to talk to.

Ruth hadn't been able to get media coverage when she'd been doing a major crowd-funding campaign to replace the money that she had lost when the federal government cut funding to clinics that provided the full-range of services for women's health because those full-range services included abortions. But threaten the clinic with a bomb, and everyone showed up.

The robot was nearly set up. The bomb squad was talking on microphones. The second ambulance had shown up, without its sirens blaring, and had to park behind the news vans.

Edie was about to shake off the blanket to change that scenario when one of the police officers walked over.

Everyone seemed calmer than she wanted them to be. She wanted them to rush in, get the bombs away from the clinic, and save the people who had disappeared around back. (Save that security guard.)

But she stood stoically behind Ruth, watching everything that was going on.

Finally, Edie saw movement on the left side of the clinic. Slowly, all the observers turned that way. A few reporters started to run forward, only to be held back by a handful of police officers.

The chopper changed direction suddenly and then hovered overhead.

Clearly something was happening in the back, and it had nothing to do with the robot because that thing was still being assembled or automated or whatever it needed to get itself behind the building.

If they needed to respond fast with that thing, they clearly couldn't do it. She didn't want to know that, either.

The group of people half-ran, half-walked from the side of the building. Some were in uniform. Two weren't. She squinted. Not all of the uniforms matched.

Her breath caught. They were getting out. They were making it out. Somehow, she had thought she would see carnage today.

Conversations rose around her—reporters, on air, talking to their producers or camera people, something; cops telling everyone to stand back; the paramedics coming forward so that they could see if anyone needed help.

No one was assisting anyone else, that she could see. And then she saw two cops dragging someone along, head down, body limp, like she'd seen in those TV reports of protestors. She looked at the dragee for a moment, saw plaid shirt, trooper hat, black pants, and realized it wasn't the security guard.

She didn't see him at all.

Edie swallowed nervously. Ruth was standing at attention beside her, clutching her arm. The blanket was sliding off them, but only Ruth hung onto it. A wind had started up, frigid, with some ice pellets in it— not quite snow, not quite rain.

Edie eased out of Ruth's grasp, out of the blanket, around the barricade, searching for the security guard. Somehow, everything would be all right if the security guard showed up. Edie knew she was being irrational, but she didn't care.

And then she saw him, coming around the building, his arm around a small woman—the woman with the iPad, what was her name? Jade. That's what he called her. Beside them, another man in the same uniform as the security guard.

They weren't running, but they weren't walking either. They were hurrying, but not panicked. Some of the police had panicked, but not those three. They acted like it was a normal, everyday occurrence to deal with a bomber.

Maybe it was.

The two cops with the plaid-shirt man lifted him bodily into the back of a squad car. As they did, she realized his shirt was unbuttoned. His pale stomach jiggled. It almost looked bruised. And he might have had a bruise on his face as well—or maybe that was just his skin reacting to the cold.

The cops slammed the car door closed, and one of them leaned on the vehicle. Another came over—the man in charge, it seemed—and spoke to them briefly. A member of the bomb squad peeled off his helmet, joined the threesome, and gestured at the car. The cop shook his head, but the bomb squad guy didn't seem to care. He walked to the car, and Edie stopped watching right there.

She was looking at the security guard. He was scanning the crowd as if something worried him. Then his gaze caught hers, and he smiled.

He *smiled*. She smiled back, her heart fluttering a little. God, she felt like a schoolgirl. Hormones and excitement from all of the events of the afternoon. It had to be.

Still, she wanted to run across the icy street and fling herself in his arms, telling him how glad she was that he was all right. Hero complex or something. She had it bad, whatever it was.

Because she didn't even know him. She'd barely exchanged three sentences with him.

If she acted on these emotions, it would be bad—for her and for him. In the morning, or next week, after some reflection, she would actually see him for what he was, for *who* he was, and all of this connection they felt would disappear. But right now, she was half-observing herself wryly, knowing that she was experiencing something she had only read about before. She had never been this impulsive, at least with men, at least with attraction.

She'd been *impulsive* with men. She'd pick one, and enjoy him for an evening or two, and then toss him back. Like the fishing her dad used to do. It was all about the catch, the wriggling life in her hands just for a moment, and then back it went into the stream, never to be thought of again. Stress relief, she would tell Ruth, and Ruth used to agree.

Stress relief until Edie missed her period. Stress relief until three pregnancy tests proved to her that her body wasn't fooling her.

Stress relief until she realized that every kind of fun had consequences. She probably would've been better off drinking alone in her townhouse.

She sighed, fingernails digging into her ice-cold palms as she bunched her hands into fists. She was going to stand here, and not embarrass the crap out of herself by running over to him and exclaiming over him.

Too many people heading toward the group already. The reporters, the camera operators. The police were pushing them back, *again*.

Ruth came up behind Edie and wrapped the blanket around her. Edie didn't jump this time, but she was getting irritated. Yes, she wasn't wearing a coat. Why were people treating her like she was incapable of thought? *Handing* her the blanket would work just fine.

She glanced at Ruth. Ruth had that serious expression on her face, the one she usually reserved for bad news.

"I need you for the next ten minutes," she said. "And then you can get to the hospital."

Edie almost snapped that she didn't need a hospital. Stress, again. And with no stress relief in the future, no matter how cute the security guard was. She didn't need a lecture to know just how bad that idea was.

She had to calm herself. So she put on her lawyerly persona as if it were a costume.

"You have me," she said calmly, even though she didn't feel calm. She followed Ruth into the crowd.

Ruth approached the officer in charge, who told her, without looking at her, to get back.

"No," Ruth said. "I need to know what's happening here."

The security guard and his team were standing off to the side. His gaze met Edie's and her breath caught. Schoolgirl. Jesus. She nodded at him.

He nodded back.

"We'll give the press a briefing shortly," the officer said.

The security guard stepped forward as if he were going to step into the conversation, maybe add his weight.

Edie tried not to look at him, but she couldn't avoid his angular face because he was in her line of sight.

"Ms. Talbot is not press," Edie snapped at the officer. "She runs the clinic."

"Oh," the officer said, and looked at Edie. "And you are?"

"Her lawyer."

The security guard's eyebrows went up. He clearly hadn't expected that.

"Christ. Already?" the officer muttered. Apparently he wasn't a fan of lawyers. That was all right. Considering how this was all going down, she was beginning to realize she wasn't much of a fan of cops.

"Ms. Bayette was in a meeting with me when our security team identified the problem," Ruth said. "She wasn't chasing—"

"You need to keep Ms. Talbot up to date," Edie said before Ruth said *ambulances*. "She knows the facility, and she knows the area. She might have information you need."

The security guard stepped forward. He was going to butt into the conversation. She didn't need him, not in this way. Then that mental observer who had been watching her reactions let a bit of amusement slip.

Apparently it hadn't taken a day or a week to take the sheen off the security guard. It only took a few minutes—with him stepping in to help the little ladies.

"There have been some very serious threats here," the security guard said. His deep voice sent warmth through her, even though she didn't want it too. "That's why Santore Security is involved."

"I'm sure that's all important," the officer said. "But right now, we need to secure the scene."

Edie began, "We're not asking you—"

"It *is* important," the security guard said. "I don't hire my people out on small jobs."

His people? Edie looked at Ruth, but Ruth was watching all of this, waiting for it to play out.

"The clinic has had five bomb threats in the past month," the security guard (business owner?) said. "A few weeks ago, someone shot at a doctor leaving the clinic."

"And one of our doctors was murdered last year," Ruth said.

Something like irritation flashed across the security guard's face. Edie had no idea why that piece of information would bother him, but it did. He hadn't listed it.

"You need to get with me to provide us with the information on the bomb threats," the officer said to Ruth.

"I will, when and if I can get back into my clinic," Ruth said.

"Besides," Edie said. "You should have the information. We've reported it to the police each time."

The security guard's (business owner's?) brown eyes met Edie's. She prayed he wouldn't say anything more. Because the clinic had hired Santore Security when it became clear that the police weren't going to do anything.

"We'll deal with it," the officer said. "Right now, we have to find out what's going on with those explosives. One of our guys is interrogating the suspect right now. I'll keep you informed."

He started to walk away, but the security guard caught his arm.

"One of my people is still missing. She had gone into those woods about twenty minutes ago—"

"That was reckless of you," the officer said.

The security guard's eyes narrowed. Edie suddenly got a sense that the man could be very, very dangerous.

"I would like," the security guard said slowly, as if he were dealing with a particularly recalcitrant child, "to go to those woods and find out what happened to my employee."

"We'll find her," the officer said.

"I'm sure you will," the security guard said. (Business owner. He said she was an employee. He was a business owner.) "But you'll probably find her dead. I'm letting you know that I am going into those woods, since your attention is elsewhere, and I would appreciate it if you let your officers know so that they don't shoot me."

The officer physically leaned back as if the business owner's words had actually slapped him.

"I'll send someone with you," the officer said.

"Good," the business owner said.

Edie wanted to tell him not to do it. That desperate schoolgirl thing. She didn't want him harmed. But she kept her lawyer on and remained calm.

"You ladies get back to the barricade," the officer said. "I'll tell you what's going on."

Ruth didn't want to head to the barricades. Edie could feel it in the tension in Ruth's body. Ruth was still feeling dismissed.

"There she is!" said the other male security guard. He hit the business owner on the shoulder, gently, to get his attention. "Mack, there's Corinne."

Everyone looked in the direction that the other security guard was pointing, everyone except Edie. She was trying on the name. Mack. It suited him. And now she knew who he was because she had vetted the contract for Santore Security.

Mack was Michael McTavish Santore, the owner of the company. His correspondence had been signed Mack, a signature with very clean lines, with his full name beneath. She remembered it because it was so unexpected. Most people signed their full names, even to cover letters.

Apparently, he did not.

He had broken away from the group, then stopped. Edie finally looked in that direction.

There was a reason everyone was staring.

A slight woman walked down the icy street, with a man in front of her. He had his hands behind his back, and she had a gun pointed at his head.

Everyone was silent. Even the reporters had shut up. Edie couldn't hear the helicopter. Apparently, it was missing this.

The woman looked like something out of a movie—the stranger who came to town, the Avenger who somehow managed to get the bad guy even when the police had failed.

"I found this asshole on a berm of snow that he had built, with a sniper rifle, ready to take out anyone who was going to get near that car," the woman said.

Her words echoed in the cold.

"I didn't shoot him then," she said. "I'm not going to shoot him now. Unless *no one fucking helps me*."

The intensity of that last sentence got everyone to move. The police came forward, the reporters as well, and so did Santore, all of them running toward the woman, questions shouted in her direction.

"Can this get any worse?" Ruth asked.

Normally, Edie would have given her the lawyer answer. The *I'm trained to tell you just how bad it can still get* answer.

But she wasn't feeling lawyerly at the moment. She was feeling—oddly enough—like cheering.

"I don't think it's worse," Edie said to Ruth. "I think things have just started getting better."

The next fifteen minutes erupted into a controlled chaos. The police taking the sniper from Corinne, reporters rushing around the barricade to get the story, police pushing them back, the bomb squad working as if none of this were happening.

Mack shoved his way past all of the people to Corinne, Lashon at his side, Jade behind them, one of the officers arguing with her, saying she had no right to drag a man into the street like that with no evidence. Corinne turning on him, and Mack grabbing her before she could say something she would regret.

Reporters shouting, the chopper overhead, a man—someone he barely recognized—moving away from the barricade, one of the officers saying that they needed to take Lashon in for questioning because of the man he had shot, and something niggling at Mack's brain. It was Corinne's voice, strong, as she said, *I found this asshole on a berm of snow that he had built, with a sniper rife, ready to take out anyone who was going to get near that car.*

Ready to take out anyone who was going to get near that car.

Had the sniper shot the other man? Not Lashon? Had the sniper been *aiming* for Lashon? Just because someone owned the sniper rifle didn't mean he was a good shot. And the people who were coming after this clinic, they were nuts. The cop in the back of the building had been right about that.

The police were trying to take Lashon into custody too, talking about dealing with Corinne, and Mack knew he was going to lose his temper. The cops in this town hated private security. The white cops in this town believed that private security companies owned by African-Americans weren't security companies at all, but licenses for theft and mayhem.

He'd run into it before, and he hated it.

He needed his lawyer.

"Jade," Mack said, "call Petruchio. Get him here as quickly as possible."

She nodded, but she looked as pissed and concerned as Mack felt. Petruchio Jones's offices were on the other side of the city, so *as quickly as possible* was at best an hour from now.

Mack needed someone else—and that stunningly beautiful lawyer might be the one to help.

"Keep him apprised of the situation," Mack said, meaning *let Petruchio know where we end up*, "and don't let them arrest anyone that we know."

Jade started, "But…"

Mack walked away before he could hear the rest of her argument. He scanned the area for the beautiful lawyer but couldn't see her. What had Ruth Talbot called her? Ms. Bayette. It suited her. A little New Orleans for this far north, and even though she didn't have an accent, she had a bit of strength that he always associated with the women of that fine city.

People had knocked over the barricades. Reporters and their film crews were talking to anyone they could find who was willing to get camera time. The chopper was still buzzing annoyingly overhead.

The ambulance was parked as far from the building as possible and still be in the middle of the mess. Its back gate was open, and Ruth Talbot stood next to it. Which meant the beautiful lawyer had to be somewhere nearby as well.

He made his way around the crush of people, ignoring the reporters who called him by name, including the one asking him if he had planned another heroic rescue—God, he shuddered when he heard that —and he reached the side of the ambulance. Lights were on inside, and he realized then just how dark it was getting. The sun, if that's what you could call that white hazy thing covered with gray clouds, was nearly below the horizon. The streetlights that still worked in this neighborhood would be struggling on any time now.

The beautiful lawyer was sitting on the side of the ambulance, wearing a pair of ski pants that were several sizes too large, and thick, thick pairs of socks. She was tugging on some boots. Ruth was handing her a bulky white sweater.

He had no idea who had provided all of that clothing, but he was happy to see it. The lawyer had been incredibly underdressed for the conditions.

"Ms. Bayette." As he spoke, he felt a pang of uncertainty. Had he remembered her name right?

She looked at him in surprise. Either she hadn't seen him come up beside her or he *had* gotten her name wrong.

He barreled on. "We haven't been properly introduced. I'm Mack Santore."

He extended his right hand. She took it. Her fingers were surprisingly warm.

"Edie Bayette," she said. "You were amazing in there."

"So were you," he said. He smiled, unwilling to let her hand go. "You were right: neither of us had time for second-guessing."

She smiled in return, which lit up her entire face, even her chocolate brown eyes.

"Well, I'm glad we didn't, then," she said. But there was something in her voice—a politeness maybe?—that urged him to stop flirting and get to the point.

Flirting. Humph. He had been flirting. He hadn't even realized it until now.

"I overheard your conversation earlier," he said. "You're a lawyer?"

She sat up straighter, as if being a lawyer was a coat she put on. "For the clinic."

"And no one else?" he asked.

"In private practice," she said, being deliberately vague, the way that lawyers did when they didn't want to discuss what they did. But he knew she hadn't really answered the question.

Ruth frowned. She moved just a little closer. Protectively. Did she not want to share her lawyer? That would be strange.

"I was wondering if we could borrow your services until my lawyer gets here," Mack said to Edie Bayette. "The police want to charge Corinne and Lashon—with what, I'm not exactly sure. Saving the neighborhood? Preventing a bombing? Doing something right while black?"

He sounded bitter. He hadn't expected all of that to come out. But it did, and now he didn't seem nearly as rational as he wanted to.

Her lips thinned. "I assume Corinne is the woman who went all *Seven Samurai* on us?"

The reference startled him. Most people would have referenced *The Magnificent Seven* if they referenced old movies at all. *The Magnificent Seven* was the American version of the *Seven Samurai*. Mack preferred the Japanese version, and because of it, he understood how accurate her reference was.

"Yes," he said.

"Oh, for God's sake. And what did your friend Lashon do?"

Mack couldn't tell if she was siding with the police here. The phrasing of the question actually implied guilt.

"They want to charge him with manslaughter, at least until all of this can be sorted out."

She didn't look surprised, but Ruth did.

"That gunshot?" Ruth asked. "It was him?"

Mack shrugged a single shoulder. "I've been a little busy and haven't had time to ask. I assumed so, but now I'm not so sure."

"But even if it was him, he shot one of the bad guys," Ruth said.

"Yeah," Mack said. He wasn't going to mention he had experienced this kind of stupidity from the local police before. He was just going to focus on getting his people out of trouble. "The dead guy was threatening the clinic. I can testify to that."

Edie didn't ask him how he could testify to that. Her expression was maddeningly calm. Then she slipped her hand from his. He hadn't realized how tightly he'd been holding her fingers.

She put her hand on the gate and started to ease herself forward. Ruth put a hand on her shoulder.

"You've had enough excitement for today," Ruth said.

"Nope, I haven't," Edie said. She looked even better in the oversized cable knit sweater. The clothes took some of the edge off her.

"Maybe you haven't," Ruth said, "but the baby has."

Mack felt like someone had poured cold water on him. Once he found out that Edie Bayette was the clinic's lawyer, he no longer thought of her as a patient. Ah, hell. He never had, not really. He had thought she looked out of place from the way she was dressed, thought she wouldn't need the services of a clinic like Sanger House.

Sometimes, he was as guilty as those idiot cops of judging by appearances. And as nice as her appearance was, she was involved with someone and he had been flirting. That violated all the rules. They were his rules, but rules just the same.

As Edie gave Ruth a withering look, he gathered himself, made himself pull back just enough so that Edie wouldn't sense him flirting any longer. And he would do his best not to. It was just that he had been so attracted...

"You know," Edie said to Ruth, "babies survive all kinds of things. Thirty-forty years ago, women didn't even know they were pregnant when they were as far along as I am. I'm sure they did all kinds of bad things, like drink or smoke or—wait! I'm not doing any of those. I'm just going to stand up and talk to some police officers. That's it."

"After a scare—"

"Ruth," Edie said. "You go all Mother Hen on me, I find a brand new doctor."

Ruth's mouth clamped shut. Mack had never seen anyone shut her down before.

Edie turned toward him. Her cheeks were flushed, and this time he knew it wasn't the cold.

"I have to put on these boots or everyone will yell at me," she said. "Apparently they agree with you about my shoes."

"You were getting frostbite," Ruth said softly. "And speaking the truth is not Mother Henning you."

"You know, Ruthie," Edie said as she slipped the boots over the thick wad of socks on her feet, "in my profession, speaking the truth is not a defense."

In spite of himself, Mack grinned. Speaking the truth wasn't always a defense in his profession either.

She pushed herself off the gate. He was about to help, but Ruth glared at him as if helping Edie was tantamount to treason. He also wasn't sure he wanted to touch her anyway. The attraction he felt toward her was strong. It was just better not to tempt fate.

She was significantly shorter without the heels. She didn't lose an ounce of power though. She stalked ahead of him as if she were going after big game, which, he supposed, she was.

They had almost reached the cars when someone yelled, "Stand back!"

He grabbed her shoulder and pushed her behind him. An explosion sounded not too far from them.

The sound echoed, and then there was a moment of complete silence. No one spoke. Even the chopper was gone. He was barely breathing. He wasn't sure Edie was either.

"Clear!" that same voice yelled.

This time, Mack could see the source. It was one of the skinny bomb squad guys, one of the guys who hadn't arrived in complete gear. He was staring at a video monitor, and on it, floodlights showed a clear containment box filled with smoke.

Apparently they had found an explosive and set it off.

"What the hell was that?" Edie asked.

"They safely detonated a bomb," Mack said.

"Did they now?" she asked, as if that were important information. "They yelled 'clear,' so I assume we can move forward?"

He nodded and took her arm. She looked down at his hand with something like amusement.

"I know you're probably one of those well-brought up guys who opens doors for women and all that," she said. "I appreciate it, but despite what Ruth said, I'm not fragile. Never have been, never will be."

He let her go, a flush heating his cheeks. That was the second time she had made him blush, and it felt weird. He didn't blush.

She walked a little faster so that she was ahead of him. She arrived beside Corinne and Lashon before he did.

Jade waylaid him. "I can't reach Petruchio," she said.

"Keep trying," Mack said, and pushed past her.

"I understand there's some question about what these folks did?" Edie was saying as he approached. Two police officers—taller, older white men—were staring at her as if she was a child who had gotten loose from the playground. Channel 25's go-to reporter, Carmen Something-or-other, was trying to elbow her way close as well.

"Miss," said the cop closest to Edie, "there's no reason for you to get involved. We—"

"No reason?" Edie said. "Are you telling me that you don't want a lawyer to talk to you? Because if that's the case, we can just head to the courthouse right now. And on the way, I'm going to take the time to tell the press where we're going. They all got that footage of Ms.—"

"Zeyada," Mack whispered, realizing he hadn't told her Corinne's entire name at the very moment that Edie was going to use it.

"—Zeyada," Edie said, as if she had already known the name, "with the terrorist in hand, asking for help in getting him into custody. And now you're going to *charge* her for doing your job?"

"It's just procedure, Miss," the officer said. "We—"

"Well," Edie said, "it's procedure in my business to get the press involved when things go awry. It seems like things are going awry to me. And what has Mr.—"

"Jackson," Mack whispered.

"—Jackson done?" Edie asked. "Something equally heroic and unapproved, I trust."

"He shot a man, Miss," the officer said. "Even when we shoot our guns in a righteous shoot, we have to go through a procedure—"

"Then by all means," Edie said, "let's treat him like a police officer, and not a criminal. Of course, there should be an investigation, but by my lights, Mr. Jackson and Ms. Zeyada happen to be heroes, and heroes should not be mistreated like this, don't you agree?"

"Miss," the officer said, sounding desperate. "It's procedure."

"*Fuck* procedure," she said with such force that everyone looked at her, including that Channel 25 reporter. "These people saved lives today, and you want to *punish them?*"

Her voice went up, deliberately, Mack realized, because her expression remained unchanged. She was good. She might even have been better than Petruchio, at least in this situation.

"Miss—"

"Who is in charge?" she asked, "because I'm getting nowhere with you clowns."

Corinne drew in a breath. Her style was vastly different than Edie's. Corinne was polite until she couldn't be anymore. Apparently, Edie was combative from the start.

"Um, Miss, he's busy, you know, we're dealing with explosives—"

"Yes, you are," Edie said. "And if Mr. Jackson and Ms. Zeyada hadn't been here, you would still be dealing with *perpetrators*, and maybe those *perpetrators* would have detonated those explosives. Mr. Jackson and Ms. Zeyada saved lives today."

The officer opened his mouth, and then closed it again. Mack suppressed a grin. He liked watching this woman work.

"Here's what we're going to do," Edie said. "You are going to uncuff Mr. Jackson."

Lashon gave Mack a panicked look. Clearly Lashon didn't like the way the lawyer was handling this.

She was very combative, which Mack admired, but was also worried about.

"Miss—" the cop said.

"*Now*," she said.

The other cop, who was holding Lashon's arm, tilted his head a little as if to say, *Let's just get this over with.* The cop raised Lashon's wrists enough to deliberately hurt him, and made a show of taking the handcuffs off.

The cop even showed them to Edie, who looked spectacularly unimpressed.

She nodded when she saw the cuffs, but she didn't compliment the cops for letting Lashon go.

"My clients are going to come, voluntarily, to the station, with me or one of my colleagues, and they will give a statement as long as their lawyers are present. They will not speak to the press before they speak to you, and you will treat them like citizens rather than criminals. The *moment* anyone talks about custody or procedure or arrest, we leave, we talk to the press, we create a *shit storm* in the media."

"Miss, this is above my pay grade," the officer said. "I'm just—"

"And the way I'm leading off the shit storm," she said, "is by informing the press that you all *knew* that Sanger House has been receiving bomb threats for *weeks* and you refused to even have patrol cars drive by twice a day. That was all we asked. Twice a day. The clinic had to take funds away from important programs to afford Mr. Santore's security service here, and thank God they did, because his people saw a perpetrator, called you, and when you did not arrive in anything close to record time, Mr. Santore's employees went after the perpetrators, and from what I can tell, caught them. And now you want to save the city from the *good guys*? Is there some kind of agenda here that I need to know about? Because all of this is just where I *begin*. I go deeper than that, faster than that, if you give me or Mr. Jackson or Ms. Zeyada any more trouble."

God, she was brilliant. And beautiful despite being wrapped in clothing three sizes too big. Two reporters had caught every word she said, and two separate camera operators had drifted over, boom mics within range.

The police officer finally noticed. He looked miserable.

"Well," he said, "if you promise to bring them to the station..."

"Cross my heart," she said, and made the little childish sign against her cable knit sweater, above the left breast rather than below it. Mack looked at her breast a nanosecond too long before he caught himself.

The police officer was staring at her, stunned. She put her hands on both Corinne's and Lashon's backs.

"Let's move," she said in a completely different voice. Deeper, softer, not nearly as strident.

Mack stepped between the three of them and the officer, just in case he changed his mind. One of the reporters jogged alongside Corinne.

"Ms. Zeyada, could you tell us—"

"I just promised the police that Ms. Zeyada would give the press a statement *after* she gives a statement at the precinct," Edie said. "That's how we're going to deal with this situation. I'm sure you have more than enough for the eleven o'clock news. Do us a favor and show Ms. Zeyada's heroic arrival on this street this afternoon, and we'll be even more likely to grant you the very first interview."

The reporter gaped, trying to recover, but by then Edie was already past her. Mack let out a small chuckle. The near-arrest had gone from a near-disaster to some kind of golden moment.

The streetlights had come on, and so had all of the floodlights from the police equipment, bomb squad, satellite vans, and that damn chopper. It was lighter than it had been all day on the street, and Mack just noticed.

The reporters couldn't keep up with the four of them. He suspected that was deliberate on Edie's part.

He had to get his people to the vehicles. But he didn't feel comfortable leaving the scene just yet.

He said to Corinne, "Do you think there are any more perpetrators in those woods?"

She had explored part of them, at least. She would know.

She smiled at him, which surprised him.

"*Perpetrators,*" she said and actually giggled. Stress. Corinne giggled when stress eased. He found it both endearing and annoying.

Edie looked at her in surprise. Lashon just rolled his eyes.

"He's picking up police lingo," Corinne said to Edie. "Or yours. Great show back there. Thank you."

"You're welcome," Edie said, with that same low, businesslike voice. "But we can discuss pleasantries later. I'd love to hear your answer to Mr. Santore's question."

Corinne's smile faded. She took a deep breath, realizing—like she always did—that her giggles and amusement were inappropriate.

"I didn't see any more 'perpetrators,'" she said to Mack. "If there are more, and they're smart, they're long gone. They left when the sirens started."

He agreed with that. Or they faded into the crowd, watching but looking innocent somehow.

"Here's what bothers me," Corinne said. "The two men we saw weren't very sophisticated. But the equipment was."

Lashon nodded. Apparently he had noticed that too.

"You think someone's funding them?" Edie asked. She clearly didn't speak their language.

"No," Mack said. "She thinks that these two were patsies. This isn't some group that got its shit together in the last two weeks and decided to attack Sanger House. She thinks—"

"She thinks she can speak for herself, thanks," Corinne said, her tone still inappropriately light. "She thinks—*I* think—that this event might be tied to some of those national organizations, the pro-life ones that also have a militant wing."

"Like that church that protests funerals?" Edie asked.

"For all the press it gets, that church is pretty small," Lashon said. "There are some very big hate groups in this country, and we've taken our eyes off the ball with them, focusing on terrorists from overseas. Some of the politicians have even co-opted the hate groups because those groups go after 'suspected' terrorists—"

"Like us," Mack said bitterly.

"You?" Edie sounded surprised.

"We have dark skin," he said. "That means we also have an agenda."

He hated the accusations that had come his way the past decade or so. Before that, the accusations had never been to his face, and if he or his team got arrested, it was always for some kind of coded reason.

He wasn't sure this change had been for the better.

Both things infuriated him.

"Mack," Corinne said warningly. "You might be wrong in this case."

For all her toughness, she preferred to give people the benefit of the doubt.

But Edie's gaze met Mack's, a small frown creasing her forehead.

"Well, that explains something," Edie said. "I was wondering why the police were being so harsh with you."

They had reached the blue Dodge that Corinne had been driving. One of the doors was still open, and the car was beeping, complaining, its beep sounding thready.

"Where's Aldis?" Corinne asked.

"Last I saw, he was walking the perimeter with you," Mack said.

"I saw him just before the cops dragged me off," Lashon said. "He was coordinating with Jade. She would know where he is."

Mack nodded. He knew that Aldis hadn't left the car door open— that had probably been the first responders and the patients from the clinic, too distracted to close the door when they left.

Probably. He didn't entirely like it, though.

"Aldis?" Edie asked.

"He works with us." Mack wasn't going to explain further. He shoved the open door closed, and the car stopped complaining.

It had been a mess inside. He didn't want the women in the vehicle, just in case he was wrong and one of the bad guys had gotten to it.

"I'm going to take you to the precinct," Mack said to Corinne and Lashon.

"Actually," Edie said. "I'm going to take them there."

"But Ruth didn't want you to get too involved," Mack said. "We can have my lawyer meet us there."

Edie's mouth twisted slightly. She still looked lovely, even when she was disgusted.

"Don't be like Ruth," she said.

He flushed for a third time, and was about to deny that he had been, except that Edie wasn't done.

"I'm pregnant," she said. Lashon and Corinne looked at her with surprise. "I'm not on my deathbed. This pregnancy is so new we don't even know if it's going to be a difficult pregnancy. I haven't had morning sickness yet. I actually feel pretty damn good. So all that this fussing does is piss me off."

Mack had no idea how to respond to that. Lashon looked at Edie with wide eyes. And then Corinne giggled, breaking the mood.

"I assume fussing always pisses you off," Corinne said. "I assume the pissed-off has nothing to do with hormones."

What a nice way of asking if the pissed-off actually did have something to do with hormones. Mack would never have been able to finesse a question like that.

Edie looked at her and then grinned. Apparently, she understood the sideways question.

"You assume correctly. I am permanently pissed off. Except when I'm *really* pissed off."

Corinne slipped an arm through Edie's.

"That's my kind of woman," Corinne said. "So let me guess. You want to take us to the precinct."

"I do," Edie said. "I promised you would be there. And your lawyer is nowhere nearby. I trust she's en route?"

"He," Mack said.

"Great," Edie said. "Have him meet us there. Until he gets there, these two are my clients."

"You have a car nearby?" Mack asked. "Do you still have your keys?"

"Shit," Edie said, then shook her head. "My keys are in my purse, which is in the clinic. After the little standoff I just had with the police, I don't want to ask them permission to go inside."

"I doubt they'd grant it to you anyway," Mack said.

He didn't add that he didn't want her—or anyone he knew—inside that clinic until the bomb squad cleared it. He wasn't exactly unnerved by the fact that the bomb squad had found a live bomb, but if he had any doubts about the nature of the threat, they were gone now. This threat had been real, and it had been narrowly averted.

"I'll drive you all to the precinct," he said.

"All right," Edie said, then she glanced down at her clothing. "I look so professional." She eyeballed the police, still dealing with reporters and the scene. "Let's stop at my place. I'm going to get some appropriate clothing—"

"Not those shoes again," Mack said.

"No, actual boots," she said. "That fit this time."

"You look fine," Corinne said.

"I'm sure I do, for a homeless person," Edie said. "But there is a very real chance we might go before a judge today, and I'd rather not look like I came from the scene. It's better if I look like a high-powered attorney. In this instance, clothes actually do make a difference."

Corinne nodded, and quietly, Mack agreed. People saw what they wanted to see, and while some older high-powered male attorneys could get by with a sloppy sweatshirt and ill-fitting pants, having just been at the scene of a major incident, younger men, women, and people who didn't fit the lawyer stereotype probably couldn't.

He was liking this woman more and more as each moment went by.

"My car's in that lot over there." He nodded toward a lot a block away. It was full, something he had never seen before. He suspected many of the cars belonged to the media personnel who were still crowding to the scene.

He checked his pockets surreptitiously, making sure he had his keys as well. His fingers found them, and his phone. He needed to let Jade know where they were going, but as he pulled the phone out, his curiosity got the better of him.

He extended the phone to Edie.

"Do you need to let your husband know you're all right?" he asked.

"Oh, I suppose I should, if I had a husband," she said.

Then she peered at the lot. The lights from the crime scene behind them filtered through the grayish ice-mist, providing the only illumination. The streetlights in this part of town were mostly out of order.

"Which car is yours?" she asked.

"It's not really a car," Corinne said. "It's a gigantic SUV. Just come with me."

She led Edie toward the lot. Lashon dropped back half a step and said quietly, "Nice try, boss."

"That obvious?" Mack asked.

"Nah," Lashon said. "I just know you, man. Scrappy, pissed off, and beautiful is like your version of heroin."

"Nice," Mack said, tone dry.

Lashon shrugged. "Truth isn't always pretty." Then he grinned. "Although she is."

"Yeah," Mack said. "Pretty, brilliant, and pregnant."

"No husband, though," Lashon said.

Mack let out a small laugh. "As if that matters these days."

He hurried so that he could get ahead of the women before they arrived at the SUV. He was going to check it over before he let anyone get inside it.

Normally, he would say someone who did something like that was operating from an excess of caution, but today wasn't normal.

For anyone.

11

The SUV was pristine. Edie hadn't expected it. She would have thought that it was a rental, but it didn't have that sharp chemical odor most recent rentals had. And there were fingerprints along the dash and the steering wheel. Otherwise, the vehicle didn't look used at all.

She was glad they weren't taking her car after all. It definitely looked used.

She sat in the backseat with Lashon and watched as the dark and shadowy neighborhood disappeared behind them. She could always tell when she was leaving the worst part of the city because the streetlights glowed yellow as the neighborhoods improved, and the streets were not covered in ice.

She knew that some of the city counselors complained about the treatment the poorer sections of town got; she also knew that little would improve until a new government swept into all areas of the city, not just certain council seats.

Mack Santore drove the SUV as if it were part of a military convoy. He sat up straight, had one hand on the wheel and the other at his side, maybe even near the weapon she had seen on his hip.

That question he had asked about her husband, that was odd. Or maybe it was just considerate. She couldn't tell. But she had felt a spark of attraction between them, not that he was going to act on it.

She could tell that from the disappointed look he had given her when he realized she was pregnant. She couldn't tell if that disappointment was because she was pregnant or because he thought she was involved with someone else. Or maybe she had been projecting her own opinion of herself on him. *She* was disappointed with herself for the behavior that led to the pregnancy, even though she had done everything right, birth control wise.

As Ruth had said to her during their conversation, there was a reason that failure rates were listed on birth control pill packages. *Someone* had to make up the four percent. Lucky her, she was one of them. And her pills would have to fail on her the night that the condom broke.

She felt her own cheeks heat. She rubbed her hands on her knees. If anyone looked, they would think she was trying to keep warm.

Instead, she was thinking about herself and, oddly, worrying about what condition she had left her townhouse in. Sometimes the front rooms were clean, and sometimes they looked like a hurricane had hit.

She had been so focused on the pregnancy tests the last few days that hurricane might be an option, although she seemed to recall picking up clothing and doing dishes within the last forty-eight hours.

Her building loomed. When she bought her townhouse, it had been in a transitional neighborhood. Her building was one of the first to undergo an extensive rehab. The building had been a group of row houses, some of which had been burned out in a devastating fire fifteen years before. There had been some controversy over the rehabilitation of the neighborhood since entire families of squatters had been thrown out of the lower floors.

What the complaining press did not know—and what she had worked very hard to keep quiet—was that the redevelopment company also had a grant for low-income housing, and helped several of the families qualify. The reason the company didn't want anyone to know was because they were afraid of being inundated by applications should they ever do another project like that again.

This city had lost much of its economic base, and lower middle-income families and poor families had been hit hard. The depth of the problem was overwhelming, even for groups like the ones Edie was affiliated with. Sometimes it looked like nothing would ever get done, no matter how much everyone tried.

Driving into this neighborhood did improve her mood, though, despite all that had happened today. The streetlights on all four corners did a little to dispel the darkness, but the lighting the architects had placed on the sidewalks and walkways made the neighborhood seem safe and pretty. Even with the snow and ice, the landscaping looked terrific.

Her townhouse was in the center of the entire building, but she only shared a wall on one side. The other side butted up against an archway that led into a communal garden.

She had left lights on in her living room in her haste to leave that morning, and she hadn't drawn the shades. As the SUV pulled into a parking spot in the circular driveway near the archway, she saw a sweater tossed casually on the back of the couch.

Oh, well. So much for impressing the short-term clients.

At least she had food for them. They had said they didn't need anything, but she knew better. Sometimes going through the system—even if they were innocent (especially if they were innocent)—could take twelve hours or more.

On the way, she had borrowed Mack's phone to call the property manager. She could see him standing near the archway, waiting for them, shifting from foot to foot in the cold.

The SUV had barely stopped when she got out.

"Thanks, Hank," she said. "Appreciate this."

"Saw you on the news," he said, pulling a wad of keys out of his pocket. One of those keys was the master. He said he kept the wad to confuse anyone who decided to steal the keys from him.

"I hope I looked all right," she said.

"I'm hoping you are all right," he said. "Scary times."

"They are scary," she said. "And I'm fine."

At least she knew he wasn't asking because she was pregnant. He was asking because he was worried that she had been at a crime scene.

He unlocked her door. She thanked him again, and then he disappeared through the archway to his own townhouse in the back.

She hadn't realized until she turned around that her three guests were still waiting in the SUV.

"Come on," she said, and beckoned with her hand in case they didn't get the point. Mack shook his head, but Corinne got out. Then Lashon did, and finally Mack shut off the SUV, clearly reluctant.

They trooped down the sidewalk to her place, and stepped inside along with her.

It wasn't as bad as she feared. It didn't smell like stale milk as it sometimes did when she let the breakfast dishes pile up for a few days. It actually smelled of the vanilla candles she had lit last night when she had tried to take a soothing bath. (Nothing was soothing her, though. Not with the worry about the possible—now actual—pregnancy.)

Her living room set was relatively clean. Only that sweater on top of the couch, which made the up-to-date furniture look lived in, instead of something out of a style magazine.

The place's design wasn't quite out of a style magazine, but it was close. She had been in the middle of three complicated cases at work when it came time to decorate the townhouse, so she had hired one of the best firms in town, spent a frustrating Saturday morning with them, pointing at pictures of furniture as they tried to get a sense of her style.

They'd been sort of close. Some of the chairs were too Louis XIV for her, with their foo-foo legs, but she didn't have to sit in them. Mostly, she used the oversized couch, which faced the real fireplace, one she had used repeatedly last month when she'd been snowed in.

The kitchen and dining room were just off the living room, and they were clean, only because she'd been too busy to eat at home. But she had supplies.

Before going into her bedroom to change, she opened the fridge, pulled out some fresh bread she had bought the day before, two different kinds of salami and three different cheeses, as well as some carrots, celery, and a fruit salad that had looked interesting in the store.

"Plates are in the cupboards," she said. "You have to eat something or we're not leaving here. Because the police are going to keep you for hours."

"Shouldn't we get there as fast as possible?" Corinne asked.

Mack gave her a withering look. "No one knows how long it will take us to get to the precinct. Especially in this weather. We're going to beat the officers anyway."

"I know they called ahead for a detective," Lashon said.

"The detective can wait," Mack said. "Ms. Bayette is right. We all need to eat something."

She liked that he agreed with her, but hated the "Ms. Bayette."

"Edie," she said, and grabbed a slice of cheddar. "I'll be back in a few minutes."

She slipped away before anyone could stop her, and climbed the stairs to the master bedroom.

Here was where the hurricane had hit. Unmade bed, clothing tossed every which way, and plates on the floor. Her television was still on, with the sound muted. Apparently, she had forgotten to shut it off that morning.

And the bathroom was worse. The pregnancy test, with its stupid announcement, still sat on top of the box, where she had compared the word *pregnant* to the image that the marketers had designed, hoping that maybe both parts of the test said *pregnant* as some kind of joke.

She sighed and changed, placing the clothes she had borrowed in a bag to return to the ambulance crew. She put on tailored wool pants, a gray and black designer sweater, and thick socks. In deference to Mack, she pulled actual boots over her feet, not a thin pair of high heels. In deference to herself, she made sure the boots had heels too.

She stopped in the bathroom to wash her face, comb her hair, and dust her skin with just a bit of makeup. Her image in the mirror caught her: she was too pale, and her eyes had deep shadows underneath them.

She looked like a woman who had been through a trauma. No wonder everyone was fussing over her. She placed her hands beside the sink and bent over for just a moment, gathering herself.

If Mack and his crew hadn't been on top of everything, the part of

Sanger House that she had been in would have exploded. People would have died.

She might have died.

And then this whole pregnancy thing would have meant nothing. She would have died having never been married, having had only one close relationship, and no one truly close to mourn her. She had a will, of course, but all her money—and she had that—would go to the various charities she did pro-bono work for.

Her friends would miss her, but that was it. They would miss her. Her death wouldn't have a huge impact on their lives.

"Stop having a pity party," she whispered, then gathered herself. She had people to attend to, arrests to prevent.

Time to be super-bitch lawyer, a persona she actually loved. It was as much a part of her as her slightly crooked nose.

She stood up, washed her face, and applied makeup, paying close attention to those shadows.

If the police didn't cooperate, maybe she would give another press conference right there. Her secretary—

Crap. She suddenly realized the one place that had to know what she was doing was the office. And she hadn't contacted them.

So she left the bathroom and grabbed her backup cell. It was, in theory, her personal phone, but she didn't make a lot of personal calls on it, so rarely carried it.

In fact, of late, all she had used it for was booty calls.

She glared at the phone for a moment, as if it were the reason for her pregnancy. Of course. Because *she* couldn't be culpable in it.

Then she shook her head at herself, grabbed another purse and her extra set of keys, and started downstairs, the phone dialing the office as she walked.

She couldn't do anything about the pregnancy today.

She couldn't do much about herself.

But she could keep these people out of jail, all for doing their jobs.

And she could do that better than anyone she had ever known.

*S*he came down the stairs like a teenage girl dressed for prom, each movement elegant and controlled. Only she was more elegant and controlled than a teenage girl would ever be, and she had none of the self-consciousness that a teenage girl would have. She was on the phone, talking to someone she worked with, judging by her tone, and yet someone who knew her, because she was reassuring that person that she was all right.

Mack held the last half of the salami and cheese sandwich he had made between his hands as he watched her.

"Better eat it," Lashon said under his breath. "Because right now, you're outing yourself as a man in lust."

Mack wasn't sure he was in lust, although that was part of it. He was a man entranced, though. And he was a man confused. Because this townhouse had no second-person presence whatsoever.

He recognized the setup. It was a one-person home. The couch was used, but none of the chairs. The tall chairs around the breakfast bar had been pushed in, as if they were posing for a photo shoot. Only the chair across from the TV had been tilted crookedly.

Nothing in the dining room was out of place, and the back door, which led to a little garden area, was closed and locked. The coats that hung near that entry were all women's and so were the boots and shoes that had been set aside for the garden.

This woman was pregnant, but not closely involved with the father. Whether the father lived elsewhere or whether he was even in her life, Mack couldn't tell.

And the fact that his brain was working on all of this instead of finding whoever went after the clinic or protecting his own people told him that neither he nor Lashon were right.

Mack wasn't a man in lust, exactly, nor was he entranced, exactly. He was more a man enchanted. Because there had to be some magic here, something that made his connection to this woman so very strong.

He made himself look away from her before she got off the stairs. He finished the sandwich and put his plate near the sink. He had been hungry. Corinne was nearly done as well, and Lashon had made himself two sandwiches.

Corinne had also made a sandwich for Edie. Corinne extended the plate now.

Edie waved a hand, dismissing the food, and hung up from her call before dropping the phone into her purse. She had extras of everything, it seemed. She was a woman prepared.

"Let's just go," Edie said. "We have to get to the precinct. Thanks for indulging me on the clothing."

"Thank you," Corinne said. "We were hungry."

She grabbed her coat, and so did Lashon. But Mack didn't grab his.

"You need to eat," he said.

"And you need to stop taking Ruth so seriously," Edie said.

"I don't care about Ruth," Mack said. "You're defending my people, and you've had as stressful a day as we have. You're eating too."

"I'll be free to come and go," Edie said, clearly bristling at his tone.

"And I'll be free to do the same," Mack said. "More free than you will be, since you might be talking to detectives and judges. Corinne made you a sandwich."

Edie glared at him. It was a powerful glare, a masterful glare. The kind that would make most strong men weep. He found the glare more attractive than he wanted to think about.

After a long moment, she took the plate from Corinne and ate, quickly and surprisingly delicately. Edie didn't finish the sandwich. Instead, she opened the fridge, put the plate inside, and pulled out a bottle of water.

All of that took maybe three minutes. She wiped her mouth with the back of her hand. Mack half expected her to burp just to prove she wasn't intimidated by him. But she didn't.

Her gaze met his again. This time, she had a similar glare, but this one contained a warning. *Don't try that again.* And he barely suppressed a smile.

He liked her. Too much.

"Let's go," she said.

And they did.

13

The precinct was old and filthy and built of stone so thick that Edie doubted the car bomb those men had devised would have even chipped the exterior. The stairs leading inside were marble but had been walked on so much that they were actually worn down just a bit in the middle.

The entire place still smelled of cigarettes even though smoking had been banned here for more than a decade. Someone really needed to wash down the walls, but no one ever would.

Still, she had forgotten how much she liked it here. It made her heart rate go up, in a good way, bracing her for the challenge—whatever that would be—ahead.

A metal detector less fancy than the one at Sanger House greeted them. Edie handed the cop manning the thing her cell phone, dumped her purse and coat on the x-ray mechanism, and then walked through the little archway.

No beeping, which was a good thing. She'd gone through that nightmare one too many times.

She waited for her group, watching Mack, wondering how he would react going through a metal detector at the police department since he had to man one at Sanger House.

He had reached into his pocket and pulled out his wallet. His coat was back, revealing his gun. He handed the open wallet to the cop, who looked at it, and then at the gun, and then waved Mack around, calling him by name.

Of course, he knew the cops. Of course, he had a license to carry. Of course, she hadn't thought that through.

Lashon's gun was long gone, as was Corinne's. They walked through just like Edie had.

Once she was certain they were inside and she wouldn't have to fight just to get them through the door, she turned her attention to the rest of the entry.

It was tight here because the department had cut the entry in two. Bullet-proof coating covered the wall behind the desk sergeant, and the door beside the desk had an automated lock that had to be opened either with a passcode or by someone like the desk sergeant.

She had always thought the arrangement—which she still considered "new" even though it was almost six years old—left the poor desk sergeant out in front, undefended and a potential victim of whichever angry asshole decided to ruin someone's day.

She leaned her arms on the desk, grateful for her heels. If she hadn't been wearing them, she couldn't have faked this relaxed pose.

"Edie Bayette, with clients Corinne Zeyada and Lashon Jackson, and their boss Mack Santore. I believe someone in back is expecting us."

The desk sergeant grinned. "Someone is, and someone ain't. So *you're* the lawyer? Because the someone that ain't says he's their lawyer, and he has more up-to-date credentials than you do."

Edie tried not to sigh with exasperation. She had gotten ribbed mercilessly when she first came to the police department as a defense attorney after she had done one year as a public defender. The cops accused her of going to the dark side. And now that she no longer practiced criminal law (unless she couldn't help herself—as in this case), she got ribbed as well.

And she didn't even recognize this desk sergeant.

She wasn't in the mood for teasing or sarcasm or vague pronouncements. She also wasn't going to inform him that she had an idea who was waiting. It was probably the lawyer Mack had called first.

"You gonna let us in?" she asked the desk sergeant.

"Oh, Miss High-and-mighty, already on her high horse," he said, and pushed some button behind the desk that made the door buzz.

Mack pushed it open, his gaze meeting hers as he did so. He seemed to look at her quizzically all the time, as if he didn't understand her or as if he wanted more from her or something.

She wasn't able to figure it out.

She probably would have tried if she wasn't dealing with new clients, an ever-changing body, and the stresses of nearly getting blown up.

Her clients followed him through the door, and she brought up the rear. The second part of the entry was where the lawyers with their supposedly not-guilty clients, visitors with some other business, and actual criminals waiting to be processed waited in one large, often smelly, mass.

As a young defense attorney, this part of the entry had freaked her out. Until she realized that cameras were on everyone, and there were guards everywhere. Plus a lot of police officers usually waited with the minor offenders they had cuffed to the benches.

Mack was already talking to a tall, well-dressed man in a black silk suit. The man's bald head caught the light just like the threads in the suit did. In spite of herself, Edie grinned.

She'd recognize that bald head anywhere. Petruchio Jones. They had worked together as young attorneys and helped each other survive the early dark times in their budding careers.

"Hey, Petruchio," she said, "have you come to wive it wealthily in Padua?"

He whirled, a grin on his face. "Ah, Edie! Of course not. We're not in Padua. Your only fault, and that is faults enough, is that you are intolerable curst."

"And shrewd and forward, so beyond all measure," she said. "But you also are no prize, sir."

And then they both laughed. He came over to her, and enveloped her in a hug.

"Ah, Edie, I missed you," he said. "Who else can I misquote Shakespeare with?"

"Just about anyone who knows where your name came from," she said, squeezing him tightly. Hugging him felt good. It had been a long time since anyone hugged her from sheer affection.

Over his shoulder, she could see Mack, watching with a frown on his face. Corinne smiled, and Lashon simply looked perplexed.

"Well, clearly you two know each other," Mack said drily as Edie and Petruchio separated.

"And clearly, you don't approve," Petruchio said.

Now, Lashon did smile, as if he knew something no one else did. Mack shook his head.

"I just—never mind." Mack's gaze met Edie's. "I guess this is where we part company, then."

"I don't think so," Petruchio said. "I heard you on the drive over here, Edie. There are reporters using your clips. This story has already gone national, and for that reason alone, kicking you off it right now would be a mistake."

She opened her mouth to argue with him. She was involved. She was nearly a victim of the bombers, and that wasn't good.

But she'd known Petruchio forever, and he could read her objection. His posturing vanished.

"Besides," he said softly, "I have no real idea what's going on."

She laughed again, which actually felt good. Laughing let out some of the stress.

"All right," she said. "With luck, we can take care of this tonight."

At that moment, a detective she didn't recognize came out of the back. "I understand Corinne Zeyada is here? I would like to speak to her and her attorney."

They were dividing up the defendants. Mack's face flushed. He looked like a man about to go to war. Edie put her hand on his arm and felt a zing of inappropriate lust. Damn the baby hormones.

She ignored that and said softly to him, "Let us handle this."

"Which one is in the most trouble?" Petruchio asked her under his breath.

"Lashon," she replied in the same way.

"He's yours, then," Petruchio said. "Mack can catch me up."

He stepped forward without letting her answer—not that it mattered, since she agreed with him.

"Give me one minute to consult with my client, detective, and we'll be right with you."

"What are they doing?" Mack asked.

"Nothing unusual," Edie said quietly, still watching the door. And, just like she expected, another detective came through it.

"Lashon Jackson?" the detective asked.

"Mr. Jackson is here," Edie said. "I'm his counsel."

"This is informal, counselor," the detective said. "I'm sure you understand."

She gave him her most feral smile. "I'm sure you understand that I'll be sitting in, informal or not."

The detective's gaze met Lashon's. "Is that what you want, sir?"

Sir, Edie thought. *How manipulative.* But she didn't say that.

"Yeah," Lashon said.

"Let's go, then," the detective said and held the door open. Corinne and Petruchio were already heading down a different hallway.

Lashon started to follow the detective, but Edie caught his arm.

"One second," she said, and turned to Mack.

His gaze was wary.

"We're out of attorneys," she said so softly she could barely hear herself. "You don't have one and that's a problem. They're going to try to provoke you. I want you to leave this building and wait for us at a Starbuck's or something."

"Starbuck's is going to close soon," he said, knowing he sounded petulant.

"I don't care where you go," she said. "I care that you're not here. We'll call you. I want to see you leave before Lashon and I go back."

"Mr. Jackson," the detective said.

"One minute," Lashon said. Edie wasn't sure if he could overhear the conversation or not.

"We don't have a minute," the detective said.

Edie nodded forcefully at Mack, as if she could shove him out of the precinct with her forehead.

"Fuck," he said softly. "You better end this stupidity."

"Trust me," she said.

He shook his head once, said to Lashon, "You know where to find me," and pivoted, leaving this part of the entry. Edie watched through the closing door as he let himself out of the other part of the entry as well.

"Think he'll stay away?" she asked Lashon.

"Yeah," Lashon said quietly. "He knows what's at stake."

Then Lashon walked over to the detective. Edie kept pace with both of them.

He knows what's at stake.

Everything for Santore Security, for Corinne, and for Lashon. In this city, the police had indicted on less. The national news had called some white shooters who killed African-Americans vigilantes, and the local press was trying hard to prove that the community wasn't racist.

What better offering did they have than two people of color, who brought down some major criminals near what the press billed as an abortion clinic?

Yeah, Mack wasn't the only one who knew what was at stake.

Edie did too. And she needed complete focus to make sure she was up to the task.

14

*E*die was right—Mack knew that she was right—but he hated leaving the precinct. His people were there, and they could possibly be charged with crimes just because they were doing their jobs. Jobs he had hired them for.

So while he waited, he decided to make himself useful. He had to find out what was going on at Sanger House. He needed to make sure Ruth was all right. And he needed to get some of his own investigators on this case.

It already looked like the cops were going to make a hash of it.

He made a number of stops in the three hours after dropping everyone at the precinct. He went to the hospital first because Ruth was there, advising, helping with the patients that had been brought in, and trying to pretend she wasn't upset.

He promised her he would find whoever did this, if they hadn't been found already. He also promised her he would be back at Sanger House as soon as the police released it as a crime scene.

"I already told the police that we were opening up at the usual time tomorrow," she said to Mack. "They told me we couldn't, and I told them that we'd climb over their damn crime scene tape if we had to. Because people need us and they can't get our services elsewhere.

So if you want to be there first thing in the morning, I'd appreciate it..."

Of course he had agreed. And as he left the hospital, he realized that in most ways, Ruth Talbot was stronger and more courageous than most men he had ever met. It seemed like nothing could stop her.

So he was going to make sure nothing would stop him.

He ended up at the crime scene next. It was still well lit, with reporters prepping for their eleven o'clock newscasts in less than an hour. The police were still combing the premises, and he couldn't get permission to go inside.

But he did note that the police had a perimeter up this time. No one was going to get close to the clinic right now, which was both good and bad for the following day.

He wished he could trust the police to do a proper investigation, but he couldn't. Not with them wasting resources on Lashon and Corinne. Aldis and Jade were still here. Jade was recording everything the police were doing, and Aldis was walking the neighborhood, just to see if he found anything out of the ordinary.

Mack spoke to them briefly. He offered to replace them, to let them go home.

"Are you kidding me?" Jade said. "I nearly got blown up. This is personal, man."

He grinned at that. He had felt the same way.

Aldis, on the other hand, had finished his walk through the neighborhood.

"I don't think anyone's coming tonight," he said. "Not with the cops here. If you don't mind, I'm heading home for some shut-eye. I'll be back around six."

Six a.m. was early, but Mack agreed. Six was that kind of in-between time that some smart criminals might take advantage of. If Aldis got here at six, Mack would arrive an hour later and start the fight for Ruth so that the clinic could open on time.

As he walked away from Aldis, Mack mentally worked the schedule in his mind. He needed to pull some guards from some of the lighter jobs. He would refer to the news coverage as his reason. He had a few star-fucker clients who really only hired Santore Security because famous people hired them as well. Those clients would feel like they were part of a big national news story if they let their guard disappear for a few days.

He might have to partner with another firm to get coverage, but he would handle that in the morning, as long as he had a full staff on the clinic.

He walked back to his SUV, shivering just a little in the cold. The temperature had gone from *God it's cold* to *holy shit is this kind of cold even natural?* As he climbed in the SUV, his cell rang.

He glanced at the screen. Petruchio. A stab of disappointment went through Mack, and he smiled at his own ridiculousness. For a moment, he had hoped he was hearing from Edie.

Although, now that he thought about it, he doubted she even had his phone number.

Mack started the SUV as he answered the cell. He also turned the heat on blast-furnace.

"We're as done as we're going to be tonight," Petruchio said without preamble. "You want me to take these people home? Or you want to meet us?"

Judging from the tone of Petruchio's voice, Mack knew the answer.

"I want to meet all of you," Mack said. "That diner on third, you know which one."

"The one you live in half the time?" Petruchio said. "Yeah, I know it. We'll all be there."

And then he hung up before Mack could insist that Edie join them, in case she wanted to bug off. He would have said that he wanted to hear about the legal side of Lashon's case from her, but he would have been lying.

No sense in lying, at least at the moment.

He put the SUV in drive, spun around, and drove a little more recklessly than he should have on such thick ice to Ray's All-Night Diner.

There was no Ray, and there was no need to say the diner was open all night, not any more.

But there had been a Ray, back when the diner opened in the 1920s. And in those days, "all-night" was something special. The diner had gone through hard times in the intervening decades and had been slated for demolition several years ago.

Mack had grown up eating at Ray's, and he couldn't let it die. He invested money he didn't have to buy the place and hire an old military buddy who had mad cooking skills. He let his old friend manage Ray's, and now it had become so successful that no one could imagine the neighborhood without it.

Technically, Mack no longer owned the business. He'd sold it to the friend who helped him save it, for his initial investment back plus 10 percent. His friend hadn't finished making all the payments, but he'd made enough so that Mack no longer thought of Ray's as his.

Still, Mack felt proprietary every time he pulled into his own personal parking spot. Ray's was a square, squat building on what was once a large parking lot. Mack had divided up the lot. Not all of it belonged to the diner. He'd kept those properties, and eventually he might do something with them.

He got out and walked up the handicapped access ramp, which had not one speck of ice on it, despite the weather. Ray's had windows on three sides. Only the back was windowless, because that led into the kitchen. The design was very art deco—lots of chrome and black, which Mack had played up in the remodel.

He'd even made the interior retro—checked floor, black and silver tables, black booths with silver trim. He opened the door to the smell of frying onions, baking bread, and hundred-year-old coffee.

He felt right at home.

He took the booth in the back. To call it a booth wasn't quite fair, because the table was shaped like a kidney and had a booth on one end and chairs on the other. But it was the largest booth in the entire place, and it had the benefit of privacy—more or less. It was awfully close to the counter and the side door to the kitchen, but hardly anyone ever sat over here, and the staff rarely used that door, except when serving customers at this booth.

Mack had just settled in when Petruchio entered, followed by

Corinne and Lashon. Mack's heart stopped for a half second. He didn't see Edie. And then she walked through the door, head tilted sideways, hand near her ear.

She was on her phone.

She finished the call as the door closed behind her. Then she looked around. Clearly she had never been in here before.

Petruchio, Corinne, and Lashon had been in this diner more times than they could count. They even knew where Mack would be. They trooped over to the booth. Edie followed slowly and took a chair at the outer end of the kidney, about as far from Mack as she could get.

"Well, you're here," Mack said as they all got settled. "I take that as a good sign."

Petruchio shook his head slightly, and Edie's lips thinned. Corinne got up as Mack spoke and went behind the counter to grab a coffeepot. She poured for everyone except Edie, who put her palm over her cup.

Lashon wiped a hand over his face.

Mack didn't like the silence, but he had to endure it for a moment longer as one of the regular waitresses showed up. She pointed a pen at Mack, Corinne, and Lashon, and asked, "Late night usuals?"

Mack nodded, not wanting to think about choice at the moment. Lashon added a steak to his usual platter of eggs, and Corinne changed her order to a veggie omelet. Edie studied the menu as if she was going to be quizzed on it, and Petruchio said, "Don't I count as a regular?"

"Only if you order the same damn thing every time, honey," the waitress said, "which you do not."

And he proved it by ordering a bacon burger with cheddar. Edie got a BLT and a plate of fries. The waitress grabbed her menu and vanished through the side door to the kitchen.

Edie glanced at everyone. No one seemed to want to answer Mack's off-hand question about whether or not everything had gone well. He was about to pose it differently, when she sighed and sat up straight.

"Petruchio has been very kind since we left," she said. "He claims we got as much as we did because I played hardball in front of the press."

Corinne and Lashon both nodded, and Petruchio, who hated taking a backseat to anyone, started to speak.

Edie held up a single finger, silencing him, something Mack had never seen anyone do before.

"But," she said. "The downside to what I did is that this incident has national attention now. And that puts pressure on the cops to solve everything in a neat and tidy little bow."

"Which is good for us," Petruchio said to Mack. "They can't fit in charges against Lashon or Corinne, particularly since Edie here got the press to broadcast video of Corinne walking down the street like a comic book heroine, having captured one of the bad guys all by her little self."

"Not so little," Lashon muttered, and Corinne whacked him on his biceps with the back of her hand.

Clearly, everyone was just a bit punchy.

"It's good for us in the short term," Edie said, looking directly at Mack, "and bad for us in the long term."

It felt like she was talking to Mack, and only to him. Maybe she was. Maybe she had tried this argument with Petruchio already and lost.

"It's good for us, period," Petruchio said, confirming Mack's supposition.

Edie let out an exasperated sigh. "It's good for Lashon and Corinne. They're not going to be charged. They might end up media celebrities for a few days, but they're not going to go to jail or be investigated too heavily and maybe not even spend a day in court."

"Okay," Mack said, grabbing his cup of coffee. "That's the short term. What's the long term?"

"That neat and tidy little bow," she said. "We have one dead bad guy and one terrified bad guy, who, from what I can tell, has shit for brains. Either the mastermind is dead or we don't have every member of the conspiracy here."

Her words reminded Mack of a question he'd had earlier.

"So you shot him," Mack asked.

Edie put her hand on Lashon's arm to stop him from answering, but he still said, "No."

"They're testing the bullets." Edie's expression told Mack that she hadn't liked his question. "Remember, neat and tidy bow. If they can show that Shit For Brains shot his partner, then everything gets even easier."

"Okay," Mack said. "I got that."

"But that sniper's nest Corinne found makes a mess of that stupid bow," Edie said.

Mack was about to correct her: Corinne hadn't really found a sniper's *nest*, more like a shooter's hangout.

"Anyone could have shot from there," Edie said. "There could be a missing shooter, or several missing conspirators."

"I was searching for more people," Corinne said, "but didn't see any."

Edie nodded. She clearly had that piece of information. "So, if the police wrap up this case, and these two aren't the extent of the conspiracy, then we're in trouble."

"We, as in Santore Security?" Petruchio asked. Of course, Petruchio asked. He worked for Mack, and Mack owned Santore Security.

"We, as in Sanger House," Edie said. "We've been getting bomb threats for weeks. Then they try this, and fail."

Mack leaned back in the booth. She was right: these yahoos would come back for another round.

"I'm convinced that they're not done," she said. "If the people running this operation are smart, they'll lie low for a few weeks, maybe even a few months, but they'll be back."

He let out a small sigh. "You don't think the police will get Shit For Brains to talk?"

"I think Shit For Brains knows less about who is planning this whole thing than we do," Edie said.

Petruchio leaned back in the booth. His fingers tapped on the tabletop. He was clearly thinking.

"I don't suppose we can call in the FBI," Corinne said.

Edie started to answer her when the waitress returned with food. Mack's stomach growled in anticipation. That sandwich Edie had insisted they all eat was hours ago, and it had been the only food he had had since breakfast.

The waitress gave him the gut-buster burger he'd ordered. The first thing he always did with that pile of food was smash it down so that he could bite it.

No one else noticed what he ordered—because it was *always* what he ordered at this time of night—except Edie, whose eyebrows went up.

"Where do you put that?" she asked in a completely different voice than he had ever heard from her. Her voice was low, sexy, almost a come-on by itself.

Petruchio's eyes widened and he pretended he'd never seen her before. Then he looked over at Mack as if to get confirmation that he and Edie were a thing.

Mack pretended to ignore them both. But he was very aware of Edie. She was watching him closely, even as the waitress gave her the oversized BLT that was one of Ray's Diner's specialties.

"Oh, my God," she said. "As if Americans aren't fat enough."

Everyone laughed at that, maybe a bit too hard. But they needed some levity after the day they'd had. Then they tucked into the huge plates of food before them.

There was silence for a few minutes. Then Edie daintily wiped her mouth with a napkin.

"To answer your question," she said to Corinne, "we can let the FBI know that we have suspicions. Since this is an active investigation, though, the police should be the ones calling in the FBI."

"And if they close the investigation?" Corinne asked.

"Then we have to wait for another bomb threat or another action," Edie said.

She was right. Mack chewed, realizing that, until this moment, he hadn't tasted his food—and someone had put too much BBQ sauce on his gut-buster. He hated the tang, but ate anyway.

He swallowed and added, "I doubt we'll get a threat next time. I suspect they'll just act."

"Me, too," Edie said. "I think the only gift we get out of this is time."

"Yeah, what good will that do?" Petruchio asked.

Mack set the remains of his burger down and grabbed a french fry. He tapped it on the plate like a tiny gavel.

"It gives us a chance to investigate," he said quietly.

"Which the police expressly forbid us from doing," Petruchio said.

But Edie was smiling. Her gaze met Mack's. Her eyes were warm. She was convinced he knew what she was thinking—and he probably did.

He liked being on the same page as her.

He liked being with her.

"Are you two going to share?" Lashon asked. "Or is this where the rest of us quietly fade into the night?"

Mack broke the gaze with Edie and silently cursed Lashon.

"The four of us can't investigate," Edie said in a tone that was all business, as if Lashon hadn't spoken at all. "But Mack can."

Everyone looked at him except Lashon, who was looking at his plate, clearly embarrassed by the lapse.

"Why can Mack investigate?" Corinne asked. "He—"

"He wasn't there when the police told us not to," Edie said.

Mack grinned at her. He had been so flummoxed when she and Petruchio had asked him to leave, and it turned out to be the right decision. He would wager they had probably even planned some of this.

"But it still does us no good," Corinne said. "Investigation is not Mack's strong suit."

He scowled at her, pretending to be angry at the comment, even though it was true. She raised her eyebrows at him in silent defense.

"Yeah, I know I'm not good at investigation," Mack said. "That's why I have people."

Corinne rolled her eyes, but Edie tilted her head, clearly intrigued.

"And I'm ahead of all of you on this one. I put an investigative team on this after I left the scene this evening. Eventually, we'll catch these yahoos."

"Or we'll get enough information to interest the FBI," Petruchio said rather pointedly. He hated the cowboy aspects of Mack's business, even though he shouldn't. The cowboy side of Mack's business usually meant more money for Petruchio.

"We just have to be careful," Mack said to Corinne, as if Petruchio hadn't even spoken. "We can't let our guard down for an instant. We plan another six months on this job, minimum."

"You think it'll take that long for a return visit?" Corinne asked.

"If the masterminds are smart, yes," Mack said. "I do."

"And if they're dumb?" Corinne asked.

"The police probably have them in custody," Mack said.

Corinne grunted. She clearly didn't believe that.

"That's going to be expensive," Edie said quietly. She almost seemed to be talking to herself.

But she was right; it was going to be expensive to keep the security team on board, and Mack had already given the clinic the lowest possible rate.

"Maybe a fundraiser?" Petruchio asked. "Now would be the time. And on a national level, citing all the work the clinic does."

Then he shifted slightly in his seat, looking directly at Edie.

"The clinic does do more work than abortions, right?" he asked.

"Ga-ahd," she said with great emphasis. "Really, Petruchio? You have to ask that?"

"I don't know," he said, clearly not upset by her tone. Lashon was. He looked at her as if she was even tougher than he had imagined.

Mack leaned back. He loved watching someone take on Petruchio. So few people did.

Edie looked eager to do so. She shook a piece of bacon at Petruchio.

"Women's health," she said. "That's what Sanger House does. And some counseling for families, and a lot of work with children. *A lot.* Because women sometimes let their health go—particularly single moms—"

And she winced slightly, which only Mack seemed to notice.

"—so that they can take care of their kids' health problems first. So Sanger House does all this family stuff, and part of the family stuff includes the occasional abortion. The number of abortions have risen at Sanger House because the conservative legislatures all over the state and in nearby states have made safe and legal abortions hard to obtain. So people are driving from all over the Upper Midwest to come to our little clinic for help that the asshole legislatures have made almost impossible for them to get. *Even* when the abortion is medically necessary to save the life of the mother."

Her voice had risen. She had gotten strident. This was clearly a speech she had given before.

A few people from booths across the diner were looking at them now. Mack wanted to gesture her for her to lower her voice, but he knew, like he had known what she would say about the FBI, that she wasn't going to.

"And," she continued, glaring at Petruchio, "it's questions like that one, which make idiots like Shit For Brains decide to save the world one unborn baby at a time, by murdering existing people. Did you *know* how many children were at Sanger House this afternoon? If that bomber had decided to strike when I got there, then at least five children—five living, breathing, *happy* children—would have been injured or maybe killed."

Her voice wobbled and then broke. She gasped, and a sob emerged. She looked shocked. She put her face in her hands, pushed the chair back, and headed away from the table.

Mack was trapped behind it. He couldn't get to her.

But Corinne was up and hurrying after her. Corinne managed to steer her toward the restroom.

The entire diner was quiet for a moment. Some music—Billie Holiday, from the sounds of it—floated out from the kitchen.

Lashon had turned gray. Apparently, he hadn't realized just how close to horrid carnage they had all come.

Mack hadn't let himself think about it, not in any real way, although that moment when he had seen the pink dog had sent him into an even higher level of diligence, which, fortunately, circumstances had calmed.

But the way that Edie had searched that examine room made him realize just how involved she had truly been, even when she thought she hadn't been.

Petruchio whistled softly.

"I've known Edie since college," Petruchio said. "I've never seen her tear up before."

Here was where Mack could minimize the reaction. He could tell Petruchio that she was pregnant, and they would have that guy moment, the one where they all half-smiled about hormones and overreacting.

But she hadn't overreacted. She had searched for a child, helped Mack clear a building, defended his people, and taken care of all of them, while pregnant. She had been exceptionally strong today.

And besides, it was amazing more of his people weren't in tears. Tears were a normal reaction to stress—at least for normal, healthy people.

"I think it just became clear to all of us how close this came to complete disaster," Mack said. "If it weren't for Lashon and Corinne—"

"And you and Edie," Lashon said. "You guys cleared the building."

"Yeah," Mack said flatly. "It took a village."

He almost made a comment about singing Kumbaya, but didn't. Because that would minimize too.

Still, he didn't like the attention.

"We were lucky," he said. "And that's all we were."

Petruchio shook his head. "I'll see what I can do to get the cops to call in the FBI."

"Don't," Edie said. She had come back from the bathroom, Corinne at her shoulder. Edie's face was pale, her eyes red-rimmed. She looked younger now that she had washed off her makeup, less iron-lady, more overwhelmed girl-woman.

"You're right," Petruchio said. "I was insensitive, and this could be bad. It will be bad, at some point—"

"You're a defense attorney," Edie said. "The police will fight you. They'll think you want the FBI because Corinne is guilty of something, not because it's the smart play."

She sat back down. So did Corinne.

Mack stared at her. Edie was brilliant. She seemed to see problems from all sides. He knew that's what lawyers did, but most were only effective in some areas.

She seemed to see *all* the areas.

Petruchio must have seen the surprised admiration on Mack's face. Petruchio leaned a little closer.

"This was why she was first in our law school class." Petruchio spoke in a mock whisper, pretending to have a guy-bonding moment with Mack, but really, wanting Edie and everyone else to hear as well. "Moot court, every damn thing that they threw at us—Edie got through it all with flying colors. The rest of us, we fell apart."

"You did not," Edie said. She was eyeing her food as if it was going to hurt her.

"We did," he said. "We all watched you and wished we could be you."

"Stop," she said curtly.

Petruchio's lips went up in the corner. He had clearly been goading her, and he was happy that he had succeeded.

She poked at her sandwich, then sighed and made herself start again. Mack wondered if she was queasy on top of everything else.

Petruchio grabbed his coffee cup. He hadn't touched it before. It seemed to be a sign that he was going to be serious again.

"So," he said to her, "you're looking at six months or more of added security at the clinic."

Edie nodded tiredly.

"And," Petruchio said, "I'll wager that Mack here has already given you a break on price."

"That's confidential," Mack said as Corinne said, "'Break' is probably an understatement. He's the official bleeding heart."

Lashon kept his head down. He knew better than to get involved in this conversation.

Edie looked up at all of them. Apparently she hadn't known that the team teased Mack for undercharging for security all the time, particularly with groups who really needed it.

"So here's what I suggest," Petruchio said. "You do a fundraiser for Sanger House—"

Edie let out a moan that was a no all by itself.

Petruchio held up a hand, stopping her this time. "Hear me out."

"No," she said. "People always suggest fundraisers, and they have no idea what they're talking about. You lose a third of the money for all the gala stuff, even when most items are donated, not to mention the time—"

"And the target-rich environment," Mack said.

Edie grew even paler. Apparently she hadn't thought of that part.

He hated fund-raisers. They were big *attack-me* signs, at least in his business.

And besides, he felt a little protective of her. She looked too tired to take on any more.

"I wasn't talking about an in-person fundraiser," Petruchio said. "I know how hard those things are. I was talking about online. You have the nation's attention. Let the nation donate. They will."

"Sounds wonderful," Edie said, "and I'll present it to Ruth, but I'll be honest, we don't have anyone who can set that up, especially right now."

"I do," Petruchio said. "I have a guy who does website work. If you let me, I'll set it up."

"Guilty conscience?" Mack asked.

"Hell, yes," Petruchio said. "I'm a defense attorney."

And that made everyone smile.

15

The conversation swirled around Edie. Somewhere in the middle of the computer and online discussion, she had lost track of what was being said.

It was after midnight, and she had been up since seven, obsessing about the possible (actual) pregnancy. And then she had gotten up, and taken the test, and been in turmoil ever since. And all of that was *before* she had gone to the clinic.

She finished most of the BLT, even though she had initially thought it too big for her. Maybe this eating-for-two hunger thing was real. More likely, though, she was responding to all the stress.

The stress was coming out in a thousand different ways tonight. Taking on Petruchio like she did, that was uncalled for. She knew that Petruchio's politics and hers were almost diametrically opposed, and for that reason, she rarely brought up politics when talking to him.

She loved him like an annoying brother, and she didn't want to lose him over political campaigns and the fact that he believed every stupid thing that came across Fox News. (She thought that embarrassing for a member of the bar, and said that to him just once. He had glared at her and said, *Not everyone has time to study the political issues of the day as if preparing for Professor Sim's Constitutional History Final.* And that was when she realized just what a touchy subject politics was for both of them, and decided not to bring it up again. Whoops.)

The political discussion wasn't the real problem though. The political discussion had simply led her to the worst moment she'd had in years, concerning her self-control.

High-powered attorneys did not burst into tears at a diner in the middle of the night while staring at the world's largest BLT. High-powered attorneys did not burst into tears when taking on the police who were stupidly charging two heroes with interfering with law enforcement—and whatever other charges they could think of.

High-powered attorneys did not burst into tears when talking to the best-looking man they had seen in years.

High-powered attorneys did not burst into tears.

Period.

And then she almost smiled to herself. That *period* was the problem. Or rather, the lack of a period.

"You okay?" Corinne asked her.

Edie suddenly realized that everyone was staring at her. And Mack— the best-looking man she'd seen in years—was looking at her as if he would have to haul her to the hospital at any minute.

Damn Ruth for telling him Edie was pregnant. Not that it would have made a difference.

If only she could have met him months ago.

And then what? She would have jumped his bones instead of Bert Collins, and she wouldn't be pregnant, but she probably wouldn't have seen him again, and—

"Yes," she said quietly to Corinne. "I'm just tired. The day is catching up to me."

"To all of us," Mack said warmly. Edie loved the timbre of his voice.

Petruchio looked at the Patek Philippe watch he had bought after his first big win. *Extravagance 'R Us,* she had said to him when he had showed it to her so that she would do the proper amount of fawning. (She rarely did the proper amount of fawning.)

"Great," he said. "It's almost midnight."

"What happens at midnight, Cinderella?" she asked.

He gave her a fond and yet somehow withering look. "I have pretrial motion tomorrow at nine, and a deposition before that, not to mention a business breakfast, which I hope to God I can change."

He slid out of the booth, and as he did, everyone else stirred too. He looked across the table at Mack. "Call me if there's more I have to do."

"*When* there's more," Mack said.

"I hope there won't be," Lashon said as he searched around his plate for the check. He was going to keep looking in vain. Edie had seen Mack pocket the check the moment the waitress had set it down.

Edie stood as well, and pushed her chair in so that Corinne could get up. Edie stepped back so that she wasn't in the way of the group as they finished the conversations and said their good-byes.

God, she was tired. The fatigue had been her first clue that something had changed inside her body. Because, just a few weeks ago, she'd been able to go nonstop on four hours of sleep and not feel tired at all the next day.

Right now, her legs felt like jelly and her brain was slowly turning into mush.

She groped for her purse, found it on the back of the chair, and felt one small measure of relief for the first time in a while over what her very last boyfriend (years ago) had called her "purse fetish." At least she had money, an extra credit card, and a secondary phone.

She just hoped that cabs would come to this neighborhood. They usually avoided anything south of the river.

"Let me give you a ride home," said a voice in her ear. Mack's voice. It sent a delightful shiver through her.

"It's all right," she said. "I can get a cab. You have to be back to work early tomorrow as well."

"I'll bet you do too," he said. "You just don't strike me as the kind of person who uses her busy-ness as a badge of honor."

He was right beside her, his shoulder inches from hers. She could feel his body heat and the slight tang of the soap he had used that morning.

She smiled slightly. "Then you don't know me very well. I am probably the busiest person I know."

"And you don't brag about it, like other excellent attorneys I know." He looked past her at Petruchio, who was arguing with the cashier. Mack smiled ever so slightly.

"You could tell them that you already paid the check," she said.

"And spoil the fun?" he asked.

She chuckled, in spite of herself.

Petruchio looked over from across the room, saw them both smiling, and then smiled himself. He mouthed *thank you*, and headed out the door. Corinne and Lashon followed.

"I can drive you home," Mack said.

"That's all right," Edie said. "I'll call a cab, and you can go home and get some sleep."

"I'd sleep better if I knew you weren't waiting here for a cab that might not show." His words reinforced her worry about the neighborhood.

She hated the way that certain parts of the city were considered just too dangerous for "ordinary folk." Especially when real ordinary folk lived in those parts of the city and managed to do just fine.

She sighed slightly. She didn't know this man, but Ruth did. And Edie trusted Ruth.

Heck, Edie trusted herself. Mack had set off none of her warning bells, and had she met him on one of her "fun" nights, she would have had no qualms getting a hotel room with him.

Hell, she would have no qualms now either.

She smiled at him. "All right, especially since I don't even have to tell you where we're going."

He nodded, then swept a hand forward, indicating that she go first. She did, grabbing her coat as she went. She started to slide it on when she realized the movement had just gotten a lot easier.

She looked over her shoulder to find him helping by holding up the coat like a gentleman. She wanted to chide him—maybe say something about pregnant women could put on coats—but she didn't want to call attention to the pregnancy anymore.

She didn't want to think about it anymore.

"Thank you," she said.

"No problem," he said, grabbing his own coat.

She led the way to the door, then stopped. "I have no idea where you parked," she said. "So you get to go first."

"Fair enough." He opened the door and let in air so cold that she was afraid her entire body would turn to ice in an instant. He held the door for her, then made sure he walked ahead of her into the parking lot.

"Careful," he said. "Black ice."

He held out his hand. She took it, startled to find his fingers warm. He hadn't put on any gloves. Neither had she, and her hands had frozen the moment the cold air had hit them.

Weirdly, she remembered his touch from earlier in the day—the strong fingers, the calluses, the only-half-casual grip.

He led her across the parking lot. He wasn't kidding about the black ice. The lot looked like it had been shoveled bare, but the late-night cold combined with some kind of moisture in the air had caused an extra, almost impossible-to-see coating to cover everything.

His black SUV looked like a military vehicle in the dark. The SUV chirruped and its lights blinked on and off as he unlocked the doors. Then he opened the passenger side and helped her into the seat.

She was grateful, even though she probably could have climbed in herself. It was a measure of just how tired she was that she was able to accept help without complaint.

The vehicle was cold and smelled faintly of leather, something she hadn't noticed that afternoon. She leaned her head back against the headrest and closed her eyes for just a moment.

He got in, shaking the SUV as he did, and then it started, humming to life like the high-end machine that it was. No radio kicked on, though, like it would have in her car. She had noticed earlier that Mack's vehicle seemed oddly impersonal, and it did even more so now.

But he drove it as if he and the SUV were old friends.

"You really think this whole thing we experienced today is a conspiracy?" Mack asked.

"Yeah." She rubbed her cold fingers over her face. Her cheeks were warm but the tip of her nose was ice cold. "I got to meet Shit For Brains briefly. He really is dumb. And there was nothing in the lead-up to all this that suggested anyone involved was that stupid."

Mack sighed. She could see his breath, even though the SUV's heater had kicked on mighty fast.

"I thought the incident today wrapped up too easily," he said. "Will you remain on board for Corinne?"

Edie nodded tiredly. "If I can."

"What do you mean?" Mack asked. "I thought her case was mostly settled."

"It is mostly settled," Edie said. "But if something else happens, then I don't know. My body has a big surprise planned for me right around Labor Day. And don't think I haven't already noticed the pun."

He was silent for a long moment. She wondered if she should have brought up the pregnancy and then decided, screw it. The pregnancy was now part of her life, and he was asking about the future.

"What does the baby's father think of all this?" he asked quietly.

A natural question, she supposed. And she could skip over it if she wanted to. There was an easy, political answer—something along the lines of *He's not too thrilled* or *We haven't had much of a chance to discuss it.*

Something about this man driving the SUV made her want to be honest with him. Maybe it was the strong attraction she felt. Maybe it was just the fact that he seemed like a good and decent human being. Or maybe it was just that she needed someone other than Ruth to talk to.

"The baby's father." Edie sighed. "He's a piece of work."

Mack swung his head toward her, startling her with the suddenness of the movement. "Is he violent? Will he hurt you?"

"No, no," she said. "Not like that."

Then she pressed her lips together. She had changed her mind. Mack didn't need to know after all.

"Like what, then?" he asked.

She let out a small sigh. "The only way I can tell you is to give you too much information."

He was quiet for a moment, as he turned the SUV onto one of the better lit streets leading out of the neighborhood.

"I'm willing to listen if you're willing to share," he said after a moment.

She nodded, just once. She was willing to share, and yet she was embarrassed about it.

"We—um—he was a one-night stand," she said. "And after the condom broke, I assured him that we had nothing to worry about because I was on the pill."

Mack's face, illuminated in the much-better lighting in her neighborhood, remained impassive.

"And I really believed that," she said. "I was on the pill. I—we—were using the condom for protection against diseases, not for birth control."

He made a small noise. She took it as an acknowledgement. Or maybe he was uncomfortable with the way the conversation was going. Or maybe he didn't believe her either. She wasn't sure.

"You see," she said, because she had to justify this to someone, "Ruth tells me that no birth control is 100 percent effective and that there are people who are part of that small percentage whose birth control fails. People like me."

Mack glanced at her. She couldn't read his expression.

But she had started into this, so she might as well finish it.

"Anyway," she said. "I called him two days ago and said there was a really good chance I might be pregnant—"

"You didn't know for sure?" Mack asked.

"I did know for sure," she said. "But I was hoping I was one of that small percentage of women for whom the home pregnancy test failed as well. But, no, I'm not."

He made a small, sympathetic sound.

"So," she said, "I called him, and told him that there was a really good chance I might be pregnant, and he said he *knew* it. Women like me only existed to take advantage of him, and he wasn't going to be taken advantage of. He said I lied to him, and I would get to pay for that lie. I reminded him that we, um, were both at fault for the situation, and he said I could have taken care of it with the morning after pill if I had just listened to him."

"Nice guy," Mack muttered.

"Oh, it gets better," she said. "I was attributing his reaction to shock, so I said we could talk later, and he said the only conversation we would have later was when and where I'd get the abortion. I said I wasn't sure I wanted one, and he said that if I chose to have a child, that child would be 100 percent mine, and all he would ever do, no matter how hard I tried to screw him, was pay for the procedure. He would have his lawyer send over papers to that effect. If I wanted to gold-dig someone, I could gold-dig someone else. He was prepared to stop women like me. So I did the adult thing. I hung up on him."

"Jesus," Mack said as the SUV pulled in front of her building. "Where did you meet this guy?"

She could avoid answering him altogether now. And she wanted to, because this was the part that embarrassed her. Not the conversation with Collins. Not the fact that she actually got pregnant.

The way she had been living.

She knew how it sounded.

Before she could say anything, even if it was just to deflect his question, he said, "It looks like there's more black ice," he said. "Let me walk you to the door."

He was coddling her because of the baby. But she didn't entirely care.

"Okay," she said.

He pulled into one of the open parking areas and then shut off the SUV. He got out, came around, and helped her down. It wasn't that far to her door, but he had a firm grip on her elbow the entire way.

His touch sent those same shivers through her. It had been a horrid day, and it would be a horrid night.

She would be alone with her thoughts.

Maybe she could get him to stay. She wasn't really his employer. She had nothing to do with his hire. And she didn't work for him either, not with the legal case. Corinne was her client.

He knew she was pregnant, and now he knew the father wasn't in the picture. Maybe she could convince him that she wasn't trying to entrap him either. Because she wouldn't be.

It was just pretty simple for her: most people drank to forget or relax. She used sex. And she didn't have a car tonight.

She couldn't go back out.

"Look," she said, "I'm tired, but wired at the same time. Would you like to come in for a nightcap?"

"You can't drink," he said, with just a touch of judgment.

"I promise to drink only fresh juice," she said. "But I can make you something."

He paused, as if he couldn't quite decide, and then he nodded once.

"All right," he said. "One drink."

She unlocked the door and stepped inside. She had left all the lights on. Their half-eaten feast still sat on her kitchen island, the cheese adding its own special funk to the air. She tossed her purse and coat in the closet, then indicated the couch.

"Have a seat," she said, and turned on the gas fireplace. She cleaned off the island, mostly by scraping the spoiling food into her trash compactor, and then opened the fridge to get herself the recommended orange juice. "What would you like? I still have a lot of booze here."

"Whatever you're having," he said.

"I'm having orange juice. Would you like a little vodka or gin in yours? Or something else...?"

"Orange juice is fine." He was sitting gingerly on the edge of the couch, looking at the blue and gold flames rising out of the fireplace's white rock surface.

She poured them both some of the so-called fresh squeezed she had bought at the market the day before, and handed him his.

She wrapped her hand around hers and sat across from him in the overstuffed chair she rarely used.

"So how did you meet this piece of work?" Mack asked again. Apparently he wasn't going to let that go.

She shook her head ever so slightly. She wondered if telling him would make him easier to seduce or if the pregnancy had already taken everything off the table.

But he asked. And he would want to know, especially if he slept with her tonight. Better to tell him now.

She let out a small sigh. "You ever hear of Tinder?"

His mouth opened ever so slightly. "That swiping app? The one that tells you who in the neighborhood is looking for a hook-up? Isn't that dangerous?"

She shrugged one shoulder. "You can control for risk," she said. "If that interests you."

He stared at her. Her cheeks were hot. She was probably the color of a tomato by now.

"I...I'm not going to apologize for it," she said. "I have a high stress job and rather than drink myself into oblivion or do drugs or something like that to decompress, I..."

She wasn't sure how to finish that sentence. She'd never said it out loud before. *I meet men for casual sex. A really good screw takes my mind off work for a little while anyway.*

But she couldn't say that to him. Instead, she said, "I don't like complications, so I prefer to hook up."

"But you had this man's name," he said.

"That's one of my conditions," she said. "They have to give me their real name. I tell them I'm a lawyer and I can check everything on the spot, and believe me, that chases half the men away. The rest—they're looking for the same thing I am. A few hours of..."

She almost said *comfort*, but most of her hook-ups had nothing to do with comfort and everything to do with mindlessness. For an hour or so, she was just a body, doing things with her mind shut off. Completely off. And she usually liked that.

She'd like it now, but she wasn't sure she wanted to tell him, not with the expression he had on his face. He looked shocked and hurt, somehow.

"Anyway," she said. "I met him like that. So it's no surprise he thinks I changed the rules of the game."

"So," Mack said a little more quickly than she would have expected, "are you going to keep the baby?"

What an odd question to ask next. She wasn't sure why it was his concern?

And his phrasing startled her. She hadn't really thought of what was happening with her body as *the baby.* She thought of it as *the pregnancy.* *The baby* was a little too real for her right now.

The pregnancy was young—only a few weeks old. Probably not even enough to show up on those sonogram tests that everyone ended up pasting to their refrigerators as *My baby's first picture.*

The orange juice threatened to come back up. Heartburn. Pure heartburn.

"Am I going to...?" She couldn't even finish the question. "I'm not having an abortion, if that's what you're asking."

"Why not?" he asked, his voice oddly dispassionate. "It would make things easier for you."

"In theory," she said. "In practice, it's just hard in a different way. I've helped a lot of women through theirs. It's hard. Hard in a way that I don't want to experience. *I* don't want. It's right for other women, at times. It might even be right for me years from now. But right now, I'm exercising my right to choose, by choosing not to."

He didn't nod or move. His gaze was on hers.

He was almost acting as if it was his child, not someone else's. Or maybe she was just misreading him.

Given how tired she was, she was probably misreading him.

She had probably been misreading him all day.

Damn hormones.

"Look," she said. "I know I have a lot of options, even with abortion off the table. And I know people who can help me."

She said that to forestall anything more in this conversation. She wanted to change the subject. She wanted to touch him, and have him touch her.

She had a hunch that wasn't going to happen now.

"Raising a child alone is hard," he said, as if he knew.

"Are you married?" she asked, because it was a better question than *do you have kids?* As a childless person, she hated that question. Because it was always filled with judgment.

Do you have kids? Because if you don't, you have no idea what I—we—our family is going through.

"No," Mack said. "I'm not married. And before you ask, I don't have kids. My mom was a single parent. I was the oldest. My father was a son-of-a-bitch who left all of us. Mom was a teacher, and she made okay money, but it was unbelievably hard on her. On us."

He said that last so softly she almost missed it.

"I know." Edie sipped the orange juice. It tasted a little bitter. But she hadn't been able to trust her taste buds for the last few weeks either. They were giving her all kinds of mixed messages. "There's adoption too. I've thought of that a few times. It's just—I'm such a control freak. I might spend the rest of my life wondering if I had given the baby to the wrong people."

He nodded, just a little. "You have to trust."

"Yeah, that's going to work," she said and stood. "I'm a lawyer. We're trained to trust no one. Ever. And I was good at not trusting *before* I went to law school."

She went into the kitchen, poured the orange juice down the sink, and rinsed her glass. Then she stood with her palms braced on the stainless steel lip.

"The question is," she said to the faucet, "am I going to be a better parent than someone who actively wants a child? I've helped the clinic with locating adoption services. The good ones vet every single couple that comes through the door. And they're all couples. Any kid I keep will just have me. Any kid I give away will have two parents—at least at the start."

Mack didn't respond again. Damn, that man could use silence as a weapon.

Her cheeks were still warm. She had really embarrassed herself, confiding in him. He now knew a goodly number of her secrets, and she knew none of his.

She turned around. He was staring at the fire again.

She still wanted to seduce him, but she couldn't figure out how it would work. How strange for her. She usually knew how to handle herself around men.

Honesty would work. Probably. Something like, *Look, I invited you in here because I was thinking of jumping your bones. No strings attached.*

But she was getting the sense he wasn't that kind of man.

Getting the sense. Yeah, right. She *knew* he wasn't that kind of man. The way he had looked when she said Tinder, the fact that she had gone down a measure in his estimation.

She didn't like that. She liked being the best at everything she did, being the best person, at least according to all her friends.

And this—this revealed her for the fraud she was.

She looked at his broad shoulders, at the muscles running down his arms. If she put her hand on those muscles ever so lightly, then asked him if he wanted another drink, he would probably get the message.

But that felt wrong too.

So, instead, she sat back down in her chair.

"They're my problems," she said. "I'll figure it out."

He raised his head, his gaze meeting hers. His expression was vulnerable, his eyes soft. The attraction was back, and it hummed between them.

Then he stood, cutting it all off as if it had never been.

He held up the orange juice as if he were going to make a toast.

"Thanks for this," he said.

She didn't stand. She didn't need to. He was making himself very clear.

He walked the three steps it took to get to the island and set the glass on that. Then he headed to the door.

He stopped just as he put his hand on the doorknob.

"You'll figure this out," he said softly. "You're one brilliant lady. You'll figure out what's best for everyone."

She nodded. There was nothing she could say to get him to stay. Nothing she could say that would allow her to respect herself in the morning.

Especially since it was clear she had destroyed any respect he might have had for her.

"Thank you," she said. "And thank you for driving me home."

"My pleasure." His voice rumbled, and she felt that attraction again. God, she loved hearing him talk. She wanted to be his pleasure. She wanted to share pleasure and show him pleasure.

She threaded her hands together.

"Good night," he said, and let himself out the door. It snicked closed behind him.

She didn't move until she heard the SUV start. The lights illuminated her window shades for just a second as he backed out of the parking spot.

And then he drove away.

How ironic. She had finally met a man she liked, one she wanted to talk to as well as screw, one who felt like an equal, who had an interesting job, and who seemed quite kind, and the life she had led until this day had made him think less of her.

It made her think less of herself.

She'd been going through the days mindlessly, performing her best for her clients, doing great work for everyone and then coming home here, where the loneliness ate at her. Ruth had said to volunteer, to give herself time, to trust that she would meet someone, and Edie had said she didn't need to meet anyone. She could go it alone.

She never planned on marriage, never thought she would have a family, never really wanted anything except her career.

She still wanted that career.

And she wasn't sure how to have it—and the baby—without changing everything.

She stood up, swaying with exhaustion. Maybe she would be able to sleep after all.

Maybe there were benefits to the fatigue that had been plaguing her with all these physical changes.

She grabbed her phone, set the alarm, and headed upstairs, hoping sleep wouldn't elude her this night.

Because Mack already had.

16

*S*he had put him in a terrible position.

Mack drove carefully down dark, ice-covered streets. The streetlights only worked on the corners in his neighborhood—if then. Not for the first time, he wondered at his own sanity: building a business and rehabbing a historic home and all without the right amount of capitalization. He had enough money to get through the next two months without selling something or getting a big job, and with all of his people on the Santore House matter, he didn't have enough personnel for the big job.

He certainly had more than enough to worry about. He didn't have time for a relationship. And yet, he had found himself considering one as he looked at Edie across that table in the diner tonight.

And then she told him how she got pregnant.

To say he was surprised was an understatement. He was shocked. He had thought he had seen everything—and nothing could shock him.

But she had.

She made him question his own preconceptions.

He knew that dating apps, particularly the swipe-and-fuck apps as Aldis called them, deliberately derisively, existed. Mack had just assumed that the people who used them were young twenty-somethings at their first jobs straight out of college, or losers who had no other choice.

He had no idea that a highly competent attorney—one of the best he'd ever seen—would routinely use the app for casual sex.

Which wasn't exactly true. He wouldn't be nearly as shocked if the attorney were a man. In fact, he knew a lot of high functioning professional men who did exactly what Edie had been doing. He'd worked security for some of those men and advised them to stop the behavior because it was dangerous.

Not physically dangerous the way he would think it was for a woman, but dangerous in other ways, opening the men up to blackmail, fraud, and theft.

Surely, Edie was smart enough to consider all of that.

He smiled ruefully to himself. He had no idea that double standard existed inside of him. He thought he was a very open-minded man when it came to women and their capabilities. He believed he wasn't bigoted about women at all. And yet he was judging Edie much more harshly than he would judge any of his male friends in a similar situation.

He turned the SUV onto his block. The entire block was dark. The single working streetlight was at the other end of the block from his house, which was also dark. He'd learned that if he kept his porch light on, it was an invitation to theft.

Three Fires had once been one of the largest cities in the entire country. A hundred years ago, it was *the* city in the Midwest, the place where everyone wanted to go. It grew and grew and grew, with more and more industry coming in. Then, fifty years ago, the industries shuttered, many of them moving overseas at the same time that white flight occurred because the civil rights movement made it impossible for whites to exclude people of color from their neighborhoods any longer.

Add to that the early 1970s oil crisis, and Three Fires's urban landscape resembled a ghost town. The gorgeous mansions of his grandmother's day had become ruins, filled with squatters.

Not that his grandmother had ever lived in any of these houses. The people who lived in these houses would have thought her only worthy of cleaning them, even though she was a doctor's wife who raised five children and sent them all to the best universities in the region.

He bristled with anger every time he thought of things like that. Only he had a hunch the anger he felt tonight had nothing to do with the history of his neighborhood and everything to do with the woman he had spent time with this evening.

His house was a six-thousand-square-foot Victorian marvel that resembled a mini-castle. He had fallen in love with it as a boy and had even played in its ruined first floor. His mother would have been appalled to learn that, because the floor boards were rotted, the roof was caving in, and the man who squatted in the place during those years had some kind of mental illness that made him unpredictably violent.

Mack now suspected that man had been a Vietnam vet and had PTSD. When Mack tried to trace him, all those years later, he couldn't. No one even remembered him, except as the crazy smelly guy who once lived at "the palace."

Mack used the garage door opener and pulled the SUV into the garage. It had once been a carriage house, large enough for two carriages. One wall had been falling in when he bought the place and so he replaced it at the same dimensions, deciding that a one-car garage would do him just fine.

He'd also added a shop and heat, for nights just like this one, so that his engine block wouldn't freeze in the ridiculous cold.

He closed the garage door without getting out of the SUV. He rubbed his hand over his face.

He couldn't get her out of his mind. He had seen so many sides to her today: that fierce and frightened woman searching for the child in the exam room. The competent woman who helped him clear the building. The brilliant attorney who took apart a poor cop in a matter of moments and suggested a national media narrative, all while wearing borrowed clothing and looking like a lost child. The passionate advocate who burst into tears at the dinner table.

The flustered pregnant woman who wasn't sure where her future lay. And the flushed, defensive woman who confessed to using sex as recreation and nothing more.

He found all of those women attractive, all of them intriguing, and all of them desirable.

But the last one, the one who had confessed to sexual habits that made him realize what a prude he was, she confounded him.

Because he would have taken her hand once they got inside her townhouse. He would have stared at that fire with her, arm around her, holding her close, comforting both of them.

He would have kissed her ever so gently and spoken of tomorrow— if she hadn't just told him about her Tinder history.

He was thinking, as he stared into that fire alone, that anything he did after that confession would reflect poorly on him. If he touched her, she might have thought he was taking advantage of her vulnerability and her sexual history.

If he told her he found her attractive, she might think all he wanted was a one-night stand.

And if he told her that she intrigued him, she probably would have dismissed him.

That was what he had been thinking then. Now, though, he was wondering if he had simply been making excuses.

He had been shaken by her, down to his very core. Shaken by her pregnancy, shaken by her courage, shaken by her sexual history.

He had no real sexual history, not like that. He had slept with five women in his life—his high school girlfriend for the entire summer before college; his two college girlfriends; and the woman he lived with for four years, the woman he thought he was going to marry.

And when they broke up, he had his one and only one-night stand. He remembered every bit about that experience—how erotic it had seemed at first, and then, midway through as she screamed and scratched and moaned her way through their encounter, how empty it felt. His body helped him through it, but as she slipped out of bed to use the bathroom, he got up and got dressed. He hadn't wanted her to see how disgusted he felt—not at her, but at himself.

He had been celibate for five years now. He'd dated, but he never wanted to feel like that again, like a man who used someone else simply to fulfill his needs, not to have a mutual relationship. So he waited.

He hadn't exactly been saving himself, but he hadn't been in a hurry either.

Except tonight. Tonight, he would have considered it. Before their talk,

He opened the door out of the garage. The garage on this property had been a standalone, but he had built a breezeway between it and the house. Even though he had remembered to heat the garage, he had not remembered to heat the breezeway, so the cold hit him like a slap in the face.

Everything had been a slap in the face tonight. Including—or maybe most especially—his own thoughts.

He let himself into the house. The kitchen was warm, the light over the stove comforting. He had remodeled the kitchen and the bathrooms before he moved in, knowing those were the most disruptive remodels, and he was glad he had. Because this kitchen made him feel like a king every time he walked into it.

It was square, with custom cabinets and a matching table in the center of the room. The appliances were white, which meant they glowed in the half-light, along with the farm sink.

He hadn't eaten much more than breakfast here in almost a week, and he felt the loss. He also realized, as he stood in the darkness, how much more he liked this kitchen than that open-concept, marble and gray metal kitchen that was in Edie's townhouse.

The entire place was very modern and impersonal, the kind of design he'd seen on a hundred different design shows. Yet it had suited her. When she came down the stairs in her business attire, she looked like a powerful woman who belonged in that home.

Of course she had.

He let out a small breath. That alone should have told him that his reaction to her had little to do with them, and everything to do with the events of the day. The adrenalin, the survival, the moments of sheer terror. Going through those things with someone was an aphrodisiac.

He'd know that forever. He'd seen it at his job and when he was in the military. People slept together when they were celebrating being alive.

He grabbed a glass from the cabinet near the sink and poured himself some water.

Then he leaned forward just a little, his reflection showing ghostly in the window overlooking the back yard.

If all that were true—if he only wanted her because she was pretty as well as his partner in survival—then the attraction would slowly fade. It should have faded when she told him her history.

And it hadn't.

If anything, her vulnerability made him want her more.

And he had fled. Of course, he had fled. She wasn't going to be a one-night stand for him. And that would be all he would be to her.

So he was protecting his heart.

Because he knew, deep down, if he had asked some all-powerful being to create the perfect woman for him, she would be brilliant and beautiful and tough and vulnerable and passionate and a little bit wounded, all at the same time.

She would be a lot like Edie Bayette.

Hell, she probably was Edie Bayette.

And he had no idea what to do about it.

17

*P*etruchio Jones hadn't been the only one with early morning meetings and a deposition from hell. Edie's started at 8:00 a.m. At least she managed to avoid the breakfast meeting, because she probably would have spent the morning puking.

Either the stress had attacked her cast-iron stomach or the morning sickness decided to rear its ugly little head. She ate a lovely breakfast, then wasted it before she ever left the townhouse.

She took Ruth's admonition for nutrition to heart, however, and when the nausea finally fled, around 10:00, Edie ate some kind of breakfast sandwich that her secretary picked up for her.

Good thing, too, given the tenor of the morning. Petruchio hadn't called his morning the morning from hell, but Edie had known going in that her morning would be.

The woman Ruth wanted Edie to see had backed out of coming to the clinic, but somehow Ruth had convinced the woman to meet Edie at the law office. Edie had spent the first half hour of her morning with a terribly nervous, completely frightened woman who was afraid to go near Sanger House after what happened the day before, although she agreed with the plan: have the abortion now.

Edie drove her to one of the nearby hospitals, where Ruth had admitting privileges. The procedure would happen there instead of Sanger House. Unusual, yes, but the woman felt safe enough, and when Edie left, Ruth was talking the woman into going to one of the women's shelters in town. Ruth promised to help her get in.

Edie had no idea how Ruth managed to be so warm and kind, considering the stress she'd gone through the day before and probably was still going through.

But Edie had felt compassion as well. That woman had been terrified. Edie, at least, wasn't in that circumstance.

And she had other things to think about, like the way that the Three Fires Police Department had treated Lashon Jackson. He didn't want to file a lawsuit, but she thought he had a case.

She also had to make sure they weren't going to charge him with anything. They seemed pretty angry that Jackson had done their job for them.

All of that came out of yesterday, and she still had other cases to deal with, bread-and-butter cases for the law firm.

So by the time lunch rolled around, what she wanted was a nap, and what she had to do was get her purse, her phone, and her car, so that she could function like a normal human being again.

Besides, she wanted to know what was going on at Sanger House on the day after.

She trusted Mack and Ruth to get rid of the crime scene tape. Or, she figured, someone would have called her. She had left their names with her secretary along with instructions that she be interrupted should anyone call.

No one had.

So, she bamboozled a cab driver into taking her to Sanger House. She had had troubles with cab drivers taking her to that neighborhood before, and she had worked up a system. She got in the cab, gave an exclusive downtown address, then searched her purse for a moment, swore, and said, *I'm sorry. I've changed my mind. I need to go to Sanger House. Do you know where that is?*

She always said "Sanger House" because it sounded much more legitimate than the clinic's address. A handful of cabbies knew where it was. Most didn't. None had balked once she was in the cab, although several bitched about the change in direction or let her know that they usually didn't go into the neighborhood.

This guy, who smelled faintly of vinegar and clove cigarettes, had merely grunted, turned his cab around, and driven the shortest route to the clinic.

Bully for him. Clearly, that meant he wanted her out of his cab. He'd take her there quickly and get out just as quickly.

The sky was overcast again—early February in Three Fires was always unpleasant, but this week was even more so. The gunmetal gray sky, the occasional ice sleet, the temperatures so cold that they set her teeth on edge.

This morning, she had given up and put on a black wool suit that made her look like she was trying to impersonate all the male attorneys at the courthouse. At least the suit kept her legs warm. The skirt she wore yesterday had been a mistake.

As she slipped on some high heel dress boots before leaving the townhouse, she actually heard Mack's voice in her head, chiding her for her impractical shoes.

She had mentally answered him in the same tone, saying the chances of being in a crisis situation two days in a row were between slim and none.

At least for her. Maybe that was how he lived his life.

As the cab headed toward Sanger House, she wondered if he would still be there. It was unusual—she thought—for the guy who owned the company to be manning the metal detectors at the front door of a women's health clinic.

But what did she know?

Well, a little more than she had the day before, because she had Googled him over breakfast. Mack Santore was one of those decorated military types who had come back to civilian life with a vengeance. He had started Santore Security, he said in one interview with the *Detroit Free Press*, to give people with government-given skills the best jobs they could possibly have.

It was code, she realized, for people with military training who, for one reason or another, couldn't or wouldn't get hired anywhere else.

In an interview with the *Chicago Sun-Times*, he had been a little clearer, saying that he preferred former military to ex-cops because former military had a sense of honor.

She wondered what was behind that statement, which bristled with animosity.

He had given no interviews to the local paper, even though the *Three Fires Telegram* was just as big a paper as the other two. Santore Security was often in the news here, though, and everyone seemed to treat it with kid gloves.

And when Mack Santore showed up at one or two fundraisers, usually for vet projects, it made the news because he was considered one of Three Fires's most eligible bachelors.

Maybe if she had spent her time at society functions, she would have known that.

But she hadn't.

She'd spent her scarce free time in upscale hotel bars, meeting men she hoped to never see again.

She sighed and felt her cheeks warm, again. The cab turned onto the block leading to the clinic, and she rubbed a hand against her face. At least the street was not full of police or ambulances or TV satellite vans this afternoon. There was one unmarked police car parked haphazardly in front of Sanger House's parking lot, which was empty.

One of the crime lab vans was parked behind the building, and techs, in their white suits, looked like ghosts against the gray sky. Another car was parked near the front door, and Edie thought she caught a glimpse of Corinne inside it.

Lashon was walking the sidewalk, helping a very pregnant woman across the ice. That probably wasn't in his job description, but it warmed Edie nonetheless.

It meant that the clinic was open, and even though the day was clearly an unusual one, business was proceeding as usual.

She paid the cab driver and got out, wrapping her heavy dress coat around her. Her leather gloves kept her hands warm, but she wasn't wearing anything on her head. She hated messing her hair, but more than that, she hated that tight feeling around her skull.

She was a hot mess these days, and it was only getting worse.

Someone wearing a Santore Security uniform watched her from the trees. None of the crime scene techs noticed her. She couldn't see inside that car where she had thought she had seen Corinne, and the police car was empty.

Weirdly, her stomach clenched at that thought, and she hoped that she wouldn't have afternoon sickness on top of everything else.

She made herself take a deep breath of the ice-cold air. It felt like little needles heading down her lungs. Her heart was pounding. She was rather astonished to realize going back to the clinic was scaring her.

The events from the day before had had more of an effect on her than she realized. She usually liked going into the clinic and seeing the families, the women who found just a little bit of hope at a difficult time, the efficiency of the staff.

Today she was nervous as hell.

She pulled open the door to the clinic and felt the wave of warm air envelop her. A man she didn't recognize sat at the metal detector, and disappointment filled her. She had been expecting—she had been hoping—to see Mack.

She smiled at the new man. He was older, balding, but looked like he could take pretty much anyone in a fight.

He passed her through without a comment, and she went into the clinic itself.

The waiting room was not full, which surprised her and shouldn't have. Patients who could probably canceled appointments after the news yesterday. It would take a while for everything to settle down.

Darcy sat behind the reception desk and grinned when she saw Edie.

"I have your purse and coat," she said. "I think everything's inside, including your phone."

She bent over to get it all, then handed it to Edie like an offering.

Edie took it all. The purse was heavy compared to the one she was carrying, and the coat felt too thin.

Darcy grinned at her, either unconcerned about the day before, or past her initial reaction to being back at work.

"Someday, you'll have to tell me how you survive without your phone," she said.

"Easy," Edie said. "I have two, and I can access information from both of them on my computer."

"You're smarter than I am," Darcy said with clear admiration. "I would never have thought of that."

Your job doesn't require you to be available 24/7, Edie thought but didn't say. It would sound ungrateful, and she was grateful to Darcy. Besides, Darcy's job was as hard as hers, just in a different way.

Edie sometimes thought of what she did as after-the-fact work, but Darcy's job was in the thick of it. People bled and cried and nearly died in Darcy's office. If someone nearly died in Edie's office, she clearly wasn't doing her job.

"Is Ruth here?" Edie asked. "I'm hoping I showed up during her lunch break, and that she actually has a moment to talk."

Darcy's eyes grew wide, in a Yikes kinda way. "She gave up on lunch breaks almost a year ago. Now she has lunch moments. I do get her to eat, though."

Edie nodded, feeling disappointed. No Mack, no Ruth.

"However, I think she won't mind if you crash her meeting. She's with Mr. Santore. They're hammering out the schedule for the next few weeks, given everything that happened. You want me to call ahead?"

"Please," Edie said. "But I'll start back in case she says no. If she yells at you, you can blame me for being the pushiest person you know."

Darcy laughed as she picked up the phone. "But you're not the pushiest person I know."

"Damn," Edie said as she let herself into the back. "I need to try harder."

Darcy's peeling laughter followed her through the maze of corridors. Doors closed, with the flags of many colors flying, showing the patient status. Redundant folders sat in the holder on the doors, redundant because Edie had helped find a donor for the laptops the doctors used to update patient files on the fly. The laptops *and* the software.

That had been an expensive proposition, but not nearly as expensive as hiring Santore Security would be.

If she didn't believe in this cause, if she didn't know what kind of good the clinic was doing, she would tell Ruth to cave in to the protestors and the violent nutjobs who wanted to destroy this place.

But Edie personally knew a dozen children who were alive because of the clinic and their presence in the neighborhood. She'd successfully defended almost thirty women on all kinds of minor criminal charges, women she'd met through here. And she had no idea how many lives Ruth and her doctors had saved over the years, but once Darcy had estimated that they were saving at least three per week—and those were the ones Darcy had known about.

A couple of the nurses waved at Edie as she went by. Since her extra coat was draped over her arm, all she could do was nod and smile, but she found herself doing that all the way down the hall.

Her heart rate went up again as she approached Ruth's office, where she had been less than twenty-four hours ago before her world got turned upside down. She wondered if she'd have trouble sleeping tonight and for the rest of the week because of everything that had happened.

Last night, she had just been too exhausted.

Ruth's office door was closed.

Edie grabbed the doorknob and knocked at the same time. She pushed the door open as Ruth told her to come in.

Ruth was sitting behind her desk, hands folded over some files. She looked very prim as she faced Mack. He leaned against the wall, arms crossed, expression somber. Energy crackled from him, almost as if he couldn't quite stay still.

His gaze was on Edie, his expression guarded. That flush she had felt earlier got worse. She had embarrassed herself the night before. Clearly. He no longer respected her.

Ruth raised her eyebrows, as if silently asking what Edie wanted.

Edie had to force herself to forget Mack. Attraction was good and fine, but it wasn't everything in the world. There were a lot of other things to focus on.

Like keeping this clinic around.

"Just checking in," Edie said. "I'd like an update, and I wanted to know if you needed my services for anything."

"Update is simple," Ruth said. "We managed to get the cops to let us open the clinic, as long as we don't use the parking lot for the next few days. We don't need your legal services right now, but I could use some fundraising ideas later in the week. I understand that Mack's lawyer friend offered some web services so we can do something like a crowd-funding thing, which is about as much as I understand of the offer."

"That's right, he did," Edie said, "and I think you should take him up on it."

Ruth closed her eyes and put a hand to her forehead. "I can't, Edie. I can't take on any more."

Edie had never seen Ruth like that. Mack's gaze met Edie's over Ruth's head. He looked concerned as well.

"I'll talk to Petruchio," Edie said. "I'll make sure it works."

Ruth nodded, but didn't open her eyes. "Thanks," she said wearily.

"No problem," Edie said, her gaze still on Mack's. It felt like he was actually holding her hand, compelling her forward. "It looks like you should get a few minutes of shut-eye, Ruth."

"Yeah," Ruth said. "If only I could."

"She's still seeing potential disaster," Mack said.

"I don't blame her," Edie said. "This whole thing has us all stressed."

"And Mack says it's going to continue." Ruth opened her eyes and smiled tiredly. "I can usually handle ongoing problems, but this one..."

"I called a buddy at the FBI," Mack said. "There's a hate group that's targeted private clinics like Sanger House. The group believes that because these places receive government funds to pay for some health procedures, the clinics are making the government complicit in murder or some such nonsense. He explained it all to me, and I still don't understand it. I mean, the government expressly does not pay for the abortions. I asked."

Edie slipped inside the office, even though there wasn't much room, and closed the door behind herself. She didn't want the patients to hear this.

"You don't understand it because these hate groups make no sense," Edie said.

Mack shook his head slightly as if he still couldn't believe what he had heard.

"Well," he said, "we have a list of names now, and some faces to watch for. I'm going to set up some cameras and hook them to a security system with facial recognition software so we can watch the neighborhood."

"Is that legal?" Edie asked, then wished she hadn't. She had learned long ago that she could ignore certain things if she had no "actual" knowledge of them. She was an officer of the court, after all, and was duty bound to report criminal activity. In theory, what was considered criminal wasn't up to her, but in practice, it sometimes was.

"The way we do it will be legal, counselor," Mack said, with just a hint of a smile. He apparently knew what she had been thinking.

And that hint of a smile cheered her. The connection remained, at least on his side. She had thought it gone.

"Are you all right today?" Ruth asked her. "You look a little green."

"I'm fine," Edie said. "I wish you two would stop coddling me."

They looked at each other. Ruth raised her eyebrows at Mack, apparently surprised he was included in the "coddle" statement.

"Do me a favor," Ruth said to him. "Coddle her all the way to lunch, will you? Because I can guarantee that this is her lunchtime, and she's not going to eat anything."

"Says the woman who has lunch moments," Edie said.

"At least I have lunch," Ruth said. "You're going to have to now as well."

Edie shook her head slightly. Apparently, the coddling statement had made no impact at all.

"Yes, Mom," Edie said. "I'll be a good pregnant woman, Mom."

"You better believe it," Ruth said. "Because this child is probably as close as I'll ever get to one of my own. So, you're going to treat it right from the start. Now, both of you leave me. I need a lunch moment and a nap moment, preferably not at the same time."

Edie opened the door to the office, feeling slightly relieved that Ruth could at least attempt humor. Edie stepped into the hallway, Mack behind her. Two nurses stood at the nurses' station, pouring over a computer file. A little girl sat in the middle of the hallway, playing with a blond Barbie and whispering to it about a new baby sister.

Edie walked around the little girl toward the patient exit.

"Hey," Mack said from behind Edie. "*Do* you have time for lunch?"

"I do," Edie said, "but I didn't think you would, given everything that's going on here."

"I have a good team on today," Mack said, "and I doubt we'll see any more of our so-called friends this week. I tried to brief Ruth, but she didn't want to hear it all. She said sometimes she likes swimming in that river in Egypt. Took me a while to understand what she meant."

"She loves De Nile," Edie said. "And sometimes it even works for her."

Mack sighed. "The things you don't want to know about doctors."

Edie smiled. She'd learned that doctors were all too human years and years ago.

"So," he said, "care to join me for lunch?"

And with that sentence, her heart rose just a little. Maybe last night wasn't as bad as she feared. Maybe she could have a friendship with this man.

She certainly was going to have a professional relationship with him, for as many months as it took to put the bad guys away—whoever they were.

Still, she wished she could stop the attraction she felt. She wanted to take his hand and lead him out of the building. She wanted to take him home, which surprised her.

Because most men never got within a mile of her townhouse, and he'd already been there twice.

"I've got about an hour," Edie said, trying not to sound too eager.

"That's lawyer for yes?" he asked.

"That's lawyer for yes," she said.

18

This time, he didn't take her to the diner. This time, he met her at a pub a few blocks from her office. Not that anyone could walk in this cold. But she seemed pressed for time, and he wanted to be understanding.

He wasn't pressed for time so much as in need of organization. He had to move staff from jobs, figure out if he could find enough money to bring on at least one more person, and redo all his books with the new facts in mind. He relished none of those tasks. He enjoyed the job more when he was doing things like yesterday, rescuing people and making certain that creeps went to jail forever.

Which was not the job, not really. But days like yesterday always spoiled him for weeks afterward.

The pub was on the ground floor of a building that had stood in Three Fires for more than a century. The exterior was a white stone that actually gleamed. The gleaming white didn't help the eye on days like today; gleam gave just a hope of sunshine that he knew would never come.

The pub was buried inside the lobby of a boutique hotel, a mistake he hadn't even realized he made until he walked inside. He almost face-palmed, he was so appalled at himself.

She had made a confession about her life, one that had shocked him, and the first thing he had done was invite her to a hotel for lunch.

But, he would say to her if she asked, the Pontiac Pub was one of his favorite places in the city. He usually arrived through the side entrance, under the sign that said *No Entrance*. The pub always filtered its non-regulars through the hotel, past the fancy restaurant and the tiny coffee shop that closed at two.

He had simply chosen the main entrance on this day because he had parked across the street.

The hotel was upscale, catering (probably) to the kind of clients that Edie (probably) had. The hotel was 100 percent locally owned and managed, one of those rehab projects that had seemed so impossible ten years before.

Back then, the building had been mostly unrented offices, with the ground floor empty and lonely. Once upon a time, before the go-go nineties, the building had been a local bank with a storied history. Then the bank got bought out by another bank, which then got bought out by another bank, which then got bought out by a banking conglomerate who felt that Three Fires' downtown was too scary for a bank, and they closed the banking part and rented the offices for more money than anyone in Michigan could ever afford.

Eventually, they tried to sell it, and then they wrote it off, and finally it became affordable enough for the rehab project.

Now it was the downtown's Example Building, the one everyone pointed to when they wanted to say how easy it would be for Three Fires to become the most important city in Michigan, as it had been before.

Still, the hotel. He shook his head at himself as he crossed the lobby, his feet clacking on the black marble tiles. The pub's main door stood open, revealing the dark woods of the interior.

The entire pub—like the building itself—had been rebuilt with locally sourced materials. The woods here had come from Michigan forests. The tables were polished to a shine, with some kind of coating to make them easy to clean, but the walls had layers of unretouched wood running through the paneling like a seam of gold.

The pub's bar was a thing of beauty, with its polished surface and its old-fashioned gold railing. There was even a gold boot hook railing along the bottom.

He looked longingly at the bar itself. Just once he wanted enough free time to spend an afternoon here, nursing a local brew and watching the Red Wings beat the crap out of anyone they played. Or losing, which they seemed to do a lot lately.

He didn't care. Sometimes he just wanted to be someone else.

He took two menus off the side of the bar and went to his favorite booth. It was beneath the long plate-glass window, with the pub's name calligraphed in gold. From that window, he could see the entire street, which was usually busy in the summer, but which looked like a ghost town today due to the cold.

The thought of a beer made him want one, but he was working. Besides, Edie couldn't drink right now, and he always thought it rude when someone ordered alcohol in front of someone who, for whatever reason, couldn't currently imbibe.

He ordered coffee, got ice water for both of them, and folded his hands over the menu, waiting.

He didn't have to wait long. She came in through the same door he had used—through the hotel, dammit—and scanned the pub before seeing him. She smiled, and goddamn if the expression didn't warm him down to his core.

Either she was the most beautiful woman he had ever seen, or pregnancy agreed with her, or both. Probably both. Ruth had said that Edie looked a little green, but he hadn't seen it then, and he didn't see it now.

She looked vibrant and alive, her hair swinging free as she approached him, pulling off her gloves as she walked.

When she reached the table, she slipped off her coat, her movements graceful. He watched avidly, even though he shouldn't have. She wasn't showing yet, at least that he could tell. But he hadn't known her before. Her breasts did seem large for a woman of her size, but some women were built like that, slender and curvy in all the right places.

He wanted to slide his hands up from her narrow waist, cup the bottom of her breasts, and feel their weight in his palms. He wanted to take her in his arms and kiss her, slowly, until she leaned against him, moaning.

He wanted to—

"You know, I've never eaten here," she said as she sat down. "This is truly elegant."

The words weren't exactly cold water against his hot skin, but they at least focused his attention away from her body. His gaze met hers, and he smiled.

"It's one of my favorite places," he said, getting that out of the way in case she thought he was trying to take advantage of her confession from the previous night.

"Well, I have no idea how I missed it considering how close to my office it is." Then she grinned. "Of course I know. It's more impressive to hold lunch meetings at Squire's than it is to eat in a pub."

Squire's was the upscale restaurant he had passed.

"I think I might have to rethink that strategy," she said.

The waiter came by with their waters and Mack's coffee. Edie ordered a coffee as well, and a French Dip sandwich. Mack ordered his usual burger.

He was beginning to realize that he had a lot of "usual burgers" at the restaurants he went to.

"So, tell me," Edie said, "what had Ruth so freaked out?"

"You'll have to ask her to find out for certain," Mack said, "but I think she's having trouble with two things. The first is that the attacks might continue for another year or two. And the second…"

He let his words trail off. He suddenly wondered if it was wise to tell Edie his theory on Ruth or not.

"Go ahead, tell me," Edie said, clearly understanding the reason for his hesitation. "I'm tough."

She was a lot tougher than she seemed to realize. And a lot more composed than he expected, especially considering all they had gone through the day before.

And so pretty. He longed to tell her, to reach out and brush a strand of hair away from her eyes, to speak softly….

He shook his head slightly to get the thoughts out of it. He shouldn't have brought her here. A pub said relaxation to him, not business, and this was a business meeting, even though he didn't like to think that.

"I think Ruth is having trouble with the fact that these attacks aren't personal," he said.

"Against *her*?" Edie asked, and in her tone, he could already hear the dismissal of the accusation.

"No, no," he said. "Against the clinic. I don't think, deep down, she likes the fact that Sanger House isn't the primary target."

Edie frowned. "Why on Earth would Ruth want Sanger House to be a primary target?"

He'd seen this before, with other clients. And he'd given it a lot of thought.

"Because it's easier," Mack said. "If the attackers are focused on Sanger House, then they'll be easier to catch. They did something or had some kind of bad interaction with Sanger House or know something about someone who works there. The investigation will head down a recognizable and logical path."

"But if it's not Sanger House per se?" Edie asked.

"Then we have a long road ahead of us. We're dealing with zealots, and zealots aren't just hard to catch, they're often in the business of recruiting other zealots." He paused as the waiter showed up with their sandwiches. "Ruth is smart. I spoke to her about some of this when she hired me."

"We hired you," Edie mumbled, as she moved the bun around on her French Dip. The thinly sliced prime rib was layered on a Kaiser roll, which made the sandwich another of Mack's favorites.

He ignored her correction. From his perspective, Ruth had hired him.

"There was the murder of the doctor some time ago, which might have been personal and might not have been. The threats, which the police didn't take seriously but you all did. And Ruth has had a feeling of being watched for some months now."

"She did?" Edie seemed shocked. "She hadn't told me that."

"I'm sure she didn't want to worry you."

Edie let out a loud breath, as if that was the stupidest thing she had ever heard.

"I asked her if she would rather spend the funds on hiring her own investigator," Mack said, "to see who, exactly, was going after her, and she said she would rather have the security."

"Patients first," Edie said.

He nodded. "Patients first. And then I asked her if she thought the problems were being caused by one of the well-known hate groups. A few of them are based in Northern Michigan. Another one has its roots in Southern Wisconsin. And there's one more in Illinois. And I swear, if she could have put her hands over her ears, closed her eyes, and sung 'Lalalala,' she would have."

Edie had taken a bite of her sandwich. She finished chewing before she said anything.

Mack almost thought that was a ploy to give her a chance to consider her words a bit more carefully. He took his own burger and ate while waiting for her to finish.

She swallowed and said, "Over the years, it's gotten progressively harder to operate women's and family clinics. The religious right and the politicians they own, people who claim to have family values, are undercutting families everywhere, especially poor families. They lump everyone in one big pile, as if every family is the same. Just because a clinic performs abortions doesn't mean that's the only thing it does. People like Ruth are standing at the barricades, brandishing swords, and hoping that no one shows up with an army carrying machine guns. Because that's what it feels like."

He studied her for a moment. He'd heard her talk about these things a few times over the past twenty-four hours, and each time, she'd been very passionate about them. It didn't jibe with her job.

"How come you're a defense attorney?" he asked.

"How come you work in security?" Her response came so fast that he knew he had hit a sore spot. He hadn't meant to.

"No, no," he said. "I mean, how come you're not one of those left-wing attorneys who handles the political causes."

"I like to make money," she said dryly. But clearly that wasn't it either.

"Seriously," he said. "Be honest with me."

She studied him for a moment as if trying to figure out if she could trust him. This seemed more important to her than her lifestyle choices had the night before.

"Have you ever met those people?" she asked. "Ineffectual idiots who rail against the unfairness of the laws instead of trying to serve their clients. Most of those lawyers have no clout at all, and don't know how to use what they have."

"Not all of them," he said. He knew a few good attorneys, and used them to help some of his indigent friends.

"Not all of them," she said. "But enough of them that that entire side of the profession smacks of hopelessness."

She set the remains of her sandwich down, then wiped her fingers off with a napkin. She had clearly learned a lot of stalling tactics in conversations, to keep herself from blurting out everything that came to mind.

"Better to have money and power," she said, "and do this kind of work on the side. People will actually listen to you then."

His breath caught. People didn't usually admit to that kind of attitude. They mumbled something about balancing the scales or trying to develop a conscience. That's what Petruchio always said. He never admitted to doing anything out of the kindness of his heart.

Her hand, clutching the napkin, was resting on the tabletop.

Without thinking, he reached over and placed his hand on hers.

The electricity crackled between them, the sparks so powerful he thought everyone in the pub could see them.

Then her gaze met his, her eyes half open. He thought that sensual, and then a worry crept in—was she waiting for him to remove his hand? Would she say something about how inappropriate he was being?

He started to slide his hand away when she turned her own underneath it, her forefinger rubbing the tender skin under his wrist. His heart rate increased. His mouth opened slightly as his penis hardened so fast it almost made him dizzy. He felt like a randy teenager, his body outside of his control.

Not that he wanted it in his control.

He had no idea that the skin on the underside of his wrist was an erogenous zone, but it clearly was.

"This is a hotel, isn't it?" she asked, her voice husky.

He nodded.

"Come with me." She emphasized the word "come" ever so slightly, accenting its double meaning. Come with her. Cum with her. Jesus, he'd come ahead of her if she kept stroking his skin like that.

With her free hand, she reached into her purse, opened a wallet, and put a fifty dollar bill on the table.

That would probably cover the cost of lunch along with a hefty tip. Not that he cared. She could lead him anywhere

She didn't release his hand, holding it above the table as she slid out of the booth. He slid with her, grabbing his coat only when she grabbed hers. She seemed in possession of her faculties more than he was.

They walked out of the pub hand-in-hand. He draped the coat over his arm, hiding his pants. He was a randy teenager again with a hard-on so powerful that the slightest thought might set it off.

She led him to the registration desk and that was when he realized she had done this a hundred times before. The thought should have cooled him down. Instead, it excited him. He wanted to find out what she was like, what she had learned, if that intoxicating scent she had underneath a faint layer of rosewood perfume got even stronger when she was naked.

She never let go of his hand as she got them a room. The desk clerk didn't even look askance, which made Mack wonder vaguely how many other business professionals used part of their lunch hour in an upstairs room.

The elevators were only a few yards from the desk, but they were behind a series of pillars. Edie stood just a little in front of him. She pushed their clasped hands backwards, hitting his draped coat, and then brushing—not casually—against his hardness.

His mouth went dry. Torture. Sheer, exquisite torture.

The elevator door opened. A middle-aged man got out without looking at either of them. Edie led Mack inside and stood calmly while waiting for the door to close.

No one else joined them. Then the door closed, and as it did, she eased his hand upward, and inside the back of her pants, against her naked buttocks. They were firm and smooth, and warm. He stroked, and she leaned into him, resting the back of her head on his shoulder, then nuzzling his neck.

Nothing that would show up on the elevator security camera, except a couple who enjoyed each other's company. So easy, so delicate—

The elevator door opened, revealing an empty hallway. He had never been up here. He wondered if she had been, and then decided he didn't care. His hand remained inside her pants, and she pulled him along, the movement of her flesh exquisitely arousing.

They got to the door of a room, and she opened it with the key card as if she had done this a million times before—*she had, oh, she had*, his traitorous brain thought, as if expecting him to pull back.

There was no pulling back. He didn't want to pull back—or maybe his body didn't—or maybe none of him did.

They staggered inside the room, the lights off. It smelled faintly of cleanser. He got the impression of a bathroom on the left, a closet on the right, as she kicked the door closed, and dropped her purse and coat onto the floor.

Then she tossed his coat down with them, turned, and wrapped her hand around his penis. He was so startled that he felt himself swell even more. It took a bit of concentration to keep himself together.

She slipped her free hand around his neck and pulled his head toward hers. She didn't have to pull very hard because he dipped in. Their lips touched, sampling. She tasted of au jus and strawberries and something he'd never tasted before, something so intoxicating that he wanted more of it.

He wrapped his arm around her back, his hand still inside her pants. She was wet, and he was hungry.

She fumbled with his zipper and he was too preoccupied with her mouth to help her free him. Then she did, and he realized what she had done. She had left his pants up, but his penis free. She pulled her mouth away from his and he moaned in protest until she crouched, wrapping that mouth around his penis, and doing things no one had ever done to him before.

God, he was going to come like a boy with no control at all.

He staggered backwards, his back hitting the wall, and his hands were free now. He used them to raise her up, and lead her to the bed, which the hotel had piled with a stupid amount of pillows.

He swept them away, kicked off his shoes, pulled down his pants, and ripped off his shirt.

She stopped, staring at him as if she'd never seen a naked man before. For a second, he worried that she was having second thoughts (*he* should have been having second thoughts) and then she peeled off her own clothes. Those breasts—not as large as he had thought—pointed slightly upward. Her stomach was still flat. Her pubic hair was as dark as the hair on her head, only curly.

He sat down and gathered her toward him, except that she pulled away and sat at the same time.

On him.

His penis inside her warm wetness, the most erotic moment of his entire life.

He wrapped his arms around her and eased her onto the bed so that they were side by side, moving in unison for the longest time, for a half a minute, for a second, really, and then time stopped. All that they were was skin and nerve endings and erogenous zones.

Her mouth found some he never knew he had, and his fingers found some that made her arch, and moan, and beg, and somewhere in that timeless eternity of a single minute, she pushed against him, crying out in pleasure, her entire face flushing, her body pulsing.

He couldn't hang on any longer, so he didn't, pulsing with her in an orgasm so powerful he felt like he was being turned inside out.

Slowly, he became aware of the bed. His own sweat-covered skin sticking to high-thread count sheets, a pillow jammed into his shoulder blade, a blanket halfway up his thigh. She nestled under his arm, her heartbeat matching his.

Never had he experienced anything like this. Never. Not in any of his years or any of his relationships. Not drunk, not sober, not even as that randy teenager he had so briefly reconnected with.

This was beyond anything he had ever experienced before.

And it was her. It was all her.

"My God," she said, and rose on one elbow before she leaned down and kissed him. His penis, flaccid a moment ago, stiffened again. It had been years since his body volunteered to go again so soon after an orgasm.

She laughed against his mouth, then slid a hand down and caressed him, even though he was sticky with fluids from both of them.

"We forgot a condom," she said with something like surprise.

"Don't need one," he said. Had she forgotten she was pregnant? And then he realized what she meant, and how many lovers she'd had, and just like that, his interest flagged a little.

"Don't worry," she said, that uncanny ability to read his mind showing up again. "I tested clean."

He had no idea if he had anything. He doubted it; he'd been cautious his whole life. But she was pregnant, and—

Her finger touched his mouth.

"We'll test at the clinic tomorrow, okay? For both of us." And then she kissed her way down. The lovemaking would have ended as it had begun, except that he was in no mood to finish. He wanted to please her, and must have said so, because she made some kind of sound that indicated he already had.

"Still," he said, as if that were an argument.

She slid back up, wrapped a leg around him, and raised her eyebrows.

"Let's do it again," she said, and grinned.

So they did.

19

The spherical alarm clock on the end table beside the bed told her she should have been back at the office an hour ago. Maybe those bursts of music she had heard since she got into the room weren't in her head, but were her phone, reminding her that she had Duties and Clients and Obligations.

Screw them, she thought, and stretched out languidly beside Mack. He had the most beautiful body she had ever seen, perfectly toned, actual abs that hadn't come from a gym, muscles that looked like they came from a medical textbook of the adult male specimen, and just a smattering of dark hair that trailed from his chest to his hips.

She had never had sex like that. She'd heard it was good in early pregnancy, but Jesus. More orgasms than she could count, shudders that had gone from her nipples to her knees and back again, her tongue playing with his body making hers even wetter than she ever thought possible.

It wasn't the man, was it? It was the pregnancy hormones, right? That was what made him smell so good, feel so very right.

God, if he were up for it, she would be again. A third time. She'd never done that. With anyone.

But his eyes were closed, his skin damp. His heart fluttered under her right hand.

But he wasn't smiling. In fact, he looked pained.

He was already regretting this. A man who liked his women a lot purer than she was. Than she *ever* was.

He opened his eyes, his expression sad. She was still aching for him. She toyed with mounting him again and taking his attention away from whatever thought was going through his mind, but that wasn't fair.

He had to have his say.

She braced herself.

"I hope you don't think I planned this," he said, a comment so out of left field that she didn't even understand it.

"How could you have planned this?" she asked. "I seduced you."

"The pub," he said. "The hotel."

Bars. Tinder. Her late night confessional.

"Oh," she said, and with that one word, all good feeling left. "No. I hadn't thought that."

But she did now, just a little.

"I've never done anything remotely like this," he said.

She couldn't say the same thing, except that it felt different. It felt completely different.

He wouldn't believe her. Would he?

She had no idea what to say to ease his mind, so she kissed him. Her kiss was gentle and so was his response, wistful almost.

"I'd love to do it again," she said against his lips.

"I don't think I can," he said.

She laughed, surprised that he even considered it.

"No, I mean, you, me. Maybe I buy you dinner next time."

"And a movie," he said. "Don't forget the movie."

She smiled, cupped him in her hand, and squeezed just a little. She almost said, *I never ask for seconds*, but that would remind both of them of who she was.

"I'm late," she said, and rolled out of bed. "I get firsts in the shower."

She padded across the room, leaving her clothes. She was past the point of modesty with him. When she got into the bathroom—which was the size of her first apartment—she looked in the mirror. She had love bites on the side of one breast, and her lips were swollen. Anyone who looked at her as she went down in the elevator would know exactly what she had been doing.

Then she turned sideways and looked at her belly. She ran her hands down it. She wasn't showing yet. The baby was still theoretical, except for all the hormonal changes—the nausea, the swelling breasts, the late-night fatigue.

The increased sexual desire.

The bathroom door opened and he came in, still naked, and slipped his arms around her, his hands covering hers. His skin was so much darker than hers. She loved the contrast.

She wanted to lean into him, but she wasn't sure what that would mean for either of them.

"You're stunning," he said.

"I'm pregnant," she said.

"I know." he turned her to face him, then he traced her skin, kissed her right nipple, and touched her belly.

Then he half-laughed and stepped away.

"I was so willing to make love to you," he said, "and yet, I'm not willing to be honest."

She wanted to close her eyes against his words. She didn't want to hear them. She knew that he would now reject her. He *should* reject her —a woman who knew her way around hotels, who thought about condoms as STD protection not as birth control, a woman who was going to have another man's baby, who had had sex with that other man not three weeks ago.

But she held Mack's gaze, and to her surprise, he kissed her. The kiss was not a dismissal.

"I want to see you," he said, touching his forehead to hers.

"You are seeing me," she said.

"Date you," he said.

"What an old-fashioned concept," she said, unable to help herself.

"I'm an old-fashioned guy," he said, holding her.

This time, she did close her eyes. "That's what I'm afraid of," she said.

Instead of saying anything, he kissed her again, his hands cupping her jaw, his body against hers.

"Not that kind of old-fashioned," he said. "Not Old Testament old-fashioned. I just want to get to know you."

"You already know a lot about me," she said.

"I want to see you every day," he said. "I want that dinner and that movie and I want to do this again."

He slid his hands down her back, pressing her against him.

"And I want to make love to you slowly, at least once," he said. "Can we do that?"

"Slowly?" she asked, remembering how combustible they were. "I'm not sure."

He smiled. And waited.

She wasn't sure what he was asking. She thought of dating as something you did to meet people, not something that you did once you'd already had great sex with them.

"Why would you want to date me?" she asked, her tone registering her confusion.

"What I really want to do," he said, "is woo you."

"Woo me," she repeated. Then she shook her head. "What does that mean, exactly?"

"Court you," he said, using another old-fashioned term. "Prove myself worthy of you."

She let out a nervous laugh. "You're worthy of me. And, Jesus, who asks these things?"

He was making her uncomfortable. She got sharp-tongued when she was uncomfortable.

He ran his hand along her cheek and kissed her again, slowly, sampling her. Her breasts, already sensitive, pushed against his chest, and the arousal came back, just as strong. God, was she addicted to this man?

"I want," he said when he was done, "to know everything about you. Why you have a tiny scar on the inside of your palm—"

He had *noticed* that? Already?

"—what else causes you to make that soft little sound in the back of your throat—"

"What sound?" she asked.

"The one you made when I kissed you just now," he said. "It's almost like a purr."

She closed her eyes. She had no idea she made sounds when she was that turned on.

"I'd like to see what you look like in the morning—"

"No, you don't," she said.

"And when you're having a bad day—"

"No, you don't," she said again.

"And when you're so happy you could burst." He kissed her again. "I want to know what you look like when I surprise you—"

"You're already surprising me," she said.

"—with flowers," he finished.

She stepped back. She couldn't think with him that close.

"That's all really romantic," she said. "I love romance as much as the next woman, but this is just the beginning."

"I know," he said. "That's why I want to woo you."

"Have you ever been around pregnant women?" she asked. "They're bossy and hormonal and cry at the drop of a hat. Then they get fat. Some women are delicate when they're pregnant—I mean, they only show in front—but most gain weight everywhere, and that last month, they're so cranky…"

"I'm the oldest of five," he said. "I remember that last pregnancy of Mom's because Dad left in the middle of it. I remember some of the others too. I know what to expect."

"From a kid's perspective, maybe," she said. "But you're talking about a new relationship. You're talking about *romance* when there won't be any at all."

He tilted his head slightly. "Why not?"

"Because there's nothing romantic about pregnancy," she said.

"Really?" he asked. "Bringing a new life into the world isn't completely awesome?"

"No," she said. "It's life-changing work."

"What if I prove you wrong?" he asked.

"You can't," she said. "Life-changing work. That's a fact."

"Life is work," he said. "And there's room for romance."

She didn't know why this was making her so uncomfortable, but it was. She walked over to the shower. It was beside a deep tub that looked inviting. Only she didn't have time for a tub. And the shower's controls seemed confusing.

Plus, there were two showerheads. At different heights. For two people.

"I don't believe in romance," she said, her back to him. "And wooing."

"Just good sex," he said.

She could half see him in the floor to ceiling mirror. He still had his head tilted as if he couldn't quite figure her out.

"Yeah," she said, and wondered why that one word made her so sad.

He was silent. The silence stretched on for at least a minute. Apparently, he wasn't going to answer her. She slid the glass shower door back and looked at the controls.

Good Lord, it looked like the cockpit of a jet in there.

"Who hurt you?" he asked quietly.

Her heart hammered instantly, and she felt a little dizzy.

"No one," she said so fast that she surprised herself.

"Someone," he said. "To make you not believe in the good things in life."

"Sex is good," she said.

"And so is romance," he said.

She turned, her mind racing. She had never dated anyone, not the way he talked about. And she'd discovered sex early, and was smart enough to learn birth control at the same time. Sex had been fun, and usually impersonal. It had been the guys who had gotten hooked, at least when she was in college. She'd had to break it off with two of them.

No one had hurt her, and she had had to learn how to be cautious with other people's feelings. She didn't want to hurt them either.

"No one hurt me," she repeated.

"Yeah," he said in a tone that said he didn't believe her.

He was leaning against the marble sink, which had to be cold all by itself, but he didn't seem to notice. He looked lean and gorgeous, all GQ, yet without the clothes.

"How come you're not in a relationship?" she asked, and the question didn't come out as belligerently as she had thought it in her head. She had thought of it as a push-away question, when it actually sounded like an informational question.

He smiled like he had just won the lottery. "How about I tell you on our first date?"

She froze. She liked him. She liked him a lot. He was sexy and smart and successful and nice.

This was the moment she could push him away for good. She could say no, and shut everything down. Or she could say yes to this dating thing he wanted to do.

She had no idea how to achieve a compromise here. She wasn't sure what a compromise would be.

Because she wasn't sure what she wanted. Besides him, in bed again.

He wanted something she'd never had before. A man who wanted to spend time with her and who wanted to fuck her. She had men friends whom she never slept with, and men that she fucked blue, and no one in between.

Mack seemed to want something else, something she didn't entirely understand.

If she pushed him away now, she would never have sex like that again in her life. She had no idea why she knew that, but she just did. And more importantly, she wouldn't see him again—except at the clinic, in passing, or if some company she worked with needed the services of Santore Security.

That would disappoint her. Just the thought of never seeing him again, like this, or talking to him, as she had done for the past twenty-four hours, disappointed her. That visceral connection seemed very real.

And yet...it made her want to research. Were her hormones dictating her relationship here? Helping her find someone to assist her with the task ahead?

She wasn't that easily manipulated by her own body, was she?

She realized she had been quiet for a long time. His gaze was on her. It hadn't varied at all.

He was watching her think, and judging by the ever so slight smile on his face, he was enjoying that.

He clearly knew he had confused her, maybe even boxed her in. Was he trying to control her? Force her into some kind of relationship that suited him but didn't suit her?

As soon as she had that thought, she dismissed it. No one forced her to do anything. No one ever had.

She took a deep breath, then smiled at him. It was her best smile. It was the *meeting a new man across a crowded room* smile. It was the *charm the scared client* smile.

"All right," she said lightly. "Show me this dating thing of which you speak."

His upturned lips hadn't moved, but his eyes squinched a little, changing his entire expression. He had gone from looking bemused to looking just a little confused.

"Are you sure you want to date?" he asked, as if he hadn't come up with the idea himself.

Clearly, she had been wrong earlier. Clearly, they didn't think in unison most of the time. Apparently, they only thought in unison in times of crisis.

Or in bed.

"I have no idea if I want to date," she said, "considering I've never done it. So I'm trusting you on this one."

And that was part of her problem. Trust. She had never been very good at it. Which was why she took control of almost every situation she found herself in.

She could trust herself.

He grinned. "You look scared. You didn't look this scared in the clinic. It's a *date*, Edie."

"I know," she said. "And that worries me more than I can say."

20

*M*ack was nervous. He never got nervous over dates. *What could go wrong?* he used to ask himself, back when he dated a lot. *You have a bad meal or a bad conversation, and you end up with a great story you can tell years later.*

He'd had a lot of bad dates, starting with his second prom, junior year. But he'd never had a date that felt more important than this one.

He adjusted the sleeve on his gray merino wool suit. The suit had cost more than his first car. He got it when he had to find clients for Santore Security, back when he discovered that he had to hobnob with the right people, the people who could actually afford private security in the first place.

He had other suits that he liked less than this one, suits he had to wear on the job, particularly when a few of those clients requested his personal services as a tryout for the entire company.

He could have set up the date as a jeans-and-T-shirt affair. Pizza at one of the best joints in town, or that movie he had teased her about.

But he wanted a grown-up date with the most beautiful woman he had ever met. She was stunning, and he wanted to show her off. He had a hunch that if this worked—big if—then he wouldn't have a lot of opportunities to show her off in the next year. She had already made it

155

clear that she was worried about the upcoming weight gain and the changes to her body.

Her body—lithe and athletic, with those lovely breasts and a beautifully curved ass. She clearly did something to stay in shape, and he had no idea what that something was. He had no idea about most things concerning her.

He hadn't lied to her when he said he wanted to get to know everything about her.

He did.

He was taking her to The Flame, the fanciest restaurant in Three Fires. The Flame had a waiting list for reservations that was months long. Celebrities who came into town to promote some movie or to show how charitable they were by rescuing a building or donating some money to Three Fires' revival, couldn't get in, not even on a good night.

He'd had to call in six favors just to get the reservation, and another favor to get one of the primo seats near the glass windows that overlooked the city itself. He knew that Edie had upscale clients, and he had a hunch she had been here before, but he wasn't going to ask.

He was simply showing her how much he valued her *yes*.

He also insisted that they act like this was a modern first date, not a 1950s first date. First dates in the twenty-first century meant meeting at the location. He asked her to join him in the Flame Thrower, the bar attached to the restaurant, at eight.

He arrived early because he actually wanted to have a seat at the bar while he waited for her. He didn't want to be standing, eagerly, near the door. The Flame Thrower shared the top floor of the Buhl Building with The Flame Restaurant. Floor-to-ceiling windows here had a view of the entire city, and the Burnt River's widest spot, near Burnt River Park.

If you didn't like sitting outside, this was the place to view the fireworks on the Fourth of July, the place to watch the City Days Fireworks in September, or the place to have a quiet drink, alone on a late weekday night. He wondered, in passing, if he had ever seen Edie here on her way to meet one of her men, and then made himself dismiss the thought.

One other reason he had deliberately chosen The Flame over some of the other restaurants in town was this one was nowhere near a hotel. He didn't want her to think he was taking advantage of her confession —again.

He slipped inside. The bar was active, the crowd switching from the one-drink-after-work folks to the serious daters, partiers, and wealthy Friday night revelers who showed up here to impress themselves and their friends.

He took his usual seat at the horseshoe-shaped bar, his back to the open gas fireplace, its base made from sandstone reclaimed from some of the old buildings that had gotten torn down in the bad years. Couples sat on that base right now, flirting and clicking drinks together.

He ordered a Jameson on the rocks but didn't touch it, not wanting his breath to smell of alcohol when he first saw Edie. He was entranced; he knew he was. He hadn't been able to get her out of his mind since that explosive lunch two days before.

It wasn't just the sex. It was the mystery of Edie as well, a woman who claimed to have never dated, a woman who seemed so in control of herself, and yet so wild in bed. A woman who apparently had had no real long-term relationship.

All of that should have red-flagged him. It *had* red-flagged him. He kept thinking he was playing with fire, no real pun intended. He had never been involved with a woman like Edie before. All of the women he had known had been completely conventional.

If she hadn't had long-term friendships, he would have walked away, no matter how mind-blowing the sex had been. Not having long-term relationships—of any kind—would have shown that she didn't know how to make a commitment and that she couldn't attach emotionally.

But she had known Petruchio for years, and Ruth even longer.

Her relationships with both of them were obviously affectionate, and her closeness to Ruth showed a real emotional depth.

Mack had almost asked Ruth about Edie as they worked on security for the clinic, but stopped at the last minute. Edie and Ruth were tight, and anything he said might find its way to Edie.

He thought about asking Petruchio as well, but Petruchio, for all his charms, was very protective of his friends and would have clammed up, lips pressed together, eyes accusing. Mack had seen that look on Petruchio's face before, and it never boded well for the future of the conversation.

Maybe, after both of them knew that Mack was actually dating Edie, he could ask for more information. At the moment, though, he hadn't felt comfortable doing so.

He saw her enter the bar through the reflection of the floor-to-ceiling windows. She was superimposed over the lights of the city, looking like the starring actress in a high-gloss Hollywood film.

She carried a long coat over her arm, the arm at her side. She wore a black dress that clung to every curve. His mouth went dry. He remembered how each curve felt beneath his fingers, how he had kissed the underside of those breasts, how his hands had held her still-narrow waist as he pulled her against him. His penis stirred, remembering with him, and he made himself take a deep breath, trying to get himself under control.

Good God, the woman intoxicated him.

He spun the bar stool toward the door. She smiled when she saw him, and crossed the crowded room, not seeming to notice that she had the attention of everyone and that the bar had gone mostly silent. She wore shoes that mimicked the dress's crisscrossing blackness, with heels so high that they added another six inches to her already imposing height.

She wasn't dressed for winter, and she didn't seem to care.

He was breathless, and he hadn't even said hello yet.

She swayed when she walked, a woman who knew how to handle shoes like that. Every move she made suggested power, sexual power, and he realized, as she drew closer, she had put on the dress like a uniform, to remind both of them that she could take control of this evening with the brush of a finger.

She sidled up against him. She smelled faintly of jasmine mixed with some kind of rose, a scent he'd never noticed on her before. She must be one of those women who didn't have a single perfume, but wore different ones for different occasions.

He wanted to bury his face in her neck, breathe deeply, and lose himself in her.

Instead, he stood, placed a hand on her hip, and kissed her lightly on the lips. She did not lean into the kiss. The dress was made of silk, so soft and fine beneath his fingers that it felt like part of her skin.

"Hello," he said, his voice huskier than he had planned.

She smiled. "Hello."

She looked at his drink, then at him. "Do we eat here?"

"No," he said, not willing to move away from her just yet. "We have a reservation. Let's give them your coat."

His was already checked. He held out his hand so that he could take her coat, but she didn't let him. She walked ahead of him toward the coat check room, which had been discretely placed between the entrance to the restaurant and the back of the fireplace.

The fact that she knew where the coat check was proved she had been here before. He felt a small surge of disappointment. Part of him had hoped he would be the first to bring her this experience.

She moved just far enough ahead of him that he couldn't put his hand on the small of her back, like he often did when he walked with a woman he was seeing. She didn't even seem aware that he was following her.

By the time he reached the coat check, she had already handed her coat to the man behind it and received her ticket. Mack normally would have handled that part of the date, paying for both of their coats.

But he didn't say anything.

She turned. "Now what?" she asked. "Do we wait in the bar?"

"No," he said, feeling quietly pleased. Maybe she hadn't eaten here after all. Because if she had, she would know that once one member of a party checked in, the table was set aside, and they could all proceed the moment everyone arrived.

He extended his right elbow just a little, offering it to her. She glanced at it, then at him, bemusement in her dark eyes. For a moment, he thought she would reject it, then she slipped her hand inside his elbow, her hand so cold he could feel it through the fabric of his suit and his shirt.

He escorted her to the door of the restaurant as if they were parading down a red carpet. He felt that way, like the man lucky enough to take the most beautiful woman in the kingdom to the ball.

He stopped at the maître d's podium, and handed the maître d' the gold token he'd been given when he arrived. The maître d', a thin man dressed in a suit so formal it could have passed for a tuxedo, bowed slightly, grabbed two leather-bound menus, and without a word, led them to the best seat in the house.

The Flame had the same basic design as the Flame Thrower, only without the horseshoe-shaped bar. A lovely and large gas fireplace dominated the center of the room. Even though the base of this fireplace was made of reclaimed sandstone, just like the other one, the top was made of glass so that nothing blocked the view of anyone in the restaurant.

The table the maître d' led them to was one of three built into tiny alcoves that extended out over the side of the building. They were private rooms without being private rooms. And to say that they were completely private was wrong—because the alcove was open to the restaurant on one side, and surrounded by glass on all the others.

The glass was triple-reinforced and heat radiated from specially made heaters along the side of the floor. A remote, placed near the floral display at the center of the table, allowed the diners to adjust the temperature in the alcove. That little remote did other magical things as well, such as changing the music to something the diners preferred, and summoning the waiter should the diners need anything immediately.

Before the maître d' could do so, Mack pulled out Edie's chair. She gave him a funny sideways glance, as if she couldn't believe what he was doing, then she smoothed her skirt over that perfect bottom and sank into the chair. He helped her scoot it in and sat down, just in time for the maître d' to hand them their menus.

A waiter, wearing a similar suit, had somehow appeared beside the maître d'. The maître d' introduced them, as if they were all going to have a dinner party, and then returned to his duties.

"May I bring a cocktail or some wine?" the waiter asked.

Mack found the wine list and pulled it out, handing it to the waiter.

"We would love to celebrate," Mack said, "but since the lady is expecting, we will need something bubbly and non-alcoholic. Do you have anything?"

Edie's mouth opened slightly as Mack spoke. She shook her head just a little, apparently not wanting him to say anything about her pregnancy, and then stopped when it was too late.

"Indeed we do, sir," the waiter said. "I shall bring you our best."

And then he took the wine list and left the table without discussing any specials. Apparently, Mack had flustered him.

"I don't want the entire city to know," Edie said.

"I didn't tell the entire city," Mack said with a smile. "Just the waiter."

She sighed heavily. "All this—do you do this for every first date?"

"What's that?" he asked.

"The fancy restaurant, the perfect-gentleman routine?"

He had expected questions, just not so soon.

"It's not a routine," he said. "And yes, I do that for most women. The fancy restaurant, however, no. I've only been here once before."

"I've been here dozens of times," she said. His heart sank a little as she said that, "and never once have I managed to get one of these tables. Do you know how hard they are to arrange?"

"I do," he said primly. "I have friends."

"I would say." She was clearly impressed. Good. He wanted her to be impressed. "So how do we do this date thing?"

"There really aren't rules," he said, "although there are accepted patterns."

"And they are?" she asked.

"Get-to-know-you conversation," he said. "A few laughs. Sometimes too many drinks. Occasionally deciding that you have nothing in common with the very nice person across from you. Or deciding that a second date would be worthwhile."

"Hm," she said, opening the menu. "Seems like a lot of work to get someone into bed."

"Such a cynic," he said.

"Well," she said, "that's all I've ever heard about dating. It's all about finding someone to sleep with."

"If that were the case," he said, "I wouldn't think this dinner necessary at all."

She looked at him over the menu, her gaze hooded and filled with heat. "We could forgo the expensive meal," she said huskily.

"We could," he said, trying to ignore the way his heart was hammering in his chest, "and I would never get a reservation like this one again."

She laughed, then shook her head. "I'm beginning to think you're incorrigible."

"Ah, see?" he said. "It's working. You're getting to know me."

She laughed again, just as the waiter brought a bucket of ice and what looked like a magnum of champagne. It wasn't, of course, but he opened it with the same elaborate fanfare that he would have used had it actually been champagne.

He handed them each a full champagne flute. The amber liquid sparkled and bubbled just like champagne. Mack held his until the waiter left, then lifted a glass to Edie.

"To our first date," he said. "May it not be the only date."

She clanked her glass gently against his and then sipped. She made an eh-not-bad face, then set the glass down.

"I still don't think dates are necessary," she said. "Why not cut to the chase?"

"Because," he said, "otherwise I would never have gotten to see you in that dress."

She shook her head, clearly amused. "That's probably true," she said. "I suspect this is the last time I'm ever going to be able to wear this dress."

"Ever?" he asked.

"The body changes with pregnancy," she said. "I just don't know exactly how mine will be different, after."

"However different it will be," he said, "I'm sure it will still be just as delightful."

She flushed, then looked down.

"I'm really out of my depth here," she said, more to the menu than to him.

"I know," he said, putting a hand on his menu's burnished leather. "But that's only because you're thinking of this as a date. If we were having a business dinner, you'd be making excellent small talk right now."

She looked up at him in horror. "That's what we're supposed to be doing right now? Small talk?"

"If we want," he said. "Or serious talk."

She paused, clearly contemplating what he said, and then she nodded as if accepting the challenge.

"All right," she said. "Serious talk. You talked me into this date because you were going to tell me why you're not in a relationship."

Well, she wasn't kidding about cutting to the chase. Sometimes he forgot she was such a good lawyer. She knew how to ask the right question.

The waiter showed up, which would have saved Mack on any other date. He would have used the recitation of the specials to allow himself to consider what else to talk about, deftly move the conversation in that direction after the ritual of the ordering was completed, and never answer the question she asked.

But after they ordered—fresh lake trout for him (ice-fished, the waiter said, because apparently someone had asked him how lake trout could be fresh at this time of year) and a well-done steak for her—Mack decided to answer her question.

"I didn't plan to be relationship-free," he said, rolling the champagne flute of whatever the sparkling liquid was around in his hands. He was guessing some kind of apple juice, but he couldn't tell with all the effervescence. It was too sweet for him. "It just happened."

"Yeah," she said, as if that was what had happened to her as well. "Too busy?"

"No," he said. "I got tired of small talk and desperation."

She frowned at him.

"Some people want marriage more than anything. They'll marry anyone, just to have the ring on their finger," he said. "I want a companion, someone to share my life with. But that someone has to be special, really special. She can't just be a woman that I like."

Edie's eyebrows twitched as if she had started to frown and then made herself stop. He'd seen Petruchio do something similar. Mack wondered if they taught frown-suppression in law school.

"You sound picky," she said.

"Yes," he said, and nearly stopped. But he had told her that he wanted to get to know her, and some of that was being as honest with her as she had been with him. He wasn't used to that kind of honesty, though.

Her fingers played with her champagne flute. Her nails were painted a gentle white. They looked recently manicured. She had prepared for this date, even if she hadn't wanted to come on it.

"I nearly got married five years ago," he said. "I lived with a woman for a year. We were comfortable."

"So what happened?" Edie actually sounded interested.

"I kept putting off the important stuff, the real conversation about setting a wedding date, about a future. When she asked, I backed off." He wasn't sure how to put his feelings into words.

He moved the champagne flute aside and picked up his water glass, sipped, and set it down.

"I was driving to Detroit on business, heading down the interstate, listening to one of those dumb talk radio shrinks who talked about people doing things on rails," he said. "You know, doing things because that's the path, not questioning the path, not thinking about what was best, just what was normal."

"You were doing that?" Edie asked, her tone incredulous.

"We both were," he said. "After I finished my meeting, I went home, and we sat down to talk about it. She had been thinking something similar. We liked each other, a lot, but we didn't love each other—not in that passionate this-is-forever way."

"I doubt anyone has that," Edie said.

There it was again, that cynicism. Only he wasn't going to poke at it this time. He was going to let her reveal where it came from on her time.

"I want that," he said. "I believe it exists."

She stared at him for a moment. The look was a challenge.

"And if it doesn't?" she asked.

"Then I guess I'm shit out of luck," he said, and grinned.

She didn't grin back.

"You know," she said, "for hundreds of years, relationships were simply transactions. The union of two families for business, political, or personal reasons. Yet children got born, families were formed, people survived."

"I know," he said.

"This true love thing, it's a modern myth," she said.

He felt sad. He hadn't realized how much he'd hoped she felt the same way he did.

He decided to put all his cards on the table.

"I don't know," he said. "I feel a real pull toward you that I've never felt with anyone else."

"It's the pheromones," she said. "They're probably stronger in pregnancy. Everything else is."

He shook his head. "Maybe. Maybe it's all science and chemicals. But I don't think so. No woman has ever interested me the way you do, not from the start."

She stared at him, silent. She almost looked like she was going to get up and run for the coat check.

But she stayed.

"You think that's true love," she said after a moment. It wasn't a question, not really. And yet it was.

"I think it's a precursor," he said. "Enough that I'm willing to take chance, to do this right."

"You think a date is doing it right?" she asked.

He almost pushed back—*Do you think screwing yourself silly is doing it right?*—but he didn't.

"I just want to get to know you," he said quietly. "And I want you to get to know me."

She took a deep breath, then raised her head. One of the junior waiters or whatever they were called showed up with a bread tray and another tray filled with crudités. Mack took a warm piece of dark rye bread, slathered it with butter, and placed it on his bread plate.

She took some sliced carrots, placed them on hers, and then grabbed a roll and some butter for herself.

The junior waiter left.

"All right," she said. "Let's do just the facts. I'll start. I don't believe in love and romance and mushy stuff, but you know that. I believe that human beings do need a connection with each other, and they can find it in marriage. They can find it in friendship, and sometimes they can find it in families."

He took a small bite of the bread, listening. There were caraway seeds in it, accenting the rye.

"I never dated, had a few serious relationships before I figured out that was how the other side perceived it, but me, I thought it was steady sex. I learned how to satisfy all kinds of needs and urges without hurting anyone, and that's how I ended up at thirty-five, a lawyer on a major career track, living alone, and surprising myself by becoming a mother to be. You want the C.V. too?"

He liked that sharp tongue. He liked the way she used it, not just in conversation, but also in bed. A flush built in his neck, and he resolved to ignore it.

"Steady girlfriend in high school. Two steady girlfriends in college. The woman I told you about, and no one since," he said. "I did sleep around for a while, decided I didn't like casual sex. I like a connection. I probably would have been one of the guys who misunderstood your intentions had we met in college."

Her eyes widened at that.

"I'm thirty-six, I also live alone, and I never thought I would. The year before my mother died, I bought one of the crumbling mansions on Division and my mother teased me. She said I bought it because I wanted to fill it with children. She knew me. She was right."

"Your mother's dead?" Edie asked. "I'm sorry."

Her response didn't sound rote. She actually felt a sadness for him.

That surprised him.

"Me, too," he said. "I miss her every day."

Edie paused for a moment, then sighed. "Wish I could say the same about my mother."

"That you miss her?" Mack asked.

Edie's gaze met his. "That, yes. She's dead as well. Thank heavens. She was the most difficult person I've ever known."

Ah, maybe now they were at the root of the cynicism.

"And your father?" Mack asked.

"Sperm bank," she said, surprising him. She shrugged one shoulder. "My mother wanted a child. She didn't want a husband. She didn't have male friends. She thought you could order children the way you order a custom-made ball gown. She ended up disillusioned."

She wasn't the only one, he wanted to say.

"I don't miss her. I can't imagine what she would say about my pregnancy and how I got pregnant, not that I ever would have told her." Edie sipped some of the fake champagne, made a face, and set it aside. "So I've never really been one for convention."

"I understand that," he said.

"It doesn't sound like your parents had romance either," she said.

"My parents had a torrid love affair," he said. "Lots of sex, lots of passion."

She leaned back, clearly surprised at that.

"And that created lots of children, which my mother wanted and my father didn't. They had a knock-down drag-out fight with each succeeding pregnancy after me, and finally—when, as my father said loudly, 'they outnumber us, Lila'—he got more and more dissatisfied. The sex was less and less frequent, my father was no longer the center of my mother's universe, and he fled to a succession of younger and younger women, most of whom wanted his non-existent money."

"Is he still around?" Edie asked.

"I couldn't find him when Mom died," Mack said, and heard a bitterness in his tone that he hadn't known was there. "Not that I tried all that hard."

"What about your siblings?" she asked.

"They don't know where he is either." That bitterness still clung to his tone. "I don't even think they tried to find him. They care about him less than I do. Most of them can't remember him."

She pushed one of the carrots around, then grabbed the bread and ate it slowly, watching him. Her movement was not deliberately sensual; she was actually contemplating him.

"Is that why you want children?" she asked. "To prove that you can do better than your father?"

The question stung. That cynicism was harsh and somewhat insightful.

He made himself respond slowly, so that the small wave of anger that had hit him wouldn't show.

She had asked a legitimate question, one he'd actually asked himself.

How much truth should he give her?

"I like kids," Mack said.

"Most people do," she said. "That's not always a reason to have them."

He nodded, then took a deep breath. He had promised her truth, after all, so he should probably go all-in.

"I asked myself that very question when I did all that analysis with Bree. Because most people have kids on rails." He heard what he had just said and smiled at himself. "I don't mean 'on rails' exactly, but without thought. Most people have kids without ever questioning whether or not they should."

He added that last sentence because he realized that she could take what he was saying very, very wrong.

Indeed, her cheeks had pinked up just a little, as if she had heard *without thought* as if he had meant her.

"I like to say people marry and have the two-point-five kids because they were told to, not because they want to," he said.

"Is that what you were doing?" Edie asked.

"I think Bree and I considered it," he said. "I think we were on a road, and we just kept walking it, and it could easily have ended up in the suburbs in some nice bland house with a couple of kids neither of us had really planned on."

"But you like kids," Edie said.

He couldn't tell if she was making a point or asking a question or doing both.

"I do," he said, "and it wouldn't have been a bad life. Bree is a good woman. We're still friends."

Edie raised her eyebrows at that. Did she not believe that men and women could be friends after a breakup? If so, that was another red flag.

"So," she said, "you contemplated your decision to have kids and decided that, indeed, the decision came from—where? Your affection for children?"

"From the things I want to do with my life." He spoke quietly. "I really want a family. I want all the messy ups and downs that happen when people live together. I grew up in a large family. We struggled, we fought, we laughed, we spent time together. And I'm a better person because of it. I like that controlled chaos. I want children. I want grandchildren. I want that picture you see on Facebook of the five generations at somebody's wedding, and I want to be the wizened old guy in the middle, holding the newborn who represents the generation I won't see growing up."

She had stopped eating. She had folded her hands together and rested them under her chin, her elbows on the table in a way his mother would have complained about. Edie looked very thoughtful.

"You want that?" she asked.

His heart was pounding. He had never admitted that to anyone before. Now he told a woman he barely knew about a dream he had never articulated before. And it was so important that he was afraid how he would react if she rejected it.

"Yeah," he said, trying not to be defensive.

She frowned. "I had never given that any thought. I'd scan over those pictures."

"No grandparents either?" he asked.

"They'd disowned my mother long ago," Edie said. "I have no idea when they died. And she didn't have siblings, so it was always just me and her until I couldn't take her anymore."

"When was that?" he asked.

"College," Edie said. "I ran away to college and never came home. It looked like I was being the obedient daughter. Instead, I was running as far away as my scholarships would take me."

He nodded. She hadn't been rejecting him. She had been thinking about what he said.

"What you described is foreign to me," she said. "I have no idea what that even means, five generations of a family. How can you do that if you are out of touch with your father?"

"My family," Mack said. "From me and my wife. I don't think I'll live long enough for five generations. I'd be happy with two after ours. Kids and grandkids."

"Biological kids," she said, almost to herself.

He was shaking his head before she finished the sentence.

"Kids are the people you *raise*," he said that with such force he startled himself. "They're not the people you donated sperm to."

Her cheeks got pinker and then he realized what he had said.

He raised his hands as a small apology. "I was talking about my dad, not yours," he said. "My dad contributed sperm and a few years of his life and then just walked away. Who does that? He had an obligation. Your father didn't, whoever he was, didn't have an obligation. He had provided materials. Sometimes I think my family would have been better off if my dad had done the same thing."

"But then, you wouldn't have siblings," she said. "Or at least, siblings with the same father."

"Yeah," he said, "but sometimes I wonder if my mother would have been able to remarry and have a happier life."

Edie frowned at him. "You just said you had a great family."

"*I* did," he said. "I'm not sure how happy my mother was with her choices. She loved us, but parents are more than what their children seen."

The waiter showed up with their food. He served with a flourish, swirling Edie's plate through the air before setting it before her. Then he gave Mack his trout. The fish had a festive, wintery air, with a cranberry garnish and a side of jasmine rice.

The waiter went through the obligatory twenty questions—would you like something else to drink, anything else I can get you?—before he left. He also made Edie cut into her steak to make sure it was grilled right for her.

She proclaimed it perfect. The waiter smiled, and, after cleaning some bread crumbs off the table with some little clear thingamajig, he vanished.

Mack was going to say something about how he thought waiters in high-end places like this should be seen and not heard, but Edie spoke first.

"You took care of your mother, didn't you?" she asked as she cut the steak into small pieces. It bled onto the steak plate. Well done, yes, but clearly juicy still—the sign of a place that knew how to cook beef.

"Of course I did," Mack said.

"And after your father left, you were there for her during that last pregnancy." Edie took a small bite and gave a little—and already familiar —moan of pleasure.

The moan distracted Mack, but only for a moment. She thought he was paying attention to her because he was replicating part of his relationship with his mother.

"You're psychoanalyzing me," he said.

"Am I?" Edie took another bite of steak and half closed her eyes.

"Yes," Mack said. "You think I'm interesting in you because you're pregnant."

Edie set her fork down with a tiny clank. "Aren't you?"

He frowned. The thought had crossed his mind, but not in the way she thought.

Again, he had promised her truth. The question was, could he handle his own truth?

"Maybe a little," he said.

She raised her eyebrows. Apparently, she had thought he would deny the accusation completely.

"But only because you're not doing what I would have expected of you." He spoke quietly.

"You expected me to get rid of the baby," she said flatly.

He nodded.

"Why would that intrigue you?" she asked.

"Right away, it shows me that you're not what you seem," he said.

"What do I seem?" she asked.

He kept forgetting she was a lawyer. He kept forgetting that she was trained to pay attention to word choice and to pounce on any inconsistency.

He was friends with lawyers, not just Petruchio. They all could play this sort of game, particularly when they wanted to distance themselves from the conversation.

But she asked. So Mack would answer.

"You're beautiful," he said. "You're brilliant."

She waited, clearly braced for more.

"You like to control every situation," he said. "You handle the men in your life. You compartmentalize everything. You are a high-powered attorney, and you give to women's charities. You appear to be the kind of woman who wants nothing and no one to interfere with the way you live your life."

Her eyes narrowed.

"Children interfere," he said.

"Yeah," she said drily. "So I've heard."

And then she sipped her fake champagne as if nothing he said bothered her at all.

21

The nausea returned, ever so briefly.

Edie set down the champagne flute. Her stomach wasn't upset by the dinner or even the extra-sweet crap that was pretending to replace high-end alcohol. Her stomach wasn't even upset by the pregnancy. She was beginning to recognize what that kind of queasy felt like.

Her stomach had turned, for a brief moment, because Mack had just described her mother.

In fact, he had ended with a statement her mother made repeatedly.

Children interfere.

Yes, Mother, Edie used to say back when she was the child in question. *They do.*

She let out a small breath, focused on regaining her calm, and stared at Mack.

He looked a little out of his depth. Not because of the restaurant itself, although that surprised her. When she had first seen him in a suit that had the shine of expensive wool, she had lost the ability to breathe. It had looked as natural on him as the jeans had the day after she met him.

He'd handled the restaurant as if he had been born with a silver spoon in his mouth and had been eating in five-star Michelin dining rooms his entire life.

No, he'd been acting out of his depth with her. And honestly, she had done her best to make him uncomfortable.

He had promised he would be honest with her, and he was being honest with her. Everything he said had a ring of truth.

Even when she challenged him.

Especially when she challenged him.

He spoke calmly and evenly, without a trace of defensiveness in his voice. He had been bitter when speaking of his father, and she had actually used some of that to push him away.

But he didn't let her push. He hadn't changed the subject. He hadn't flinched.

He had actually considered everything she had to say.

And that unnerved her.

But not as much as the way he had just described her.

A brilliant, beautiful, controlling woman, who never let anything or anyone touch her. A high-achiever with an empty life.

A woman who wanted nothing and no one to get in the way of what she wanted to do.

A woman exactly like her mother.

And that very concept made her feel defensive.

She had lived her entire life trying hard *not* to be her mother. Her mother had never thought of anyone but herself. Her mother's ambition was the only important thing in the entire world. Her mother's career. Her mother's life.

Edie had never been entirely certain why her mother had even had a child, except maybe to prove the 1980s adage that a woman could have it all. Or, as her mother used to say, *A woman without a man was like a fish without a bicycle.*

It took a long time for Edie to realize that the quote wasn't something her mother had thought of. The quote was something she had gotten off a 1970s t-shirt.

He was silent. He didn't watch her. Instead, he slowly, deliberately, ate his fresh lake trout. But she had a sense that he was watching her out of the corner of his eye, waiting for her to say something.

Most men would ask if they had offended her. Or they would apologize, *assuming* they had offended her.

She wasn't sure if he had offended her or not.

He had certainly made her think.

She wasn't quite sure how to respond to him. Did she say something about children and how she could handle them? She wasn't sure she could.

She finally said, "The woman you describe should never have children."

He looked up, finished chewing a bit of lake trout, and swallowed. Then he chased it with some water.

"I didn't say that." His voice was calm, but his gaze was hooded. Had he deliberately implied that? Was he trying to get to her?

She could so easily pick a fight with him right now. She had already probed. She had a sense where some of his vulnerable areas were.

If he was like most people, all she had to do was push—just a little—and then she could make him angry.

Anger was passion. Passion, even angry passion, could be redirected into sex.

And there was that control thing he had mentioned. She would push one of his buttons, make him angry, and then move him into the bedroom —somewhere. Maybe even in her office, which wasn't too far from here.

She felt a surge of desire. This man really attracted her, no matter how much she blamed it on pregnancy hormones. She wanted to bed him, and bed him now.

"What did you say?" she asked, finally.

"You asked me if your pregnancy interested me," he said. "I said it intrigued me. But only because it contradicted what I had assumed about you. My first impressions of your character were wrong. I had thought you were a different woman than you are."

That wasn't what she had heard. She frowned.

"What's different from the woman you described?" She tried not to let that question sound desperate. She always felt desperate when she got compared to her mother. And he had compared, whether he had known it or not.

"You have a lot of compassion," he said. "You stayed and helped me get people out of the clinic."

She shrugged. She hadn't even thought about that since she had done it.

"That's what people do," she said.

"No," he said. "Most people protect themselves. They run for their lives. They don't open cabinet drawers to make sure that no child is inside of one, particularly when they hear that a bomb might go off."

"Sure they would," she said, but she was less convinced than she had been a moment ago.

"Believe me," he said. "I've been in tough situations before. People don't do anything like what you did."

She nodded, just once.

"I didn't think about it," she said.

"I know," he said. "You just did it. I admire that."

Her face heated. Damn this emotional volatility. She wasn't used to registering her emotions through her skin. She hadn't started flushing until the last few weeks. She knew that was a new side effect.

"Thank you," she said softly.

He nodded, then returned to his fish. They ate in silence for a few minutes. She barely tasted her steak. Her mind was racing. He observed her. He had thought about her.

He liked her.

She was beginning to like him too.

She had never spent this kind of time with a man. She had spent this kind of time with her friends, people she had no sexual interest in. But never with someone she had slept with.

Friendship and sex. After a disastrous relationship in college, she had kept them separate.

She had vowed never to take a friend to bed again. She valued her friendships too much, and men got a little crazy about sex. At least, that was how she had thought of it at the time.

Had she been wrong?

"You're suddenly very quiet," he said. "Is this date different from what you expected?"

"Yes," she said. She wasn't sure how she could tell him why it was different. It just was.

"What are your plans for the baby?" he asked.

She felt the conversational about-face like a sudden left turn in a fast-moving car.

"What do you mean?" she asked.

"Well, babies change everything. I assume you have enough room in your apartment, but what about your work? And I assume you'll be hiring some kind of help, right?"

She blinked at him.

She had asked him for total honesty. It wouldn't be fair if she didn't give him the same in return.

"I have only known for sure that I was pregnant for the last few days," she said.

"Meaning you haven't thought about it," he said.

"Meaning I've only just started to think about it." She was getting full. She set the plate to one side. "I don't even know what my options are. I need to research."

"Fair enough," he said, and then he smiled. The smile was small and inwardly focused, as if it were something private, something he hadn't meant to share.

"Why are you smiling?" she asked.

"Because you sound like a lawyer," he said. "You can't commit to anything until you've looked up all the case law."

She felt a jolt run through her. That was exactly how she'd been thinking.

"Is that so wrong?" she asked, then realized that did sound defensive.

"No," he said. "It actually sounds sensible. I wish more people would do that."

She felt some of the tension leave her body when he said that. She had thought ever since she had told him about her lifestyle that he was judging her. She hadn't realized that maybe he had judged her and found her admirable, not horrible.

Such things never crossed her mind.

"I've only decided three things so far," she said.

His gaze met hers. His brown eyes were very soft, and welcoming. God, the kind of look that any woman would trust.

"I decided to have the baby," she said. "That's the first decision."

He nodded. He knew that. They had been discussing it, and it had surprised him. Perhaps that was why he kept circling back to it.

"And the most important," he said.

"I don't know," she said. "I think it's a start, but not the most important decision. I think other factors have to come into play, and they're equally important. Such as what do you do with the child after you have it."

"All right," he said, as if he were withholding judgment before agreeing with her.

"I decided to keep the child," she said. "That's the second decision."

He nodded again.

"I decided to take parenting classes," she said. "That's the third decision."

He made a little sound, a humph, as if that surprised him.

"Parenting classes," he said. "I thought those things were court-ordered."

She smiled just a little. "There are the court-ordered kind, and then there are the kind that any interested parent can take at any point."

"And you're...interested?" he asked.

"I was raised by a brilliant she-wolf," Edie said. "I had no father, no other relatives, very few friends, and almost no role models. I'm terrible parent material."

"I wouldn't say that," he said.

"Think about it," she said. "I had no affection as a child. Human interactions sometimes baffle me. I have no concept of how to care for an infant or what nurturing actually is. I had no real nurturing, and I've seen enough in court to realize that people raised without proper nurturing often make the same mistake with their kids. I don't want to be cold and distant."

"So don't," he said.

"It's not that simple," she said. "They say that having children turns you into your parents...."

She let her voice trail off. Maybe he would understand now.

"And you don't want to be your mother," he said.

She nodded. Tears stung at her eyes. She didn't breathe, hoping the tears would recede.

After a moment, they did.

But she could tell, just from the look on his face, that he had noticed.

"From what you described," he said gently, "I don't think you're anything like her."

"Ah," she said, as if she were Perry Mason, catching him in a lie on the stand, "but from what you described, I am."

"Strong and capable? Caring and courageous?" he asked.

She pressed her lips together. She hadn't quite heard the caring and courageous part.

She had to change the topic before the tears returned.

"I made one other decision," she said.

He looked at her.

"I'm sending a legal document to the baby's...father..." she paused over the word, remember Mack's sperm donor remark. "I want him to sign off on his parental rights. He was going to send me something similar, so I don't think it's a problem, but I'm a lawyer, and I want to protect us."

That was the first time she had ever used the word *us* to describe herself and the baby.

"Are you sure?" Mack asked. "Some men come around."

"I'm sure," she said. "I don't want him to come around. He thinks I trapped him. I didn't. He doesn't know me, or he wouldn't say that."

She saw Mack's response in his face. Bert Collins hadn't known her because she had set it up that way. On purpose. So she shouldn't be surprised that he would act on his ignorance.

"He might want to get to know his child," Mack said.

"Then he can petition me later," she said. "Right now, he wants no part of the baby, and I want no part of him. He was a mistake."

They were all mistakes. Just a lonely woman trying to assuage her loneliness in the only way she had known how.

Those damn tears rose again, and she made herself breathe.

The men weren't mistakes. Some of them were a lot of fun. They provided release, and she had loved the casual nature of the relationships.

But now, she had to move forward, and there would no longer be a place in her life for such casual flings.

She would have thought that she would regret making that decision, but she didn't.

She didn't regret it at all.

"Be prepared for him to respond differently than you expect," Mack said.

"Because I drew up the paperwork?" she asked. "It was what he wanted, Mack. He said I should let him know if I needed abortion money. That was the only reason he hadn't sent over his paperwork yet."

"Paperwork makes it all real," he said.

"Yeah, maybe," she said. "I think physical changes make it real. Paperwork is just that. Paper."

Mack extended his hand across the table. She looked at his long fingers, with their work-calluses. Their roughness had felt so wonderful on her skin.

The fantastic sexual encounter of two days before had started with a touch of their hands across a table.

This one would too.

She took his hand, and he smiled.

She expected him to wave his hand for the check. That was how it usually happened.

The man asked for the check, they figured out where they were going, and they met there. Whoever did not pay for dinner paid for the hotel room.

If there was dinner.

Usually there wasn't. Usually it was just drinks.

He let go of her hand, and she felt the loss.

"What's wrong?" she asked.

"Nothing," he said, and moved his plate to one side. "Are you ready for coffee?"

Coffee. The question felt like it had come out of left field. She hadn't expected that. But if he had said *dessert*, she would have thought it a double entendre.

"Coffee sounds good," she said, trying not to sound disappointed. "Coffee sounds very good."

22

He ordered black coffee and she ordered decaf. They split some kind of berry confection that he barely tasted.

The conversation had somehow turned back to casual things—books, movies, the color of the sunset over the Burnt River in autumn. He hadn't enjoyed an evening this much in a long time.

Which relieved him, and worried him. He was getting along with her, and she was getting along with him. And they were good in bed.

In fact, that was all he could think of.

Bed.

The waiter brought the tab. She reached for it, but Mack put his hand over hers. The feel of her skin made his breath catch. It was as if every inch of his body came alive whenever he touched her.

He wanted her to pick up his hand again and do that thing with her mouth, the thing that had started it all a few days ago.

Instead, he made himself slide the leather case with the bill inside it toward him. He took out his credit card, and placed it inside the case, and set the case on the side of the table so the waiter could see it.

Then Mack moved his hands to his side of the table.

He had made a vow with himself. He would not sleep with her. Not this time.

He wanted to be different from every other man in her life, and so far, he had been exactly the same.

The waiter took the check.

"So," she said in a soft voice. "Where to?"

"Home," Mack said.

"Oh," she said. "Yours or mine?"

She had misunderstood him.

"Um," he said. "Both."

She frowned. Now she clearly didn't understand him. And that was all right, because he wasn't being clear. Maybe deliberately.

"This is a first date," he said gently. "I don't sleep with a woman on a first date."

"Pfuf," she said. "We already got that out of the way. First date, second date, we were pre-date. So let's figure out whose place is closer. Or did you want to go to the Fiser Inn? It's only a few blocks away."

The waiter came back with the check. Mack took his credit card out of the holder. His hands were shaking just a little—enough for him to notice, but not enough for her to.

He hoped.

He tallied the tip and realized that he hadn't paid this much for dinner in years. Certainly not on a date. A few business dinners, yes. But never on one other person.

"I can still pay half," she said, misreading the look on his face. "Or I can pay for the room."

He wasn't sure how he felt about this side of her. He wasn't sure he liked it.

Or maybe he didn't like what it represented.

Her casual attitude toward something he didn't feel casual about at all.

He took the receipt, folded it, put it in his wallet, and then put his wallet back into his pocket.

He reached out his hand. She took it, started to raise it to her lips with a bit of a smile, and he pulled away.

She looked hurt before she covered over the expression with a blander one.

"This is a first date," he said again. "I'm a gentleman of the old school. I told you that once. And I don't sleep with a woman on a first date."

"I told you I thought dates were all about sex," she said. "You didn't correct me."

"I should have," he said. "Because you've heard all the wrong things."

That bland expression had left her face. She looked confused.

"You're serious," she said.

"Yes," he said.

"Why?" she asked. "No sex on the first date seems like an arbitrary rule."

"It's not," he said. "I want to get to know you. I wanted a date."

"And," she said, with a tone that made it sound like she had realized something, "you said first dates were about figuring out if you want a second date. You don't, apparently."

"Do you?" he asked.

"I'd like to take you to the nearest bed, wherever that is, and show you want I want," she said.

Her aggressiveness unnerved him. It was the only odd moment in an otherwise pleasant evening.

It was, he realized, her defense mechanism. She was pushing him away again, because she believed that he was going to reject her.

"That would be lovely," he said. "But I'm holding to my arbitrary rule."

"Why?" she asked. "Because dinner was a disappointment?"

There it was. That thread of insecurity that he had heard from her before.

"No," he said. "Because I enjoyed this dinner more than I've enjoyed a dinner in years."

"Then let's have a nightcap," she said.

"Maybe on the third date," he said.

"That's your rule?" she asked. "Three dates before sex?"

"Or five or ten," he said. "There's something to be said for going slow."

"At this rate, I'll be in my third trimester and only interested in lying on the couch. Alone," she said.

He grinned. He liked the flashes of humor he was seeing from her.

"We know we're compatible in bed," he said.

She moved her head ever so slightly, as if she was trying to focus. Or maybe she didn't agree with him.

After all, she had had a lot more experience in bed than he ever had.

"Or," he said, "at least, *I* think we are."

She folded her hands together and rested them on the edge of the table, as if she was protecting herself.

"I just don't want sex to complicate things as we're getting to know each other," he said.

She made a small sound of disgust. "Why do men always believe that sex complicates things?"

He couldn't help himself: he smiled. "I had always heard that *women* believed sex complicated things."

"Not in my experience," she said. "Sex is sex. It's like sharing a meal. We have to eat, we have to sleep, and then there are the things that we should do, which are good for our bodies. Exercise is one. Sex is another."

His heart sank. He had thought their encounter meant more than that.

Apparently not to her.

"I suppose," he said. "But I don't see it as just a bodily function. I see it as a way to connect with someone I care about."

He couldn't hide his disappointment. Maybe he shouldn't try. And maybe he shouldn't go for that second date after all.

He liked her, a lot, but they were very different, especially on things that matter.

"Tell me," he said, leaning back in his chair. He was aware that he had moved away from her. It hadn't been a conscious move, and yet he felt it. "If you end up in a serious relationship with someone—not necessarily me—could you be faithful to him?"

She raised her chin ever so slightly. He had the impression that he had just insulted her.

"Why?" she asked.

He shrugged one shoulder. "Wondering."

"No," she said. "Why would I be faithful?"

He let out a small sigh. "Never mind," he said.

He scooted his chair back. So much for the second date.

"You're asking if I'm a sex addict." She hadn't moved at all.

"No," he said. "I was asking if you would behave according to the common practices of our society. Your question tells me you would not."

"If it's important to the person I'm with, sure I would," she said.

"That's not how it works, Edie," he said softly. "It has to be important to you."

She still hadn't moved, although her cheeks had more color than they had had for a while.

"I'm not a sex addict," she said quietly. "I have a therapist, like half the attorneys in this town. I've worked through some things, and she knows what I do. I don't have a compulsion. I have gone years without sex with someone else. My third year of law school, for example—"

"I'm not trying to put you on the defensive," he said. "I was thinking about a second date, but I'm an old-fashioned guy."

"And you require faithfulness," she said.

"If I get serious about someone, yes. I don't *require* it. I would hope that we would both want it, maybe enough to make that vow to each other in a wedding ceremony one day."

She gave him a half smile, then looked away. Then she frowned, as if an idea had struck her.

"Do you require faithfulness in other areas as well? No male friends, for example, no wandering eye when an attractive person goes by?"

"No," he said. "Of course not."

"Some people do," she said.

She had gone all lawyer on him again.

He shook his head.

"If I'm with someone," he said, "I want to be the most important person in her life. She wouldn't want to hurt me, and I wouldn't want to hurt her. We would have some things that were just ours, things we shared with no one else. I would think of sex as something like that. It would have to be for me, because I'm that kind of person."

"Except," she said, apparently still in full lawyer mode, "when people have children, they say the children become the most important thing."

"No," he said, his voice even softer than it had been before. "The *family* becomes the most important thing."

"Oh." The word was low and almost inaudible.

She had never had a family. She truly did not seem to understand the concept.

He was setting himself up for the worst hurt of his life. He could see himself getting involved with her, and she would behave in ways that would destroy him. He would wrap his heart around her and that child and then he would lose them both.

"I think you were right after all," he said gently. "I loved this date. I loved talking with you. I really like you, and I think we fit, not just physically, but mentally. We like the same things, we enjoy each other's company."

"But?" she asked.

"I'm not looking for a hook-up," he said. "I don't believe in hook-ups. I believe in relationships. You prefer to keep your heart closed. You like hook-ups and have never had a relationship. So, all I can see ahead for us is heartache. Or maybe I should be clear. All I can see ahead for *me* is heartache."

Her dark eyes seemed bigger than he had ever seen them.

He stood. He walked over to her and leaned down. She looked up, and he kissed her like he had been wanting to kiss her all night. Slowly, delving deep, tasting her and the decaf and that berry dessert. The kiss aroused him just like her touch had.

And then he pulled back.

"I really like you, Edie," he said, his mouth near hers. "But I can't afford a second date."

And then he walked out of the restaurant.

2 3

---

*E*die sat alone at the table, her lips still moist from the kiss, her body throbbing with desire. She wanted him. She wanted to follow him, grab him, and kiss him again, until he decided to go with her to the Fiser, or to her place, or to her damn car.

She wanted to convince him to stay with her, just for the night.

Only, ironically, the only way she knew how to do that was the way he had just rejected.

She felt stupid. And humiliated.

She should have gotten angry at him for making her ashamed of herself and the way she lived.

Only she wasn't ashamed of how she lived.

She was ashamed of how she had treated him.

She tapped her manicured fingernail against the cup of decaf she had barely touched.

The waiter returned, as if she had summoned him with that little movement.

"May I get you anything else, Miss?" he asked.

Miss. She smiled just a little.

"Yes," she said. "I'd like a fresh cup of decaf, if you don't mind."

"Of course," he said. "Will the gentleman be back?"

The gentleman. How accurate that was.

"No," she said. "Do you need the table? Because if so, I can move to the bar."

"Take your time," the waiter said. "We're slow on Friday nights in February. Except—you know. Valentine's weekend."

She nodded. "Thank you."

He vanished to get her more of that insipid drink. She was being cautious with everything. Caffeine, sugar. No alcohol allowed, of course, and shellfish, and god, a hundred other things.

Only the caffeine bothered her, although she realized in the past week how much alcohol she ordered at restaurants and never really drank. She just did it to be like everyone else.

Which she most decidedly was not.

If she had been, she would have understood what Mack had wanted this evening.

She let out a small sigh. She could see herself reflected in the window, superimposed over the view he had probably paid a fortune for. A thin, sharp-faced woman who was just a little too pale. The dress fit—its last hurrah, even though it hadn't been much of a hurrah this evening.

And that had been her fault.

He scared her, so she pushed him away. She had pushed hard, too. Every time he talked about anything traditional, she had made herself as untraditional—and unpleasant—as possible.

So now she sat here, alone, and wondered what she should have done.

He was the first man who interested her in a long, long time. It wasn't his fault that he had shown up shortly after her birth control failed.

That had scared her too.

The only thing that hadn't scared her had been the damn bomb threat. It had made her adrenaline pump, but she had mostly felt alive.

She put a hand on her still-flat stomach, her gaze still on herself. And she slowly realized that part of what she saw in that woman across from her was a woman she hated.

Her mother.

She looked like her mother tonight.

And she would be just like her mother if she wasn't careful. Alone, with a child she wasn't sure how to raise, a sharp tongue, a career she loved, and no friends. No lovers. No one to share anything with.

She could take all the parenting classes she wanted, but they wouldn't change her circumstance.

She could have done that tonight.

The waiter set the decaf down. She smiled at him, and picked up the cup. The liquid was too hot to drink, but she held it anyway.

Was she interested in Mack because she needed someone in her life right now? She shook her head slightly.

She wasn't. She would have been interested in him six months ago, when she was free and independent, without a large change looming in her future.

He was a match for her, and she had chased him away. Cruelly.

But she wasn't sure she could handle a relationship with him. And that very thought, the word *handle* crossing her mind, told her how she thought of other people.

She sighed and rubbed her eyes with her thumb and forefinger.

"Good Lord, how brightly shines the moon," said a voice behind her.

Petruchio. Just what she needed.

"It's actually the city," she said drily. "Not the sun, not the moon, not iambic pentameter because I'm too damn tired to think of how to cast anything in iambic pentameter."

Petruchio's reflection showed up in the window as well. He was wearing a dark suit that made his brown skin look lighter than it was. He squeezed her shoulder, then slipped around her to Mack's empty chair.

"May I sit?" Petruchio asked.

"Sure," she said. "You can even order if you want. Because I have the table for the rest of the night."

"Wow," he said. "And are you buying?"

"Sure, why not," she said.

He grinned. "That was easy." Then his grin faded. "I just saw Mack leave. You two were having dinner...?"

"Did he tell you that?" she asked.

"No," Petruchio said. "I looked into the restaurant when I first got here, just in case my party was here before me. But she wasn't."

"Where is she now?" Edie asked. She had no idea who the *she* was, and she was trying to muster up some interest in who it might be.

But she couldn't.

The fatigue had grown deep, only she didn't think it was hormonal. It felt depressive. *Great job, Edie*, she thought. *One more thing to beat yourself up about.*

"She and I—eh." Petruchio waved a hand. Then he leaned forward. "Honestly, she was a true featherbrain. I quoted some Shakespeare to her, and she asked me why I was talking weird. When I said it was Shakespeare, she asked why would I do that? Who cared about school stuff? And then I made the mistake of mentioning where my name came from and she told me she had thought my parents made it up."

"Not everyone knows Shakespeare," Edie said.

"Yeah, but everyone I date should." Petruchio flagged down the waiter, ordered some coffee and a piece of the house specialty peanut butter pie.

"You realize there are eight zillion calories in that thing," Edie said.

"You're going to help me with it," Petruchio said. "You look like you need cheering up."

She smiled in spite of herself. "Oh, why the hell not. I'm going to get fat anyway."

"Why are you getting fat? Have you decided to let yourself go?"

She realized then that she had not told him she was pregnant.

"I screwed up," she said.

"Pissing off Mack? Yeah," Petruchio said. "You should never have a business dinner with a man like him without someone to backstop you. He may work security but I think he's smarter than you and me combined."

"That's not possible," she said, unwilling to give Mack that kind of credit right now. "But I will grant you. He's smart. He's not going to see me again."

"What?" Petruchio asked. "What do you mean? Did you fire Santore Security?"

She shook her head. "This wasn't a business dinner."

"You're *dating* him?" Petruchio asked. "You don't date. You've told me that a hundred times. Every single time I try to fix you up, you say you don't date. Have you been lying to me for years?"

"No," she said, then sipped the decaf. God, that stuff was awful. She set it down. "This was my first date ever."

"With *Mack?*" Petruchio asked, as if he couldn't quite figure that out. "And you screwed it up?"

"No," she said. "That wasn't the screw-up. The screw up is that I'm pregnant, Petruchio."

He had been one second away from taking a sip of his coffee. She was glad he hadn't: he would have done a spit-take otherwise, and she was across the table from him. She had been across the table from him when he had done such things before.

"You and Mack are having a kid?" he asked.

"No," she said, and waited. Petruchio knew how she lived her life. In law school, he used to be her wingman, making sure that she didn't end up with scuzzy guys. Inevitably, he ended up with some scuzzy girl. Eventually, he decided that bars were just not his thing.

He bit his lower lip and frowned dramatically. "I don't know how to ask this without offending you, but do you know who—"

"Yes, I know who the father is," she said, without an edge. "And no, I'm not offended. He's out of the picture for good."

"Okay." Petruchio looked up, warning her that the waiter was coming.

The waiter set down a piece of peanut butter pie that was two pieces of pie wide and three pieces of pie tall. The restaurant had topped it with some kind of whipped cream and then drizzled chocolate over the whole mess.

The waiter handed her a new fork and handed Petruchio one.

"Please bring me real coffee," she said to the waiter.

"Are you sure you should have some?" Petruchio asked.

"I can have a little bit every day," she said wearily.

"No," he said. "I mean, it's late."

She shrugged. "I'm not going to sleep anyway. So why not have something that tastes good instead of crap-ass decaf."

Petruchio grinned. "There's my Edie." He looked up at the waiter and said pointedly, "Thanks."

The waiter picked up Edie's decaf without being asked (as if he needed to be asked, after what she had said) and disappeared into the restaurant.

"Does Mack know that you're pregnant?" Petruchio asked.

"Yes. Ruth can't keep a secret," Edie said.

"Well, she sure as hell kept one from me," Petruchio said. "And I gotta say, even if it's politically incorrect, you don't look pregnant."

"Why would that be politically incorrect?" Edie asked.

"I don't know. I don't do pregnancy," Petruchio said. "I'm out of my depth."

"Me too." Edie dipped her fork in the whip cream, then cut a thin slice off the pie. She took a bite. It was rich and smooth and surprisingly light.

Petruchio cut into the pie as well. "You and Mack, huh?"

"Oh, no," Edie said. "I was the bitch goddess from hell. He left."

Petruchio frowned at her. "You like him."

"You got that from bitch goddess?" she asked.

"Actually, I did," Petruchio said. "You only go full bitch goddess for two reasons—someone's an asshole in business or they're threatening to thaw that chunk of ice encasing your heart."

She teared up. Damn the hormones. Damn them. Her lower lip trembled, and she started to move away, but he was quicker.

He caught her in his arms. She couldn't remember the last time he had hugged her. Maybe college graduation? Maybe that horrid night with Larry the Idiot? She didn't know.

Petruchio patted her back as she struggled to get hold of herself. She didn't sob, not like the night before, but she was having trouble catching her breath. She was making hitching sounds, at least that was what they called it in novels. She had always thought writers had made that up.

"I didn't mean it," he said. "You're not cold. Really. I know you, Edie, and you're not."

She shook her head against his suit. It smelled of his familiar aftershave. Why couldn't she fall for Petruchio? Why didn't his touch make her all a-tingle? They were compatible, to use Mack's word. They liked each other. They thought the same way about almost everything.

But there had never ever been a spark. He was the brother she had never had. He was family, and damn that Mack for reminding her how important family actually was.

She groped the table with her right hand until she found one of the linen napkins. She wiped her eyes with it, feeling stupid. She leaned back.

"Do I look like a raccoon?" she asked. Her mascara was supposed to be tear-proof, but she had never tested it before.

"Nah," Petruchio said. "More like someone blackened both your eyes a few days ago."

"Gree-aat," she said, and tried to clean that up. He took the napkin from her, dipped it in one of the water glasses (God, Petruchio. She couldn't take him anywhere), and then dabbed off her face.

The cool water felt good.

"That's two nights in a row," he said quietly. "I'd never seen you in tears before. Yesterday I chalked it up to the thing at the clinic, but it's the pregnancy, isn't it?"

"I sure as hell hope so." She took the napkin from him, folded it, and set it on the table. She moved the water glass that he had used beside it, so she wouldn't feel tempted to drink from it.

He tapped her knee, then went back to his chair.

"Tell me," she said. "Am I like my mother?"

"Did he accuse you of that?" Petruchio asked. He sounded like a big brother now, one who was going to go punch out the school bully.

"No," she said. "But I'm heading that way, aren't I? I'm going to be a single mom, I'm ambitious, and I'm mean as hell."

He was the only person she could say that to. He was the only one who had met her mother more than once. He had taken her mother on when she had launched into Edie on the day Edie had graduated first in her college class.

And then he had run interference when she graduated summa cum laude from law school. Her mother hadn't been allowed to comment on what she had done, because her mother would have made it sound inadequate.

"Sweetie," Petruchio said. "You would have to take fucking cruelty lessons to even come close to her level of mean. You can't do it, not even when you're trying. Few people can."

Edie smiled, in spite of herself.

"You know I know this, right?" he said. "I went insult to insult with the woman more than once, and barely survived."

"I know," Edie said. "Thank you."

He cut himself another piece of pie. She hadn't even seen him eat the first one.

"You going to keep this kid?" he asked.

She nodded.

"Ballsy," he said. "Is that why you decided to turn over a new leaf and date?"

"No," she said. "I—Mack wanted to try it."

"And you let him? Wow. The Mackster has Game," Petruchio said.

"You sound surprised," she said.

Petruchio shrugged. "I can't think of two more opposite people," he said. "Mack is searching for true love. You're searching for the best fuck in the city."

Her expression must have fallen with her mood because he added, "Or is that over now?"

"I don't know," she said. "The pregnancy's new. The attempt with Mack failed big time."

"Because you were bitchy," Petruchio said.

She shook her head. "Because I asked him why anyone would want to be faithful."

Petruchio's mouth actually formed an O. Then he leaned forward and hit his forehead on the table.

She half expected one of the waiters to rush over and make him stop, but no one did.

Petruchio looked up. There was a little red mark across his skin. "Seriously? You said that to Father Mack Santore?"

"He's Catholic?" she asked, feeling even worse.

"No, but he's a prig. Jesus." Petruchio ran a hand over his face. "I mean, I like him, but God, he believes in motherhood, apple pie, and marriages that last forever. I think, had he been born a decade or so earlier, he would have saved himself for marriage."

"He definitely hasn't done that," she said, mostly to herself.

Petruchio's eyebrows went up. "Well? Did you find it?"

"What?" she asked.

"The best fuck in the city."

She laughed mirthlessly. She had, at least for her. But how could she tell Mack that? He wouldn't believe her, and even if he did, he would tell her that it didn't matter, that sexual attraction eased with time. It wasn't quite that heady thing it had been.

She was smart enough to know that. She was smart enough to know she had hormonal issues. And she was smart enough to know she had screwed up one of the best opportunities that had come her way maybe ever.

"He's not one of those guys who likes kids a little too much, is he?" she asked.

"Jesus, no," Petruchio asked. "Where did that come from?"

She shrugged.

"What, are you kicking the car to see if the wheels fall off?" Petruchio asked. "He's one of the best people I've ever met."

She let out a breath. "I was afraid of that."

Petruchio had managed, somehow, in the course of the conversation, to eat most of the pie. She had no idea how he stayed so trim.

She took another bite.

He didn't say anything.

The pie didn't taste as good as it had a moment before.

"Do you think I can?" she asked.

He frowned. "What?"

"Be faithful," she said.

He stared at her. "Are you really asking me that?"

She nodded, afraid to say anything because she might tear up again.

"Jesus," he said. "You know what you are, right?"

She didn't want to answer that. And fortunately, he didn't give her time to.

"You're like those guys we went to college with, the ones that everyone knew were horn dogs. Then the next thing you know, they got married, and they had daughters, and they became all protective and worried about the horn dogs that are out there in the world, because they know what those men are like."

"Thanks a lot," she said.

"No, I mean it," he said. "You're not listening. They *marry*. They have *families*. No one asks if those guys can be faithful. Because they're *guys*. It's considered normal for guys."

"But not for women," she said.

He pointed at her. "You got it in one."

"How do you know I can be faithful?" she asked, her voice small.

"Who practically carried me to the Revolutionary War final when I had the flu? Who found me a new apartment when Roberta threw me out of ours? Who is the only one who stays in touch with *all* of our friends from law school? Jesus, you're a walking loyalty oath, Edie. What do you mean, how do I know if you can be faithful?"

"Loyalty," she said. "That's not the same thing."

"That's *exactly* the same thing," he said. "You never let anyone down. Once they're part of your family, you'll stick with them forever. Even if it's not good for you. Like your goddamn mother, whom you should have cut off but never really did. Good thing for you that the Bitch Goddess of the Universe died, or you would have let her tear you apart for decades."

"Petruchio," she said.

"Don't *Petruchio* me, missy," he said. "We've had this discussion before. You know I'm right."

Edie opened her mouth to protest.

He shook a fork full of peanut butter pie at her. "And even if I'm making the wrong correlation, how's this? You can do anything you put your mind to. I've watched it. You're the smartest person I've ever met and the most stubborn. If you want to be faithful to someone, you will be. No matter what."

"You don't think there's something wrong with me?" she asked, her voice small.

He laughed. "Sweetie, there's something wrong with each and every one of us. We just have to figure out what that is and either accept it or fix it. You've been fixing as long as I've known you. You're like that gorgeous house that gets even more gorgeous with each remodel."

"You're just being nice now," she said.

He set down the still-full fork. "You know me, Eds. I'm never nice."

"You're always nice." She picked up her fork and poked at the graham cracker crust and what little filling was left. "Except when faced with pie."

"It's good pie," he said.

"One day your metabolism will quit and you'll balloon to the size of Texas overnight," she said.

"I will enjoy each and every bite along the way," he said.

She sopped up some of the remaining chocolate with a little bit of the crust. She felt incrementally better.

"I treated Mack abominably," she said.

"That matters to you," Petruchio said, as if he had suddenly found the perfect legal decision that would win his case in court.

"Yeah," she said. "He's a good man."

"He's that, but that's not usually enough for you."

She looked up sharply.

Petruchio raised his hands. "Not a criticism," he said. "Just a fact."

He was right. She usually didn't care.

She cared about Mack.

"What do I do to apologize?" she asked.

"How about...you know, an apology?" Petruchio said.

She gave him a withering look. "And then what?"

"I think you'll have to prove to both of you that you can be the girlfriend type." Petruchio slid what was left of the pie toward her. "Mack's okay with the pregnancy, huh?"

"Yes," she said with a bit of irritation. Hadn't she told him that already?

"Wow." Petruchio reached across the table and cut another little piece of pie. There really wasn't much left for her. "You might need that."

"Need what?" she asked.

"The one thing your mom never allowed," he said.

"What's that?" Edie asked.

"A partner," Petruchio said. "Imagine what your life would have been like if she had had a partner to help raise you."

"Lots of screaming fights and nasty putdowns, I expect," Edie said. "*Someone* dodged a bullet."

"Okay, wrong example," Petruchio said. "But there's no way you can ever emulate your mother with a man in the picture."

Edie ate the last bit of graham cracker crust. "That's not a reason to get involved with Mack."

"That's not a reason to avoid him either," Petruchio said. "It's just something to think about."

She looked at him. He had a bit of whip cream on his tie. He always ended up wearing his food, and she loved that about him.

"My life went from completely ordered to one big honking mess in less than a month," she said. "I'm not sure it's fair to bring someone else into it."

"Excuses, excuses," Petruchio said. "First, counselor, you're bringing a child into it."

"That's part of the mess," she said.

"*And*," Petruchio said, clearly not willing to let her say anything else, "your life was never ordered. It was regimented. Sterile."

"What I did wasn't always sterile," she said.

He held up his hands again. "TMI, Edie. T.M.I."

She grinned. She loved irritating him like that.

Then her grin faded. He was right. Her life had a sameness to it. The men were different, but never much more than an evening's entertainment. Which wasn't fair to them.

Or to her.

"Embrace the mess," he said. "It's either that or fight it every step of the way."

She had been fighting it. Maybe he was right. Maybe embracing it was the way to go.

Maybe she already had been embracing it, and hadn't really realized it.

After all, she had decided to keep the child, and she had known that would upset every aspect of her life.

Embrace the mess. That wasn't a half-bad slogan. She could live like that.

"Thanks, Petruchio," she said.

"What are friends for?" he asked, then clanked his fork on his plate. "Besides, I got pie. Life is always better with pie."

"Yeah," she said. Life was better with pie. And good friends.

She was lucky enough to have both.

24

The next morning, Mack decided to tackle the attic walls. He had avoided them for two years because they were so damn ugly. Some kind of cheap wallboard attached to cheap two-by-fours, separating the attic into six parts. He'd avoided it because the ceiling sloped and he was worried about hitting his head.

He'd also avoided it because there was no heat or air-conditioning up there, so it was always uncomfortable.

He could do uncomfortable today. He *needed* uncomfortable. He felt like a goddamn idiot for trying to make Edie into something she wasn't. For getting attached because of one great afternoon of sex and the fact that she was so damn courageous and smart.

And he was still hooked.

He didn't want to be. He didn't want to be attracted to a woman who wanted nothing to do with him outside of bed.

Somehow he managed to work up a sweat, even though he could see his breath up there. His back ached from crouching, and he was covered with both sawdust and pink insulation. It had stuck to his skin.

And, sadly, he didn't feel any better, even though he had pulled off wallboard and yanked at stubborn nails. Usually, destroying a room lightened his mood, got out some of his aggression.

All this did was reinforce how upset he was.

He walked down the back stairs. He planned to refinish those last, so he didn't have to worry about getting construction crap on his newly fixed flooring. He grabbed a filthy towel he'd left on the end of the dowel-shaped railing and wiped off his face. The last thing he wanted to do was breathe in some of that pink insulation. It was fiberglass and hazardous, and he'd been so mad when he woke up that morning that he hadn't bothered with the face mask.

He'd use it this afternoon when he cleaned up the rest.

The back stairs widened into the utility room off the kitchen. He'd left the utility room, even though it hadn't really been part of the original design. Eventually, he'd upgrade the utility room, but right now, he used it like the back stairs—the place where he landed after some particularly gruesome remodeling.

He turned on the water in the sink, splashed his face and forearms, then dried off with yet another towel.

After that, he figured, he was clean enough to manage the kitchen. He walked in, opened the fridge, and drank directly out of a half-full bottle of Gatorade. Then he burped and wiped off his mouth.

The perks of living alone. He could pretend like he'd never progressed past the age of twelve.

Sometimes he wished he hadn't. Then he wouldn't be all twisted up inside over a woman. He'd love to get into a good, old-fashioned fight about baseball or something, instead of thinking about the possibilities he had lost for the sake of principles.

And his heart.

He couldn't forget his heart.

Jesus, how would he have felt after spending months or a year with her, only to find her in bed with some other guy. Mack was twisted up right now, and all he'd done was sleep with her once and buy her dinner once. Imagine if he had actually committed to her.

The doorbell rang. He jumped. He hadn't heard that sound in months, not since he'd stopped ordering supplies for his high-end kitchen.

He glanced down at his shirt, saw the chips of wood and fiberglass, and hoped it all would continue to stick to the sweat stains. He really didn't want to sweep up the hallway later this afternoon.

He was halfway down that hallway when the doorbell rang again.

"Coming," he yelled, letting his irritation out. It was probably some political campaign needing a donation or some religious nutball with a tract or some homeless guy searching for the vet who used to live here.

He hoped it wasn't a homeless guy, because he'd lose an entire afternoon all over again. He always shoved those folks into his truck, bought them a meal, and then took them over to the shelter. It made his conscience feel better, but it gave his truck an odor that he sometimes couldn't get out for days.

And, frankly, he wasn't in a do-gooder mood right now. He still wanted to punch something. Or drive a hammer through an ugly and useless wall.

He reached the door. The shadow of someone shifted behind the leaded stained glass. Not for the first time, he questioned his decision to put a classic door on this place instead of something more practical with a peephole or something.

He had promised himself he would arrange security cameras on his front porch, but the head of Santore Security somehow never found time to properly rig up his own home. He had to make do with the system he had set up when he bought the place, which was, if he was being honest with himself, still better than the security most homeowners had.

He grabbed the polished, cut-glass doorknob, turned, and pulled the door open as he said in his most dismissive tone, "Yeah?"

He was braced for a Jehovah's Witness or a Mormon kid on a mission.

Instead, he got Edie, wrapped up in a fluffy blue coat, hood down, revealing a nose delightfully red with cold.

He didn't smile at her. He didn't want to see her. He was still mad at her—and himself—and the entire situation.

"I don't want any," he said flatly, using a phrase his mother used to use with door-to-door salesmen.

"I'm not here to give you any," Edie said seriously.

He hadn't realized until now how that phrase could be misconstrued. Still, he didn't move, blocking the entry with his body. The ice-cold air was freezing the sweat off his skin. In a minute, he would start shivering.

"I'd normally just have the conversation out here," Edie said. "I mean, this is a lovely porch, the kind you don't see much anymore, but the bank three blocks from here says the temperature is minus five, and God knows what the wind chill is."

He didn't know how to respond to that. He wanted her gone. He didn't want a conversation.

"Edie," he said, "we really don't have anything to say to each other."

"You might not have anything to say," she said. "But I do. Please."

He sighed a little and stepped back. She walked inside. She was carrying two large shopping bags with handles. As she passed him, he realized the bags left a scent of garlic and baked bread.

His traitorous stomach growled.

He closed the door behind her, and immediately the temperature in the foyer rose about thirty degrees.

She looked at him, as if she expected him to lead her into the kitchen or the dining room or the living room. He didn't do any of those things.

He just waited.

"I brought lunch," she said, lifting up the bags.

"I don't need lunch," he said, even though his stomach was making a liar out of him.

She stared at him for a moment, clearly at a loss. He wanted to ease things for her, to smile graciously and lead her into his kitchen, then sit across from her and enjoy a meal.

But that would mean getting involved with her. That would mean getting closer to her, and maybe even taking her upstairs to his half-finished bedroom, or stopping there on a tour of the house, just so she could see the rest of the place, and then he would sweep her into the room, and into his bed and...

"How did you know where I live?" he asked, mostly to quell the noisy thoughts in his head.

"Petruchio," she said. "But I stopped at the clinic first because, y'know, terrorists never sleep and the need for protection never ends."

"Aldis is there today," Mack said, as if Aldis were the only one. Mack had canceled some high-paying jobs to have enough staff to work the clinic. He didn't like the loss of funds, but he couldn't stomach another near-miss on his watch.

"I saw that," Edie said.

The smell of garlic bread made his mouth water, but he wasn't going to cave in. He couldn't afford to get involved with this woman, not for any reason. She would break his heart.

She swung the bags just a little, as if she didn't quite know what to do with them. "I, um, I came to apologize."

"No need." He put his hand on the door frame behind her, a not-so-subtle hint that she should leave. "I like you, Edie, but this isn't going to work, you and me."

She sighed. "I wanted to do this over lunch, but...I was a jerk. Deliberately. I got scared and I pushed and—"

"I know," he said. "I also know that you and I, we're a mismatch."

"We're not though," she said. "We agree on many things. We enjoy each other's company. Dinner last night was wonderful until I ruined it. Let me apologize properly, Mack, and—"

Something must have changed on his face because she blanched.

"*Not* that kind of apology," she said. "I understand what you're saying about five dates and going slow. I'm sorry. I really was being a jerk—"

"I didn't think you meant that kind of apology," he lied. Was he really that easy to read? Apparently so. "I just—I want the fairy tale, Edie. And I don't think that's possible for us."

She half-smiled, then moved a gloved hand, and the bag still clutched in it, to her stomach. "Clearly."

"That's not what I mean," he said. He would have loved a ready-made family. "It's just that I need a one-man woman, and that's not you. That's okay. It's just not the kind of relationship I want. That's all."

His heart ached as he said that. He did feel something special for this woman, more than he'd felt for any woman, including some he'd dated for years.

She closed her eyes, then nodded. And sighed. And opened her eyes.

"You know," she said, "I tell my clients, you can't go back in time and fix whatever it was that you've done. You just have to move forward."

He waited, leaning ever so slightly on the door, feeling sticky and filthy and sadder than he had for years.

"I—knew what you meant," she said. "About being faithful. By then, I was being so ornery that I would probably have said anything to push you away. I—I—I have no idea if I can be someone who you would want. I think I can be faithful. I've never tried it. But I've never had an exclusive relationship before either. I do have lifelong friends, though, and—"

"Edie," he said gently. "No. Much as I would enjoy so many aspects of our attempt, I just can't. Not with the baby coming."

"Yeah," she said softly. "The proof that I'm not the kind of woman you want."

"No," he said. "I'm not just risking my heart over you. I'm risking my heart over that little person you're carrying. I can't fall in love with both of you, only to lose you both."

A slight frown appeared between her eyes. Apparently, she hadn't thought of that.

"Here," she said, thrusting one of the bags at him. "Spaghetti from Antonelli's, complete with garlic bread. I guess they were prescient because they gave me two servings in two different bags. This one is yours."

"Edie, you don't have to—"

"You're clearly in the middle of something, and I interrupted, and there's more food here than I'll ever eat, even with my—passenger." She attempted a smile, but it didn't reach her eyes. "For the record, Mack. You're an amazing man, and a good-hearted one, and I treated you like shit. I'm very sorry."

He didn't take the bag, so she set it down on his shiny wood floor. Then she turned, grabbed the doorknob, and pulled.

The fact that he was leaning on the door actually meant he was holding it closed. He had to stand up to let her out.

He hesitated for just a moment, and then he stood.

She opened the door just a few inches and slipped out before he could even say thank you.

The door slammed behind her.

He put a hand on the doorknob. It was still warm from her touch. He almost pulled it open, almost told her he had changed his mind, almost gave in.

She was an amazing woman, and if she wasn't pregnant, he would have gone after her. But he hadn't lied to her.

He couldn't start down the road with her and that child, only to be turned away.

Or worse.

He leaned his head on his arm for just a moment. Outside, he heard the quiet rumble of a car engine starting.

If he pulled open the door...he would see her driving off.

He sighed.

He made his choice. He didn't like it, but it was the safe decision. It was the decision that would protect all three of them.

He let go of the doorknob, picked up the bag of food, and headed to his kitchen.

Alone.

With a meal he wasn't even sure he could enjoy, ever again.

25

*S*tupid, stupid, stupid. Edie was upset enough that she had to make sure she drove slowly and cautiously on the ice. She actually told herself what to do next: *Slow down, there's an intersection. See the stoplight? What color is it? Green? Yellow?* Because if she didn't, she'd swirl in her emotions, and she couldn't do that.

Not right now.

Especially when she was feeling so stupid.

Why had she thought that a simple apology would work? Mack wasn't that kind of man. He didn't change his mind on a whim. He wasn't susceptible to charm. He had his ideas and, in this case, he was right.

That was the hell of it.

He was right.

She hadn't thought it through. If he got involved with her, particularly now, he was taking on a pregnant woman, yes, but a pregnant woman doesn't stay pregnant forever. Eventually she delivers a child, and that child develops relationships of its own.

Stupid, stupid, stupid.

She, of all people, should have known how different a child could be from its mother.

She and hers were nothing alike. Except, apparently, in their insensitivity to others.

A car swerved in front of her, and she hadn't seen it coming. She tapped the brakes. Her car responded easily, and only then did she think to check if another car was behind her.

Hers was the only car heading north out of this neighborhood. The car that had swerved had turned left, away from her.

Her heart pounded. She slowed even more and then finally pulled over. Mack's neighborhood was being gentrified, but it still had pockets of ruined buildings and empty lots. Right now, the empty lots were piled with dirty snow and ice. The roads were badly plowed, which was what made them so treacherous.

She leaned her forehead against the steering wheel. It had been a long time since she had made so many mistakes in a relationship. One reason she usually held herself back from getting too close too fast was so that she could step back and clearly see who the other person was.

Maybe it had been the way that they had met and partnered with each other in that emergency. Or maybe she had been blinded by desire. She hadn't seen him clearly, even though he had told her who he was.

A man who wanted a serious relationship. A man who didn't have casual sex. A man who wanted—of all things—the fairy tale.

She sighed.

She didn't believe in fairy tales. She *knew* there were no happily ever afters. Even if a couple stayed together for fifty years, the relationship would end. One of them would die, and the other would be alone.

Secretly, she had always thought that would be the worst—relying on someone for decades and then, suddenly, that someone disappearing. The end of life was never a good time. Death, illness, dementia—there was no happy and no ever after.

But she doubted she could tell Mack that. He would have some kind of argument.

She shook her head, feeling the cool plastic against her skin. She was tired. Real tired and pregnancy tired. And disappointed in herself.

If she had read him properly, she wouldn't have tried that date. She wouldn't have taken him to bed.

In the past, she never messed with Romantic True Believers. She had a few times early on, and found them to be clingy and needy and hopelessly delusional.

She hadn't expected that in a man who defended people for a living, but maybe that was how he slept at night.

And then she let out a breath. She wasn't just stupid; she was cynical. Maybe he could defend people because he was a hopeless romantic, an optimist who believed people were worth saving.

She was a lawyer. She believed people did everything according to their own selfish needs.

And what were her selfish needs?

She sat up. The street was empty. She had parked behind a pile of snow that might once have been a badly parked car. Two blocks away, the bank thermometer told her that the temperature had gone up a whopping two degrees.

The bag in the passenger seat sent odors of garlic and tomato sauce throughout the car.

The first selfish need she had was lunch. The others that she had always addressed had been, simply, physical. Food, sex, sleep. Her work consumed her, and her volunteering fed her friendships.

Although that wasn't entire true. Petruchio had been right: she had always been the glue that kept their college friends attached. She had done the same with her high school friends. If she thought about it at all, she justified it—she was the one without a partner or children; she was the one with all the time to keep people together.

But it was more than that. Her friends had gotten her through. Once she realized she could survive her mother by avoiding her mother, Edie had collected friends like trophies. And she had piled those friends around her like an emotional wall, to prevent her mother from ever getting to her.

"And you think you'll be a good parent," Edie muttered aloud. Then she sighed and put the car in drive. After looking in her rearview and to the side, she pulled onto the street.

She had always liked Mack's neighborhood. She used to think that when she had time as well as money, she would buy a fixer-upper here.

The asking price for all the mansions was cheap, but the rehab costs made them as expensive as new construction. She used to dream of doing some of the rehab herself, but she had never allowed that to happen. She hadn't had time, for one thing. She had let her job consume her.

She had enjoyed letting her job consume her.

So she had purchased that condo completely finished, and she had bought the model unit. She had even bought the downstairs furniture. Only the upstairs reflected her taste at all.

If she thought of the stuff she bought as indicative of "taste."

Then she smiled. That was a *Mother* comment if any was. Her mother had always disparaged her style. Her mother had disparaged everything.

Maybe, instead of just relying on parenting classes, Edie needed to do more work than that. Maybe she had to overhaul her entire life.

Not quit her job—she loved that. But consider the rest of it. What had made her so snide about being faithful? What had prevented the long-term relationships? She couldn't blame everything on her mother.

It wasn't a question of fairness—who cared if she was fair to her mother? It was a question of responsibility.

At some point, Edie had to take responsibility for her own choices. She couldn't blame her childhood forever.

The one thing she knew she needed to change, without any counselor telling her to do so, was the sexual part of her lifestyle. She wouldn't have time to sleep around, not with a child in the house. She could probably hire a live-in nanny or something, but that seemed like a sterile option.

And a stupid one.

Why fail to take care of your own child while you were chasing hedonistic pleasures? She would have limited time to be with her child in the first place if she planned to keep her job (and she did). So, she needed to make certain that she made the most of the time she had with that child.

She would have to rethink everything.

They had said that in the promotional material for the parenting class, but she hadn't taken it seriously until now.

Before her child was born, she would have to figure out who she was.

And not just that. She would also have to figure out who she wanted to be.

She could stumble forward, let circumstances choose for her, and guaranteed, she would end up sarcastic, bitter, and alone, damaging the child she was already planning to protect.

Or she could learn how to be her best self, whatever that was.

She had no idea how to do any of it.

But she knew she had better start—and start now.

26

*M*ack paced the weird antechamber inside the clinic. For the past three weeks, he'd put in at least five shifts a week because he still didn't have enough manpower to handle the clinic's needs. He had spoken to the FBI, who were both helpful and contradictory.

The organization that attacked this clinic was a loose confederation of crazies, under the influence of an even bigger crazy named Donnie Pierce. Pierce called his organization The Fighting Patriots of America, but some of the crazies worked under different appellations, older ones like the Confederated Patriots of America and The Fighting Sons of America.

National FBI headquarters believed that all of these organizations were part of the same group, but the head of the local FBI branch claimed they were splinter groups.

Mack didn't care what the organization's internal structure was. All he wanted to know was who to guard against.

And his investigators, plus the FBI and the local police, didn't have names for the local group. The man they'd caught, Jesse Lewis, didn't supply any, because he had only worked with Bert Sessions, the man who had died. Lewis had seen other people, but he claimed he had no real idea who they were.

The FBI said that hate groups like this one generally did not attack at the same location twice. Or if they did, they would wait for years before approaching the location again.

Although a few of the agents confessed that they had seen some of these nutballs get a bee up their shorts and attack the same location over and over again.

The FBI said that Mack didn't need an increase in manpower. He just needed to make sure his people were vigilant.

His people were vigilant. But part of the vigilance included not taking anything for granted. And it sounded to him like believing these crazies would act like other crazies was frighteningly close to taking anything for granted.

Just like being in this clinic was for him. He had to pace the front area just to stay alert. The heat was on high here, and it was too hot for him, especially since he—and his entire team—wore bulletproof vests beneath their shirts.

He wore a uniform jacket over a light blue shirt because he also carried a concealed weapon. He had thought about wearing his weapon openly and decided against it.

The one thing he did know about crazies associated with hate groups was that some of those fuckers were well-trained. And one thing that they were trained well on was how to handle cops and rent-a-cops.

Mack didn't think of his people as rent-a-cops. They were too good for that. But anyone could be taken by surprise by a strong and prepared perpetrator. And unless someone took precautions ahead of time, they could lose the weapon they were using to guard people to that strong and prepared perpetrator.

Mack had never had his weapon taken from him, but he had had staff who had. They ended up on desk duty, and most moved on to other jobs. He didn't need screw-ups on his team.

He glanced at the waiting room behind that dangerous wall of glass. This morning, the waiting room was full. Three women in the last stages of pregnancy, sitting in chairs all alone, looking tired and so thoroughly through with the entire experience that they had initially made him smile when they had come in.

One woman had brought twin toddlers, and she was round with another child. Mack had no idea how she and her partner had found time to create a new child, particularly as he watched those toddlers terrorize everyone in the waiting room—until Darcy settled them down by hauling out what she considered the Big Guns—two toddler-sized bright red cars that the kids could drive all over the waiting area.

Then there was a couple—if Mack could call them that—who sat next to each other but didn't touch. The woman's face was red with tears, and the man looked quite determined. He clutched his wallet.

Mack was beginning to recognize that pattern. Either they were getting a divorce, and there was a child in the way, or they were a casual couple who had decided that abortion was the best course for them.

He couldn't ask, of course, and didn't as they had gone through the metal detector. But he had become sensitive to the upset and the level of consideration that people in crisis made.

He had seen it several times in the past few weeks, and each time, it had made him think of Edie. Not because she had decided against this choice, but because the father of her child had said it was the only choice he would support.

Mack still ran over and over that in his mind. She had seemed like the type of woman who would decide not to have a child, and yet she had decided to go through with it.

Initially, he had thought she would end up with quite a wake-up call about childcare and child-rearing as a single parent, and then he realized that she probably knew as much or more about it than he ever would. Especially considering she had once *been* the child of a single parent.

He sighed, and continued to pace on the scuffed old marble floor. If he was honest with himself, it wasn't just the unhappy couples that made him think of Edie. It was the tired-looking professional women who showed up here alone on their lunch hours or at the end of a very long day, moving slowly in some suit they had modified to become maternity clothes.

It was the women who leaned on other women as they came through the front door, and who would gamely give him a smile as he explained that he would have to pat them down before they could go in because he didn't want to risk using the wand.

It was the women, arm in arm with the men who loved them, who looked on the new baby as a new adventure.

It was every woman who came through the door because he kept hoping that, eventually, one of those women would be Edie.

He hadn't seen her at all since she brought him lunch on that cold Saturday weeks ago. He wasn't sure what he would say if he did see her. He just wanted to know how she was, and he didn't feel like he could ask Ruth.

It felt—to him—as if he and Ruth were avoiding the topic of Edie altogether, but that might have simply been his imagination. He wasn't sure Ruth even knew about their date, or his attraction, or the fact that he had decided not to get involved with Edie after all.

He stopped in front of the main door and looked across the piled snow at the apartment building across the street. Every day that he worked here, he did that. Something about the building bothered him.

He had a sense he was being watched—that they were all being watched.

And that was probably true, since the windows for the apartments on the front half of the building faced the clinic directly. That would make it the perfect place to spy on the clinic.

He had mentioned that to the police. They had checked the residents and found no connection to the FPA. Neither had the FBI. But it still bothered him.

The entire setup bothered him.

He was about to turn away when he saw a familiar form walking down the sidewalk.

For a moment, he thought he was imagining her. After all, he had just been thinking about Edie.

But the Edie he had been thinking about was the woman he had first met, who wore a stylish wool coat over bare legs in the middle of the coldest winter on record. The woman who walked down the sidewalk was wearing the same coat, but was four inches shorter. She had on sensible boots instead of heels, and her legs were encased in wool pants that seemed to match the coat.

He smiled in spite of himself. Apparently, she couldn't forgo the style just because she was going for comfort.

Or sense.

Or whatever she was going for.

She, too, glanced over her shoulder at the apartments before pivoting and coming down the clinic's sidewalk. Halfway to the building, she waved at someone—probably Lashon, who was also on today.

Then she stuck her hands in the coat, bowed her head against the arctic wind, and walked up the stairs.

Mack held the door open for her. He almost lied to himself by telling himself he did that for almost everyone who came in here, but that wasn't why. He opened the door because his heart started beating faster the moment he realized he was looking at her.

Because he wanted to see her.

"Hey, Edie," he said quietly.

She glanced at him. If she was surprised to see him, she didn't show it. "Mack," she said.

Then she peeled off the coat, tossed it on the x-ray machine along with her purse and briefcase. She handed him her iPhone, as if he were any other security guard.

Which, apparently, he was now.

He went behind the x-ray imager and looked at the purse. A few tubes—probably lipstick—and nothing else out of the ordinary. The briefcase was filled with papers. The coat had nothing in the pockets.

He turned the phone on and off, like he was supposed to, then handed it back to her.

"How are you?" he asked.

She patted her stomach, which was just a little rounder than it had been when she was with him.

"Experiencing new and delightful joys each and every day," she said.

She grabbed the phone, tossed it in her purse, then slung the purse over her shoulder, folded her coat over her arm, and took the briefcase with her free hand. She didn't say anything more to him, not anything in passing, not a see-you-later, not even a hope-you're-all-right.

She let herself into the waiting room, and, without turning around, headed to Darcy at reception, stepping cautiously to one side to avoid a toddler in a big red car. Both she and Darcy laughed as they looked at the kids, still riding around.

Mack remained beside the x-ray machine, his heart pounding. The weird antechamber smelled faintly of lavender soap and a scent he instantly recognized as hers.

She had gone past him as if he meant nothing more to her than a stranger would have. As if he were any other security guard at any other building in the city.

His cheeks grew warm.

What did he expect? He had rejected her, which was probably not the norm for her. And she had other concerns now.

Besides, why should he care? After all, he was the one who had decided it wasn't going to work.

Neither was staying inside, watching her in the waiting room, seeing her laugh, getting lost in how lovely she looked.

He flicked on the small mic on his collar, then pressed the earwig.

"Hey, Lashon," he said. "Feel like warming up?"

"Thought you'd never ask," Lashon said, his voice tinny in Mack's ear. "Be warned, though, it's starting to—heck, I don't know what you'd call this. Sleet? Freezing rain? Fresh drops of frozen hell?"

"It's all right," Mack said. He needed to cool down. "Let's switch."

So they did.

2 7

*S*he couldn't help herself. Edie turned around and looked at the elaborate entrance for one more glance at Mack. He wasn't visible, and she let out a little breath.

It had taken all of her strength to be courteous to him. She had no idea how to behave around him. She was still embarrassed at how she had treated him, and she'd felt even worse when he had rejected her a second time.

She hadn't called him and she had tried not to think about him. She had scheduled her appointments with Ruth for after-hours so that she wouldn't risk running into him. But this afternoon, she couldn't avoid it. She'd had some weird, fluttery pains that were just unusual enough that Ruth wanted to see her immediately rather than wait until after six.

And there he was, looking tall and handsome and oh, so, official in his security guard jacket. For a moment, she thought he had bulked up, but he hadn't. He was wearing something underneath the shirt, a vest probably.

The idea gave her the shivers, made her remember the last time she had seen him here. It had all gone so wrong that day, and yet it had gone so right.

She felt all of those conflicting emotions at once—joy at seeing him, curiosity about him, the fear that had come up when the bomber had gone after this place—and she didn't want him to see any of them. So she had been businesslike and curt with him, which was probably the only way she would be able to deal with him going forward.

"Have a seat," Darcy said, and swept her hand toward the waiting room. The toddlers were driving back and forth, their mother blissfully ignoring them. A woman sat in the corner, looking "pregnant everywhere" as Ruth sometimes said about women who retained too much water during their pregnancies. She had her feet on a nearby chair, either to keep the swelling down in her ankles or to avoid the toddlers, or both.

The toddlers' squeal of delight was drowning out the usual pop music that was piped into the waiting area, and Edie found herself feeling grateful. She wasn't in a pop mood.

She was in a sulky mood, particularly since that fluttery feeling had left halfway here. She had actually called Ruth and tried to bug out of the appointment, but Ruth wouldn't let her.

We're checking every little thing, Ruth had said. *Remember, this is my kid too.*

Ruth had been serious about that. She was as relentlessly single as Edie was, and didn't want to have a child on her own, not while the clinic was threatened.

And clearly that threat hadn't gone away, or Mack wouldn't be here.

Edie picked a chair as far from the toddler raceway as she could find and sat on the edge. The chair wasn't visible from the entry, which meant she couldn't see it either. Or Mack.

Still, she wanted to go out there and just catch up with him. See how he had been doing. Petruchio wouldn't tell her. He seemed to think that keeping Mack and Edie apart was his new mission in life. He had thought they were a mismatch from the beginning.

Maybe they were. But they had certainly gotten Edie to think about her life.

She had realized, she told her therapist, that she had been going through most days by rote. She had stopped heading to bars and using Tinder, and she hadn't even missed it.

Oh, she had missed physical touch, but she couldn't even say she had missed the closeness. Because those encounters had never been about closeness. They had been about heat and release, and little else.

She had less tolerance for risk now.

She couldn't tell if it was the hormones governing that or if it was her brain, or if it was a combination of both.

Or maybe it had just been time to change her life.

And she was facing major change. She was remodeling the condo—herself—while she still had energy. When there were tasks that weren't recommended for pregnant women, she hired out. Mostly, though, the remodel meant following the baby-proof instructions she had gotten from the parenting class, replacing some pieces of furniture, and covering every single outlet in the place.

The biggest change was that she was decreasing the size of her bedroom by making a small nursery off to the side. Her upstairs office was moving to the site of her massive closet, and the baby would eventually get that second bedroom all for itself—when it was old enough to sleep in its own room.

She was still uncertain about how some of these things would work, even though she had been reading everything about pregnancy she could find. She had lists—and more lists, and even more lists—as she figured out what she needed, when she would need assistance, and what kind of assistance that would be.

She had lined up her maternity leave from the office and had notified them that she was taking the full three months of parental leave that they offered. They hadn't batted an eye.

That's what happened when you worked at a place for ten years and only once took your full vacation allotment. They realized just how committed to the job you really were.

The toddlers and their mother got called to the back. The sudden silence seemed overwhelming. Edie hadn't realized how loud those toddlers had been until they stopped making vroom-vroom noises as they powered their little cars with their feet.

She smiled at one of the other women, who smiled back. Then she sighed and leaned her head against the back of the chair, closing her eyes for just a moment.

Or it seemed like a moment.

Because the next thing she knew, Darcy was calling her name from the front and grinning knowingly.

Edie stood. And, in spite of herself, she looked in the entry again.

No Mack. Lashon was guiding in a young couple, instructing them on how to use the x-ray machine.

She felt a thread of disappointment.

Mack had left, and she hadn't even had a chance to say goodbye.

28

---

*M*ack hated how high the snowbanks had gotten. Record cold, record snowfall. Record winter, even after the pundits had predicted that harsh winters were a thing of the past.

If this was good, he didn't want to see what they considered bad.

Lashon had been right: it was sleeting or subjecting everyone to freezing rain. Mack wasn't sure what to call whatever was causing icy pellets to fall out of the sky; he just knew it was damn uncomfortable.

He hunched in the parka he had purchased for just this sort of thing. He wasn't wearing a hood or a hat because he didn't want to hurt his line of sight. And he didn't wear ear muffs, because he didn't want anything to interfere with his hearing. Although he might need to do something, because it felt like the tips of his ears were freezing off.

He paced around the building, his boots sliding on the slick surface. Screw the squeak of snow, which had always irritated him. Now he was dealing with the crack of ice and keeping his balance.

The gray twilight color of the early afternoon sky made it look like a filter had fallen across Mack's eyes. The sleet only made the visibility worse, and the high snowbanks made him feel hemmed in.

He walked cautiously, scanning the area around him for movement.

Jade was walking the entire neighborhood right now, even though he hadn't seen her. Khalil was due to enter the waiting room in the next fifteen minutes, one of six rotating guards who spent part of their days inside. Never the same guards, and never the same day, in case someone was watching the clinic to figure out who all the security guards were.

Mack shoved his gloved hands in his pockets and trudged. The woods around the back of the clinic presented a problem in this kind of light. He had insisted that Ruth spend money to properly light the back parking area, but even though it was dark enough for that lighting to click on this afternoon, the lights made no difference in this gloom.

He wished he could rub his eyes and improve his vision. He hated the way the grays blended into each other.

He also hated the way they blended into his mood.

Seeing Edie hadn't made him feel better. It had made him feel worse than he had in weeks.

They had only shared an afternoon and a dinner, in actual reality, so he should have gotten over her by now. According to Lashon's Theory of Relationships, which Lashon told Mack one drunken night after Mack's breakup with Bree, the time it took to get over a relationship took proportionally as long as the relationship had lasted. If the relationship lasted one year, it took at least one month to get over it. Five years, five months. Twelve years, one year.

So in theory, a relationship like Mack's with Edie—if, indeed, it could be called a relationship—should have taken him thirty minutes to get past.

He made a snorting sound, releasing a cloud of icy breath around him. So much for Lashon's Theory of Relationships. Maybe that theory worked for Lashon, but it certainly didn't work for Mack.

It had taken him years to get past Bree, and it had already taken weeks with Edie, and he still wasn't over her.

He had a weird feeling that he would never get over her.

A movement at the edge of the parking lot caught his eye. He eased his hands out of his pockets, but didn't go for his gun. Instead, he tapped the mic attached to the earwig and said softly, "Might have something.

Need one more body in the back parking lot. Prep the interior for evac, if necessary."

Whoever joined him would have their weapon drawn. He was going to see if he was dealing with some bored kid or a high schooler taking a shortcut.

No sense in having his people get trigger happy if there was no need for it.

He did not walk quietly or cautiously toward the movement. He strode across the back parking lot, as well as anyone could stride in this weather on this ice. He was going to play the helpful security guard, at least at the moment.

As he got closer, he saw a thin man huddling near a wide oak tree. The man wore a parka similar to Mack's, but the parka's shape was weird, as if the man carried heavy rocks in all of his pockets.

Mack's vision sharpened. He could suddenly smell the wet dampness of the sleet, hear the pellets hitting the ground like an insane tap-dancer, feel the air he had just inhaled cool inside his lungs. Clearly, he had just taken a hit of adrenaline. It also made time slow down to a crawl, a feature he liked about that alert state.

He couldn't quite see the man's face. Some of that was because the man had his hood up, and the black fringe blocked part of Mack's vision. But some of that was the damn sleet. Even with Mack's heightened senses, he couldn't see through it well enough to see fine details several yards away.

"Hey, my friend," he said, his tone easy and relaxed. "Everything all right?"

The man didn't move. Not a twitch. And he should have. Mack exhaled quietly. Slowly. Bracing himself in case the man decided to attempt running in this slick weather.

"Hey," Mack said again. "You okay?"

He wanted the guy to think that he was unprepared, that he wasn't on alert at all. He wanted the guy to underestimate him. He didn't want the guy to notice that Mack was coming in slightly sideways, in an area where the piled snowbanks gave him protection against any gun the guy might decide to fire at him.

Maybe the guy was unconscious from the cold. Maybe he had walked here from somewhere else, went into the trees for shelter, and slipped into unconsciousness.

It happened.

Mack just didn't like it happening on his watch, near this clinic, at this moment.

"Hey," he said. "Buddy. Everything all right?"

He thought he saw a slight movement and knew, if he had been a jittery cop, that would have been the moment he drew his weapon.

"Mack," Jade said in his ear. "I'm at the edge of the trees. If I step onto the parking lot, he will notice me. What do you want me to do?"

"Hold," Mack said under his breath. He wanted to handle this, but he was relieved to know that Jade was there, waiting.

He had reached the low edge of the snowbank. Now it was more of a snow tumble, with chunks of gray snow toppled against each other like cinderblocks. He would have to wade through that to get to the guy.

"Hey, my friend," Mack said, deciding that buddy sounded fake. "Let's get you out of this weather. I have coffee inside."

The man shifted, the kind of move someone would make if he were reaching for a weapon.

Still, Mack relied on his training, not his fears. He wasn't going to reach for his own weapon without knowing if the man had one at all.

The man raised his head, and in the growing dusk, he looked angry, almost feral.

"Now," Mack said softly into his mic.

Ice snapped to his left—clearly Jade, stepping forward.

The man stood and looked in the direction of the sound, clearly startled. He dragged with him something greenish gray. It fell away like a mantel, and he had something in his left hand.

Rifle?

Mack reached for his gun, but stopped at the last second. The man wasn't wielding the rifle, if indeed that's what it was.

He was leaning on it, something someone who respected weapons never did.

The ice cracked and popped. The man scrambled toward the woods, then lost his balance and fell backward with an audible *whomp!*

Mack slid his hand away from his weapon. Even if the man was intent on hurting him, which Mack now doubted, he wouldn't be able to reach the weapon right away. That fall had to have knocked the breath out of him.

The ice continued to crack, and in the corner of his vision, Mack saw Jade. She stopped at the edge of the snowbank, glancing at Mack for instructions.

He nodded toward the man, not feeling the need to use actual hand signals. Jade nodded in return.

She and Mack moved toward the man in tandem, one step at a time. Jade was contending with ice, Mack with ice-covered snow, packed with what seemed like rock. As they moved forward slowly, the man struggled to get up, like people did when the wind had been knocked out of them or they were badly injured. He tried, and failed, then tried again, hands slipping and unable to gain purchase on the ground around him.

Mack reached him first. And then the stench reached Mack— unwashed human flesh, days-old urine, filthy clothing. It carried despite the cold, despite the sleet.

Mack let out a breath he hadn't realized he was holding. He tapped his mic, whispered, "Homeless," and Jade stopped.

She knew the drill. They would put the man in one of the old vans that they always brought to this job and take him to one of the shelters. First, though, it looked like he needed medical attention, which meant bringing him to the back of the clinic.

Just because the man was homeless didn't mean he was harmless.

Mack still approached cautiously. Jade was speaking quietly into her mic, informing the staff inside the clinic that they had a patient, possibly delusional, and informing Khalil that he needed to bring the ancient van to the parking lot.

Mack thought—not for the first time—that if someone wanted to initiate a surprise attack on the clinic, sending in a homeless guy first was the best way to do it. After this, he would get the team to develop new procedures because these procedures were too resource heavy. For a good five minutes, everyone except Lashon would be focused on the homeless guy, and no one would be monitoring the full exterior.

Mack couldn't change it this time, even though he suddenly felt a ticking clock he hadn't felt before. He set it aside. He couldn't change procedure midstream. He would simply have to get through it.

The man continued to attempt to get up, like a figure in a bad cartoon. Mack had finally gotten close enough to see that the thing the man had been leaning on had been a walking stick. Part of the reason he couldn't get up was because he was handicapped somehow.

Mack started to talk to him as he approached.

"Hey, my friend," Mack said in his most soothing voice. "It's just me. I'm sorry I startled you."

The man made little grunting noises. His eyes rolled, then focused on Mack.

"I'm going to help you up, and then I'll take you somewhere warm, okay?" Mack said.

Jade paused not far from them. She knew, as well as Mack did, that this was the crucial moment. The man could attack or accept help or do anything in between.

The man's lips were blue. His face was an unnatural gray. "D-D-Don't ar-ar-arrest m-m-me," he said, his teeth chattering.

He must have seen the uniform and thought it was a police uniform.

"I'm not with the police," Mack said. "I just work inside and saw you out here. The weather's pretty bad. Let's get you warm."

The man nodded and struggled to get up again. This time, Mack put his hand on the man's back and eased him forward.

Out of the corner of his eye, Mack saw Jade, remaining motionless, watching.

"Th-Th-Thank y-y-you," the man said.

"You're welcome," Mack said. "I'm going to help you up. Do you need the walking stick?"

The man nodded. He shifted. He had the cracked skin and matted hair of someone who had been outside a long time. The parka didn't look as new as it had from a distance—and it certainly didn't smell as new.

"Where are your things?" Mack asked, because he'd dealt with this before. Some of the homeless in the area went a little crazy when they had to leave their things behind.

"N-N-Not he-he-here," the man said. "Cl-cl-clinic."

For a moment, Mack thought the man kept his things in the clinic. Then he realized that the man had come to the clinic, maybe for help, maybe to get warm, and had only made it to the trees.

The man had probably had a tent or some other kind of shelter at the edge of the woods. Mack had seen it before. Some of these guys were former military and knew how to camouflage their home base.

"I'll help you to the clinic," Mack said. "They're expecting you."

The man nodded again, and this time he didn't say anything, as if he knew they were expecting him.

Jade had moved back so she wasn't in their line of sight. She would keep watching in case the man was some kind of decoy. If he was, he was a risky one because people this far gone usually didn't follow instructions.

Mack handed him the stick, which wasn't a stick at all. It was a cane, with a carved handle and beautiful workmanship, now scuffed from time and weather. The man leaned on it and on Mack, and eventually got to his feet.

Underneath the parka and several layers of clothing, the man was incredibly thin. He was shivering now.

"I got you," Mack said. "We got this."

He said that last as much for Jade as for the man.

He half-carried the man across the parking lot, making sure of his own balance with each step. Somewhere along the way, Jade disappeared, returning to her rounds. Out front, he heard the distinctive rattle of the old van and hoped that Khalil would not drive back here until Mack and the homeless man were inside the clinic.

The last thing Mack needed was to have the man startle and both of them fall.

It seemed to take forever, but they finally reached the back door of the clinic, which opened just as they approached.

Mack let out a tiny sigh of relief.

One step down.

Several more to go.

*R*uth used her thumb to end the call on her cell. She looked over at Edie, eyes haunted. Edie felt her heart sink.

"Something bad?" she asked.

She could see Ruth trying to decide what to tell her. Finally, Ruth said, "We're going on lockdown. Stay here."

"Here" was one of the exam rooms. Ruth was running every test known to man and maybe a few only known to woman, even though Edie assured her that the fluttering had stopped. Edie wasn't far enough along that the baby would cause that feeling by moving or doing something itself.

When Edie had mentioned it to one of the nurses as she pulled out the pink-and-blue stork-covered hospital gown, the nurse smiled and asked, "First pregnancy?"

Edie had said, "Yes."

The nurse patted her own stomach, which was ample, and said, "Three for me. And that flutter with each one. It's probably gas, sweetie. But you did the right thing coming in here."

Edie felt her face warm, and the nurse saw it.

"You gotta check everything," the nurse said. "We all go through pregnancy differently, and we have to figure out what's normal for us. So, no worries. I'm sure your little nub is just fine."

Edie wasn't just fine. She especially wasn't fine now that the clinic was in lockdown and she was sitting on the exam table in that stupid gown without underwear or socks or any kind of human decency.

She got up, even though Ruth put a hand on her shoulder. "You stay," Ruth said.

"In your dreams," Edie said.

She slipped out from under Ruth's hand, and grabbed her clothes off the chair. Her bra was getting too small anyway, so she left it, but she slipped on underwear, pants, and her shirt, then put her feet—without socks—into her boots. She picked up her purse, and started to leave the room, when Ruth said,

"What part of lockdown don't you understand?"

"The part where we wait for someone to rescue us," Edie said. "Besides, you have to let everyone know, right?"

"Already did," Ruth said, and lifted her phone. It had a glowing text across the screen, mentioning mandatory lockdown. And a red light had gone on over the door.

It was stupid that a clinic had to have lockdown. It was even stupider that crises seemed to happen whenever Mack and Edie were at the clinic at the same time.

Her heart started pounding. Mack. She hoped he was all right. He had been out front when she had entered, and she hadn't been very nice to him. A little flip, and no eye contact.

Was that the kind of last encounter she wanted with him?

She hoped it wouldn't be.

"I have to make sure that no one is trying to leave," Ruth said. "I would try to control you, but I know that's just plain foolish."

Edie smiled at her, and together they left the exam room. She still had some goo in places that she normally didn't allow goo—unless she was having a good time with some random guy. Not that she did that anymore.

Still, it felt a little awkward, and made her aware of the fact that she was living for two at the moment. She really did need to be careful.

No one stood in the hallway. The nurses' station was abandoned. Through the opening into reception, she saw Darcy near the door, turning the key in the lock. A few of the patients still waiting were asking her questions, and she was trying to calm them down.

Ruth had disappeared, probably making sure no one was trying to leave the back way. Edie peered out through the waiting room at that glass enclosure and saw someone standing to the side.

It wasn't Mack. It was a little too tall and broad to be Mack. The man turned, and she recognized Lashon.

Mack was outside.

Her mouth had gone dry.

She wanted to go out and see what was happening, but she knew better. She needed to follow lockdown procedure herself.

She headed to the exam room to get the rest of her things when she heard voices.

"...not quite all clear," Ruth was saying to someone. "But nothing to worry about, we think."

"...jump like that over some random homeless guy," said a female voice that Edie didn't recognize. "We're really becoming..."

The voices faded. Edie decided not to return to her room. She went to the T in the hallway so she could see the back door. But she stood against the wall so, if shots started, she would be out of the line of fire.

Ruth and two of the newer nurses stood near the door. One of the nurses was watching something on her phone, and Edie realized that wasn't the nurse's phone, but Ruth's. She had the security system on an app, and was probably watching the back door from the outside.

"Now," the nurse said.

The door opened, and Mack stumbled inside, arm wrapped around a man who clearly had seen better days. A waft of cold air reached Edie, and with it a stench so strong that her eyes watered.

Her stomach flipped, then flopped, and she realized once again that the whole increased sense of smell thing was the worst part of being pregnant.

She managed to make it to the bathroom around the corner before losing the lunch she had enjoyed not a half an hour before.

She leaned against the wall, feeling a little dizzy and a little stupid. Lockdown. If she had listened to the lockdown, she would never have encountered that smell.

The thought of it brought the smell back, and she threw up again. If anything made her reconsider the decision to have this child, it was moments like this. Nothing was worth the heightened sensitivity to odors and the attendant nausea.

Nothing.

She wiped her mouth, washed off her face, and poured some mouthwash into one of the little cups that hung from the cup holder beside the sink. She used to wonder why Ruth had mouthwash in every single bathroom in the clinic. Only dentists made that much mouthwash available for the public.

Edie used to think it was because someone was phobic about bad breath. Now she knew otherwise, and she was grateful.

She swished, spit, and took a deep breath, feeling her stomach calm. Outside, people were talking, but voices weren't raised.

She realized that had she not been in the exam room with her good friend Ruth, she wouldn't have known anything had happened at all. Only she and the people in the waiting room had any idea anything had been out of the ordinary.

She pulled down a paper towel, dampened it, and patted off her forehead.

Then she headed out of the bathroom and back to the exam room.

The hallway still smelled awful, but she willed that thought away. Her stomach threatened her again, and she mentally advised it to chill out. Because she wasn't going back in that bathroom.

She made it to the T again and saw Mack leaving the exam room on the side. His gaze met hers for a long moment. She held her breath, her heart rate increasing. She wanted to run to him, put her arms around him, and tell him how happy she was that he was all right.

Instead, she remained rooted to the spot, unwilling to break the eye contact.

He didn't smile. He stared at her as if he couldn't get enough of her either.

Then he nodded, once, and turned away.

She felt the loss of his gaze as if he had physically stopped touching her.

He pushed open the outside door and disappeared into the gray twilight.

She started to take a deep breath, remembered the smell, and went back into the exam room instead.

While she had been looking at Mack, the nausea had faded. She looked at her bra and socks piled on the chair next to that stupid hospital gown. She was done here. She wanted to go home and pull a blanket over her head, or back to the office and lose herself in work.

She was actually—startlingly enough—hungry.

And she wanted to chase after Mack, apologize again, and ask him if they could start over.

Usually she had more self-respect than that.

So she grabbed her cell phone and texted Ruth: *Exam over?*

Nooo! Ruth texted back. *Not even close. Stay put. I'll be there in a few minutes.*

Edie sighed. She looked at the crumpled hospital gown and decided not to put it back on. Ruth could ask her to do so; otherwise, Edie was done.

She slipped her boots off, put on the socks, and stuffed her bra in her purse. Then she put the hospital gown on the tissue covering the exam table. She sat on the chair, purse clutched against her stomach as if she were some prim and proper girl from the 1950s, waiting for a ride home.

A false alarm, apparently. Lockdown because a homeless man had been outside.

She shook her head. She hated that Sanger House was under this kind of threat. She also knew that it wasn't alone—other clinics went through the same thing every day.

It had become a fact of life here, especially since, as Ruth said, they couldn't resolve it quickly. They had become a target, so they had to take precautions.

Edie sighed. Mack was part of the precautions. She had to get used to seeing him, and she had to accept that she had blown whatever opportunity they had. She had to pretend to be over it until she *was* over it.

Just like she had to pretend to accept the new normal here at the clinic until she did accept it.

Funny that the pregnancy didn't bother her. Those two things did, but not the fact that some little being—a nub, the nurse had called it—had already turned Edie's life upside down.

Maybe she was ready to have her life turned upside down.

Maybe she had needed it.

She had been stuck for so long.

And now she was moving forward—into a world that she hoped would be a lot better.

At least it would be different.

And she could live with that.

30

*I*t seemed even colder than it had a few moments ago.

Mack was glad for the chill. It made the smell on his coat less severe. He was going to have to wash the damn parka, but it was too cold out here to take it off. If he didn't have to take the homeless guy to the shelter, then he would try to sponge the coat off a little later.

The freezing rain had stopped, at least, although the sky still looked heavy with clouds. And the wind had come up. Some kind of storm was coming.

Or maybe that was just his imagination. He felt even gloomier than he had before.

He had just seen Edie again, and she looked radiant. Her hair was slightly mussed, and she clearly hadn't been wearing a bra, her nipples hard from the cold. She looked like she had in the hotel room: messy, sexy, and ready for more.

In the moment their eyes met, he had thought of all of it—that afternoon, the date, the way he had walked away. Protecting his heart.

"Hey." Jade was leaning out the window on the driver's side door of the ancient van. It blended in with the sky and the ice-gray parking lot and the trees. "Do we need the van?"

Mack blinked, coming to the present. Jesus. He hadn't been paying attention to anything except Edie. And he needed to be thinking about the threats, not the woman inside.

"Not yet," he said, maybe a beat too late. "Ruth's checking him. He's in rough shape. He might need to go to Mercy General."

"Figured." Jade studied him. "You okay?"

Mack shrugged. He needed to start patrolling the area, and he was about to say so, when she added, "Because you were great out there. I would have shot him when he grabbed that cane."

"No, you wouldn't have," Mack said. "If you were standing where I was, you would have made a different call."

"I doubt it." Jade leaned back in the driver's seat. "You ever think about it? The risks we take? One split second different and our entire lives would have changed."

He stared at her. She was right: everything did change in an instant. If Mack had reacted wrong, if he had fired, if the bomb from last week had gone off—

They got paid to put their lives on the line, not the way the cops did or the way Mack did when he was in the military, but in a more muted way. To make sure everything was all right, and to be the first line of defense for people like the homeless guy and Edie and that woman with the annoying toddlers.

He took risks every day, and he rarely thought about them. He risked his life all the time, he risked getting injured or killed, he risked losing his business by taking low-paying jobs like this one instead of jobs that paid a small fortune.

He often weighed the risks versus the rewards—or rather, the risks versus what was right, what others would or wouldn't do, what needed to be done. Usually he did what needed to be done, those jobs that no one else would do.

"Seriously," Jade said. "Are you all right? because I can still call Khalil back."

Khalil. No wonder Jade was worried about Mack. He hadn't even asked why Khalil wasn't driving the van.

"You sent him away?" Mack asked.

"He's supposed to be on security detail for that hedge fund guy, remember? I told him it was okay to go because you were here, but if we need him back, I'll call him."

Mack shook his head. He was off his game, but he could get back on it.

"I'll drive the van," Mack said. "I'm the one who smells like a sewer. Unless you need to warm up?"

Jade gave him a tired grin. "I'll switch with Lashon. He has the easy duty anyway. Inside, warm and cozy."

Mack laughed, despite his mood. Then he nodded. He stepped back as Jade opened the door, and got out. She grabbed a stocking cap and some thick gloves, then swept a hand toward the van's interior.

"I think the heat's failing on this old beastie," she said, pulled on her cap, and headed away from him, beginning her rounds.

He watched her go, a strong, capable, uncomplicated woman whom he trusted like he trusted few other people. Although he wondered if he thought she was uncomplicated because he wasn't interested in her. He had no idea what she really felt about some things, and how she got through her nights when she was away from work.

Would it change his opinion of her to learn that she used Tinder the way that Edie did?

He felt a bump of emotion, a slight affirmative, and shook his head at himself. Fucking double standards. Even when you thought you were above them, they still bit you in the ass.

Would he think that Jade wasn't a valued employee because of that habit (if she had it)? Of course not. And he would consider her completely loyal and trustworthy. Although he would be shocked at her behavior.

Apparently, that religious upbringing went in deep.

He didn't quite smile at himself. If he had, the smile would have been rueful. Because he was being controlled by his emotions as much as anyone, apparently. And he hated it.

He slid into the van, pulled the door closed, and monitored the parking lot. Jade had disappeared into the trees, and he knew it would take at least twenty minutes, maybe more, for Ruth to determine if the homeless guy needed to go to the hospital and if he needed an ambulance to take him there.

Mack glanced at the closed door. Edie was probably still behind it, waiting to finish her exam, if indeed that was what she was there for. She was determined to go through this pregnancy, and he had to admire the guts in that.

She knew most of the risks she was going to take. There were the usual child-rearing risks, and then the added risk of emulating a life she had vowed she would never emulate. She risked becoming the thing she didn't want to be—her mother.

He let out a small chuff of air. It wasn't quite cold enough inside the van to see his breath, but it was damn close. He made himself monitor the woods, the edge of the parking lot, then glanced at his rearview mirror and his side mirrors, almost as if he were driving.

Edie was taking risks. He took risks every day, like he had when he confronted that homeless man. It could easily have gone wrong. The homeless man could have had an automatic rifle instead of a walking stick, or a pistol of some kind. Or he could have been carrying a knife, and he could have stabbed Mack when Mack got close.

Mack hadn't worried about any of those things—not really. He had compensated for the risk, calculated the odds of success, and then had taken action.

All things that—if someone had asked him a week ago—he did in his personal life as well.

But that really wasn't true. Because the one thing he wasn't doing in his personal life, the one thing that made every personal situation different from his job, was that he took no risks. None at all.

Not with his heart.

What he did with his heart was what he had asked Ruth to do with the patients today. He had put his heart on lockdown after he had broken up with Bree, and he hadn't let his heart out of the building yet.

Or maybe he had locked his heart down long before Bree. Maybe that was why it hadn't worked with her, why he hadn't been able to love her the way he wanted to.

Because he kept his heart locked away, protected, so that no one could touch it.

Then he had seen Edie, had watched her in that emergency, had admired her and enjoyed the way she had handled the legal situation.

He had been *working* and taking risks and she had crawled in past his protections, because he wasn't thinking about the personal. All he had been doing was responding to an emergency situation, and this beautiful woman had come up beside him and helped.

He let out another chuff of air, not liking where his reasoning was taking him.

Because if he was right—and he had put his heart on lockdown, and the only reason Edie had gotten in was because they had met in an emergency situation, while he was working—then that meant the date had been doomed to failure from the start.

A date automatically put them in the realm of the personal, not in the realm of work. It had been all about control: control of the situation (no sudden erotic moves, no way to end up in bed) and control of his heart.

No wonder he had walked away.

Lockdown continued.

And then he had seen her today. She was supposed to be in one of the exam rooms or in Ruth's office. Instead, Edie had come into the hallway to see what the emergency was.

Because that woman took risks. She ran into a crisis, just like he did, and attempted to solve it if it was within her power to do so.

He started to run a hand over his face and stopped when he realized he was wearing one of his smelly gloves.

He had accused her of being unfit for a relationship. He probably should have looked in the mirror before he made the accusation.

The question was—did he want a relationship with her?

He half-smiled. Of course he did. He couldn't get her out of his mind.

The relationship would be a huge risk, just like he had told her. Her and the baby. If nothing worked out, his heart would be shattered.

But his heart was on lockdown right now so, technically, he really wasn't using it.

He rarely thought about the rewards of taking risks. Because the risks he took were split-second ones—life-saving ones, usually. That homeless guy would have died in this cold if Mack hadn't brought him inside.

But that wasn't a reward for Mack, not technically, anyway. He got nothing out of it except a job well done.

Which was usually enough for him.

If he took a risk with Edie, the reward would be amazing, personally. It would be a ready-made family. A woman who intrigued him. A baby that he could help raise. A relationship that might—just might—last a lifetime.

Who walked away from that?

Him, apparently.

He shook his head. He was such an idiot.

And now, he had to figure out how to clean up a mess he had made—without making things worse.

31

*E*die was neck-deep in case law. The new associate had mucked up the brief he had written for Edie and Edie had to repair it. She also had to figure out how to handle the associate. He wasn't as good as everyone thought he was.

She sat in her office, scrolling through FindLaw on her computer. She preferred using the books, but right now, she wanted something she could search. She had the beginnings of a headache, and she was getting hungry. She would probably order in because repairing this brief was going to take hours out of her day that she really didn't have.

Her office, on the fifteenth floor, had corner windows that overlooked downtown. She had tucked her desk against the only bare wall, facing those windows so she could watch the daylight change over the city, particularly on days like this. She had a hunch she wasn't going anywhere.

Which was probably good, considering yesterday's excitement. She had lost half the day to her appointment at Sanger House, first because of the exam and then because of the poor homeless man. He needed medical care and, because he had been belligerent the last time he had gone to Mercy General, they didn't want to treat him.

Or they hadn't wanted to until Edie got ahold of them.

She had done that on her cell phone while Ruth was getting the results on all the tests. Which told her that the baby was fine, and the fluttering was, as the nurse expected, gas.

Such joy this pregnancy already was.

And it was just getting underway.

Weirdly enough, Ruth was more nervous about it than Edie was. Edie was worried about the months after the baby was born—the sleepless nights, the feeding schedule, handling a tiny being all by herself. She was up for it—or at least, she thought she was—but she was worried.

Glenda, Edie's kickass legal secretary, who probably would have gotten the case law right in this brief if Edie had decided not to give it to the new associate in the first place, stuck her head in the door.

"Pack up," she said in her gravelly voice. "You got a lunch."

"No, I don't," Edie said. "I have no appointments on my calendar, and I have to finish this damn thing. Just order me—"

"A new client," Glenda said. "He wants only you, and he is willing to pay through the nose. I don't think this is one you want to turn down."

Edie looked at her. Glenda had an odd expression on her face, one Edie had never seen before.

"Who is this client?" she asked.

"I am not supposed to tell you," Glenda said. "You're supposed to go to the meeting and then proceed from there."

"Hell, no," Edie said. "I don't do mysterious."

Glenda made a strange sound, rather like a cross between a harrumph, a half sentence, and a disagreement.

"You're going to want to do this," she said.

"Tell Mr. Mysterious that I'm not interested," Edie said. "If he wants a real lawyer, he needs to act like a real client. He needs—"

"He's already paid a retainer, and you need lunch," Glenda said.

"You know who he is," Edie said.

"I know what company account paid the retainer." Glenda leaned against the door jamb. "Just go. You can always leave if he turns out to be a creep. You can get your lunch to go, and then you won't have to worry, or rather, *I* won't have to worry that you're not going to eat."

"Jesus," Edie said. "Between you and Ruth, I'm going to be pecked to death. I'm an adult. I can take care of myself. I—"

"That's just it," Glenda said. "You're not just taking care of yourself any longer. We are going to harangue you. So go get lunch. The work will be waiting for you when you get back."

Edie let out an exasperated sigh. "Where's this damn lunch?"

"The Belvidere," Glenda said.

"They don't do to-go orders," Edie said. "They're too upscale for that."

"But they do doggie bags," Glenda said. "They're too eco-friendly not to."

Edie glared at her, then stood. Edie did need the break. She grabbed her purse off the chair, then took her coat, even though she really didn't need it.

The Belvidere was one building over, a remodeled hotel restaurant complex that had become one of the downtown's trendiest attractions. She liked the breakfast café inside the building, but found the upscale restaurant a tyranny of rules and ridiculousness. That just spoke to the kind of client she was going to see. One of those controlling types who had to have everything just so.

She would tell him where to stick his just-so. Maybe she would beg off because of the pregnancy.

And then she'd go to the café for a delicious gravy-smothered turkey sandwich. And she'd get fries with it, instead of mashed potatoes, just because. Maybe even some pie.

The very thought of pie made her stomach rumble. When she wasn't nauseous, she had such a strong appetite that she had to make sure she didn't eat everything in sight.

Ruth had told her that she was *not* eating for two. Edie was to be eating sensibly and shouldn't gain more than thirty pounds. All that uninhibited weight gain, Ruth told her, was dangerous for both her and the fetus. So Edie needed to monitor how much she gained.

Ruth had even given Edie a chart, knowing—dammit—that Edie would follow the freakin' chart.

That was the problem when your doctor was also one of your closest friends. She knew how to manipulate you.

Edie walked down the stairs—all fifteen flights. She knew that staying in shape was something she had to do as well. She drew the line at walking *up* all fifteen flights, however.

She crossed the lobby of the building, her heels clicking on the marble flooring. That was when she realized that she hadn't put on her boots—not that it mattered. She was only going a few steps. If the remodel hadn't been so short-sighted, she could have gone through the connector between the two buildings, but the contractor had taken it out.

She missed it.

She stepped into the blistering cold. No sleet like yesterday, but a wind that nearly blew her backwards. This winter could end right now, and she'd be one of the happiest women on the planet.

The Belvidere's doorman saw her coming and pushed the interior door open. She stepped inside, so cold that she might have been outside for hours instead of only a few minutes. She stamped her impractical shoes and clung to her coat, even though the coat check was right beside the door.

And who did she see when she got all the way inside, but Mack.

Her heart fluttered happily for a moment before it sank. She didn't need to see him right now and have him treat her like an acquaintance. That appraising stare yesterday had unsettled her, and seeing him again today unsettled her even more.

He smiled at her. The smile warmed her, even though she didn't want it to.

Please don't let him come near me, she thought. She didn't need the distraction. But he walked right at her, still smiling, and in spite of herself, she smiled back.

Then she turned away, going to the coat check, more as a way to avoid Mack than because she wanted to part with her coat. She started to peel it off, only to have it vanish from her shoulders.

She half-turned. Mack was behind her, helping her with her coat.

Dammit.

She shimmied out of it, thanked him, and then took the coat from him. The bellman behind the coat check took her coat without saying a word and handed her a ticket. She pulled out her wallet to tip him, but he had already turned away.

"They're not allowed to take tips for things like coat check," Mack said in her ear. "I already tried."

"Stupid way to treat your employees," she said, and put the ticket in her wallet, then stuffed her wallet back in her purse. "It's good to see you, Mack, but I'm on my way to meet a client."

"I know." He hadn't moved. She had to step to the side so that she could go around him without bumping into him. "I'm the client."

She felt cold all over again. She walked toward the middle of the room, near one of the plants that looked like a miniature palm tree— totally out of place in Michigan in the winter. But, at least, it allowed her to talk to him privately. Because parts of this lobby echoed, and she didn't want their conversation to be broadcast all over town.

"Is this some kind of game?" she asked. "Because I'm not playing."

"No game," he said. "Hear me out."

"No thanks," she said. "I told my secretary I don't do mysterious. I should have listened to my instincts."

"She gave you my message, right?" he asked, leaning into her. "I said I wanted only you, and that I was willing to pay through the nose."

She straightened. "If this is a legal issue, find yourself other counsel. If you are insinuating what I think you're insinuating, I don't take payment for that. I'm not that kind of woman."

He held up his hands, his cheeks darker than they had been a moment ago. "I didn't mean it that way," he said. "I'm here to apologize, and I'm willing to eat my words. That's what I meant, but I figured it might tip you off as to who you were meeting, and you wouldn't show up."

"I shouldn't have shown up," she said, and would have stalked off, but he blocked her just enough that she would have to push him aside to keep going.

"Edie," he said, touching her arm. "I screwed up again. I didn't mean for this to get off on the wrong foot. Give me a chance."

She breathed in and, in doing so, she caught that scent of his that was uniquely him. It sent a charge through her, and the attraction returned—instant and sudden.

"One minute," she said, more harshly than she had intended.

"One minute." He clasped his hands behind his back and bowed ever so slightly, like a man at a formal dance. "I am sorry for the way I've treated you, from the first real conversation we had to your kind offer of lunch last Saturday. I was being a judgmental asshole, and I hadn't thought anything through."

She frowned. "I was the one who insulted you. That whole date—"

"You were right," he said. "In some ways, it was about control. And me, not taking risks."

Her frown deepened. He expected her to understand something, and she didn't.

"I'm going to lay all my cards on the table," he said. "No misunderstandings."

Her heart rate was increasing, just because she was standing near him. She wanted to touch him, and she wouldn't let herself because she had other emotions as well. She was confused, and a little hurt, and angry, and attracted to him all at the same time.

"All right," she said, in her best lawyer voice. "Go."

He nodded. "I initially got us a reservation in the main restaurant. Then I changed it to a private room. And then I decided to have lunch delivered to a suite upstairs. If you're amenable."

She tilted her head. "What are you suggesting?"

"I'm suggesting a conversation and a meal, but I'm also saying that I've been too prudish, and if things proceed the way they did at our last lunch, I would be a willing participant."

"With me," she said.

He nodded.

"The woman who doesn't understand relationships." That came out a bit too strident.

"I'm beginning to think I don't either," he said.

One of the bellman was watching them. She wondered if he could hear everything.

She had no idea what to do here. She could go into the dining room and get them a table or ask for that private room, but what good would that do? Particularly if Mack was willing to act on their attraction again.

Was she willing to act on it? The thought of a second afternoon in bed with Mack made her breathless.

She didn't move. She didn't dare move.

"What do you want out of this?" she asked. "Lunch? Something casual?"

He reached out his hand. "A conversation. That's all. Please?"

She stared at his fingers, long, thin, rough, and callused. She could still remember how they felt against her skin, how those calluses made his touch seem more vibrant than any other man's touch had ever felt against her.

She had to put that out of her mind, though. He just wanted a conversation.

In a hotel suite.

Alone. In the middle of the afternoon.

With her.

32

$\mathcal{E}$die's gaze moved from his hand to his eyes. Her mouth was open slightly, as if she wanted to kiss him, but her expression was cold. Mack could feel how conflicted she was.

She wasn't going to take his hand. She was going to leave him standing here, like the fool he was. He had missed the opportunity with her. He had blown his chance, and now he was making things worse.

Then her fingers brushed his, and he let out a breath he hadn't even realized he had been holding.

"Where is this room?" she asked.

"Third floor," he said, sounding as breathless as he felt. He wanted to sweep her into his arms and carry her up to the suite, cradling her all the way to the bed. He wished he had a way to make this all romantic instead of businesslike.

But he knew—he *knew*—she didn't want the romance. Not right now. She had never said she wanted the happily ever after. She *had* said that she didn't believe in the fairy tale.

He did, dammit. Or at least part of it.

Because, really, what fairy tale ended with the charming prince choosing a ready-made family? Mack's fairy tale had shifted from the perfect princess to Edie, and Edie only.

He knew better than to tell her that right here, right now. That would just scare her off.

"Come on," he said, wrapping his fingers around hers. "Let's go."

He held her hand loosely as they walked toward the bank of elevators. Normally, he would have taken the stairs, but Edie was wearing high heels again, and she probably didn't do things like flights of stairs.

As he passed the concierge, he nodded. The concierge had helped him arrange a buffet lunch on very short notice. Different kinds of foods, some soup, and some other hot dishes awaited them, all in the suite's small kitchen.

Mack hadn't had time to inspect it. He hoped to hell it was all good.

They waited for the elevator. She didn't pull her hand from his, which surprised him. His heart was racing as if he had just chased a thief for half an hour. Only he was scared right now, and he was never scared when he was working.

He didn't want to do this wrong. He didn't want to lose her forever, and he knew he could.

The elevator door opened. She dropped his hand, and walked inside without him. He felt the loss. By the time he joined her in the extra-large gilded car, she had already pressed "3."

The doors closed, and he tried not to think about how close he was to her, how the faint scent of yet a different perfume (orange blossoms?) mingled with the scent of her skin. He wanted to move just a little closer to get more of it, but he didn't.

The elevator eased to a stop, then opened. She stepped outside and waited. He fumbled for the key card, praying he wouldn't drop it.

Damn, he hated being nervous.

"3641," he said, letting her know the room number. Actually it was 3641-3642—a suite—but the information was more than enough. She glanced at the numbers on the wall, turned in the right direction, and strode down the hall.

He couldn't help himself: he followed just far enough back that he could watch her move. Sturdy and feminine. She knew how to move in heels, which many women did not. And, as advertised, they accented her legs and her shapely ass.

He wrenched his thoughts away, hoping he could find something else to think about. Of course he couldn't.

At least she had come this far. That was more than he expected, quite honestly, but not as much as he had hoped.

She waited at the end of the hall, right in front of the doors to the suite. He caught up to her a moment later. She stood slightly to one side so he could unlock the door without touching her.

He opened it, then held it for her.

She walked in and whistled. "My God, Mack, are you expecting an army?"

He stepped inside and saw what she meant. Food steamers lined one wall; cold cuts, cheeses, and fresh vegetables covered the island; and a fruit plate sat at each place setting on the table near the windows.

The windows overlooked the street and the building next door—this suite wasn't high enough for a spectacular view, and, to be honest, he didn't want to spend an extra five hundred dollars for a view he hoped they wouldn't spend a lot of time looking at.

A bottle of fake champagne chilled next to the table, and a silver coffee service hovered a little too close to the table's edge.

Edie turned, her expression slightly awed. "What would you have done if I declined to come up here?"

"Eaten for a week, I guess," he said.

She smiled. "Wow. Do you mind if we eat? I'm starved."

"I am too," he said, but he really wasn't thinking of food. He was starved for her. He had craved her ever since that afternoon not so long ago, although he could barely admit it to himself.

He kept himself busy by folding up half the steel lid on the steamed food. Pasta, potatoes, some kind of beef roast, spaghetti sauce—they hadn't been kidding when they had said they were going to provide a buffet.

He and Edie wouldn't have to leave the room for a week.

She already had a plate in hand and was piling it with cold ham, cheese, and carrot sticks. He figured the carrot sticks would have gotten left, but what did he know? She seemed to want them.

As he went to the cold food, he saw dessert sitting on the kitchen counter—three different kinds of pie, some cake, and a note saying there was more in the refrigerator.

Well, at least he knew they would both end up being well fed.

She had already moved to the hot food. She was taking a bit of each, and then she went to the table, moving the fruit plate aside, as if it didn't matter. She sat down. He went into the kitchen and opened the fridge.

"We have every beverage known to man," he said.

She laughed. "Water's fine."

"Sparkling? Or plain?"

"I would have settled for tap," she said. "But I'll take sparkling."

He brought her a glass bottle after grabbing one for himself. He set them both on the table, and then went back for his lunch. The pasta didn't appeal, but the rice dish and the beef in sauce did. That plus salad plus cold cuts equaled two of his meals combined.

He slipped into the chair across from her. She reached over and moved his fruit plate so he could set his meal down.

"Well, I'm impressed," she said. "This is one heck of an apology. A lot better than a take-out dinner from Antonelli's."

"Oh, I don't know," he said, looking at her pasta. "I suspect Antonelli's spaghetti is much better than this."

"More authentic," she said, "but not necessarily better. Or maybe I'm that hungry."

She ate, so he did, trying not to watch her every move. And yet he was watching because he didn't want to miss anything.

Finally, she set the main plate aside, and pulled over the fruit plate.

"Okay," she said. "What's the champagne for?"

He didn't expect the question, although he should have. "It's not champagne," he said.

She made a face. "No more of that fruity apple-y crap, is it?"

He smiled. "It is."

Her face got more elaborate. Who knew her mouth could be that mobile?

The thought sent a rush of heat through him. He needed to get past it.

He thought about extending his hand, but didn't. Not yet.

"Look," he said. "I was wrong. I put values on you that I didn't apply to myself."

"I checked," she said. "You're not known for sleeping around. Petruchio even called you Father Mack."

He felt his face heat. "You checked on me?"

She shrugged. "I wanted to make sure—oh, I don't know. Petruchio showed up just after you left. He—"

Mack felt a sudden rush of jealousy. He thought she and Petruchio didn't have that kind of relationship.

"—thought we were a mismatch from the start." She looked down at the fruit, then stirred it with her fork. She didn't take any of it. "He also said he thought I could be faithful."

"I'm sorry." Mack truly was. "I didn't mean to make you defensive."

She shrugged again, not looking at him. "It was a fair question. I've asked it myself. I asked Petruchio. And I'll be honest. I've never done it. I've never had a long-term relationship—long-term *sexual* relationship. Petruchio reminded me that all of my friendships are long-term, more so than anyone he's ever met."

Mack let out a small breath. Petruchio had refused to talk to him, but Ruth had mentioned something about Edie being the most loyal friend she had ever had. Was that a pointed comment? Had Edie told Ruth about their date?

He didn't ask. He wasn't sure he wanted to know.

"I told you downstairs," he said. "I misjudged you."

"No, you didn't." She looked up. Her eyes were open, vulnerable. "You made me question some assumptions about myself. I needed to know too." She patted her stomach. "After all, I'm about to enter an important relationship, one I've chosen. I'm starting a family, and I need to be able to stick with it. Or I have to make other choices."

His heart clenched. "Other choices?"

Her mobile mouth flattened with disapproval. "Adoption. I already told you I wasn't going to have an abortion."

"Yeah," he said. "You gave me the political answer. Not the you-answer."

She raised her eyebrows. "What does that mean?"

"It means…" It was his turn to shrug. "It means that you made the hard choice—the for-the-rest-of-your-life choice—and given your background, I'm not sure why. Surely some sadness and pain would be worth the price of your future."

Her frown became deep. "You think I should have an abortion?"

"No," he said. He didn't want her to think that at all. "I just—well, thought maybe you had a more personal reason for not getting one."

To his surprise, her eyes welled with tears. She nodded, then licked her lips.

"It's complicated," she said. "I—You're right. It would be easy to make the other choice. Emotionally devastating, but I've had emotional devastation before."

He waited. She blinked. One tear threatened, then receded.

"I have the means to raise a child. I am sensible, and I figure I can do it. I'm also old enough to make good choices, even though I haven't." She swallowed. Hard. Her hand moved toward the coffee, then moved back. "A lot of women don't get a choice. They're not able to afford the child or the child risks someone else's health, maybe the health of the other children because they have to slip into poverty. That's why places like Sanger House exist. Not for *convenience*."

She spit out that word.

"Children aren't about convenience," she said, more to herself than to him. "They're a commitment. The most important one. I'm not having this child on a whim. It's the opposite of a whim. I know what I'm facing, and I'm going to do it. I have a lot of advantages, and I'm going to use all of them."

He got the unsaid part. She was going to outdo her mother in this, the most important thing. She was going to make her child feel loved.

He felt both humbled and schooled. He had questioned her ability to commit, missing the commitment she had already made.

"I'm an idiot," he said.

"What?" she asked.

255

"I misunderstood you from the start," he said. "It was all my issues."

"No," she said. "I'm full of issues. I'm all about issues. I just want to get past as many of them as I can. So, you can't take the full blame. We both pushed each other away. I pushed you away that lunch."

"No," he said. "You didn't."

"Yes," she said. "I did. I forced you into behavior that wasn't normal for you. Maybe even to prove a point."

He studied her. She looked very sincere.

"I didn't feel pushed away," he said.

"Yet you insisted on a date after that," she said. "And no sex."

He flushed. What was it about this woman that could make him blush like that?

"Point taken," he said. "But I don't think that was about pushing away."

"Oh?" she asked.

He grabbed the coffee, unable to look at her as he answered. So he poured instead. It was steaming.

"I—um. It was about me," he said. "It was about getting too close."

He handed her the full cup. She took it carefully. "What does that mean?"

"It means," he said, "that you scared me, Edie."

"*I* scared *you?*" she asked, as if that weren't possible.

He nodded. He set the coffeepot down, bit his lip, and then took a deep breath. *Risks, Mack*, he thought. *Take the damn risk.*

"I—um—I knew, after that afternoon, that I could—that I *was* already falling for you." His turn to swallow hard now. "I—didn't—don't—still am not sure—it's possible to fall in love that fast. It scared me. I mean, how can I love someone I don't know?"

"Indeed." Her voice was dry. That lawyer voice.

He looked up. When his gaze met hers, it felt like an electric shock. She was wide-eyed. Vulnerable. The exact opposite of the lawyer voice.

"So then I thought I should get to know you, and all I could think about getting to know you was dating you, so I suggested that."

"Insisted on that," she said.

"Insisted on it," he said. "Because I was scared."

"Of sex?" she asked.

"Of everything," he said. "You. The attraction. The feelings I have when I'm with you. The baby. The possibilities. I blamed you. I said you weren't ready for commitment. But I think I meant me."

She hadn't moved. "Are you still afraid?" she asked.

"Terrified," he said.

"Me, too," she said.

"I'm usually not afraid of anything," he said.

"I know," she said—but he wasn't sure if she was talking about herself or him.

"And when I am afraid," he said, "I usually run toward the fear, not away from it. This is all new to me."

She didn't move for the longest time. She didn't say anything either.

Then she took a deep breath. "So," she asked, "what do you want to do?"

"I want to run toward," he said.

She smiled. "Is that why we're in a hotel room?"

"I hope so," he said, then realized his answer didn't quite make any sense. He was about to clarify, but somehow he was on his feet, and she was on her feet, and their arms were around each other, and their mouths were locked, busy, unable to speak, but saying everything.

He swept her up. He had to. He had been imagining it all day.

She made some kind of sound of protest, and he pulled back just a little, expecting her to demand to be put down or to let her leave or to thank him but plead work.

Instead, she said, "You'll hurt yourself."

She was talking about his back, and he knew it. But he chose to ignore that and answer the greater point.

"Maybe," he said. "But that's the risk, isn't it?"

She blinked, then frowned. He carried her into the bedroom. The bed was huge and covered in pillows.

He set her on them.

"I'm not sure I can promise you the fairy tale," she said.

"I don't want a fairy tale," he said as he climbed up beside her. "I want you, for as long as I can have you."

Her gaze met his, hand on his chest, holding him back. She studied him as if she were seeing him for the first time.

"'For as long as I can have you,'" she repeated. Then her lips twisted just a little. The beginnings of a smile. "I like that."

She leaned back on the bed and unbuttoned her blouse.

"Have me now, handsome," she said, freeing her breasts from her bra. They bounced upward, bigger than they had been just a week before. "Have me now."

He peeled off his shirt.

"All right," he said, and so he did.

33

Three hours later, she remembered she should be back at work. There was a brief to rewrite and research to do, and God, she had never felt so sated in her life.

Mack was on his back, hands beneath his head, splendid in his nakedness. The bed was rumpled, their clothes were scattered everywhere.

She had never had sex that good in her life.

She ran a finger down the hair on his chest, following it past his belly button to his penis. It responded, and she couldn't help herself. She bent toward it, and kissed it, before wrapping her mouth around it.

"Oh, God," he said. "You're going to kill me."

She stopped.

"That's all right," he said, his voice throaty. "I'm willing to die for the cause."

She kissed him everywhere, then raised her head. If she continued, she'd be here another hour.

"I have to make a phone call first," she said, and rolled off the bed.

Her legs trembled as she walked back into the living room. She grabbed her purse, called Glenda, and said she wouldn't be back until late.

"Already figured that out, honey," Glenda said. "Have fun."

And then she hung up.

Edie stared at the phone. That didn't feel very Mother Hen-ish. That felt close to girlfriend-ish, which was decidedly not their relationship.

But, at the moment, Edie didn't care. She went back into the bedroom. Mack was propped up on one elbow.

"Everything okay at work?" he asked.

"Who cares?" she asked, and hopped on the bed beside him. "Is this what people in a relationship do?"

He tilted his head, as if he were considering it. Then he shrugged, a movement that pulled every part of his torso and then some.

"I have no idea," he said. "Who cares what other people do? It's what we do."

"More than once?" she asked.

"Obviously more than once," he said.

She crawled up next to him, and put her head on his shoulder. He had been completely honest with her.

Time for her to be completely honest with him.

"That first afternoon?" she said. "I—um—was afraid to tell you."

He froze, as if he expected something bad.

"I was afraid you wouldn't believe me." She propped herself up on one elbow. "but I'm going to tell you now."

He looked guarded.

"Best sex of my life," she said.

"Uh-huh," he said. He clearly didn't believe her.

"Until today." She grinned.

He grinned back.

"And you know why?" she asked.

He shook his head, that guarded look returning to his eyes.

"Because," she said, "I fell for you too. Hard."

"God," he said, and turned sideways. He took her hips gently in his hands, his gaze questioning. She guided him, slipped him inside of her, surprised it was so easy even after all they had done. "Is this what love feels like?"

"I suspect maybe," she said. "Let's keep testing it, and see what we find out."

He laughed, and moved ever so slowly. Teasingly. "For a week?"

"A year," she said, her voice throatier than she expected.

"Two years," he said.

"Or maybe," she whispered, before his body stole her ability for rational thought, "the rest of our lives."

"Hold that thought," he said.

"For how long?" she asked.

"Forever," he said. "Let's love each other forever."

"Deal," she said, and then decided to show him what forever would feel like, one tiny erotic movement at a time.

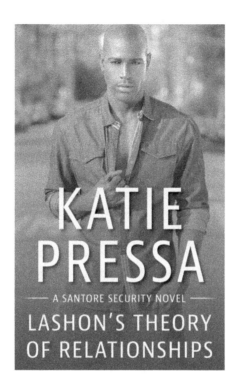

KATIE
PRESSA

— A SANTORE SECURITY NOVEL —

LASHON'S THEORY
OF RELATIONSHIPS

If you enjoyed *A Gentleman of the Old School*, pick up Book Two in the Santore Security Novel series. Here is the first chapter from *Lashon's Theory of Relationships.*

He'd worked it out on a late-night drunk two years ago. Lashon Jackson did not think of himself as the kind of man who got upset about relationships. But his sister, Latisha, finally got through to him, just before that drunk.

Your problem, Baby Brother, she had said, using the nickname he hated, *is that you are so damn macho, it's a handicap. Anger and courage— they're okay. The rest, the soft squishy emotions, you pretend they don't exist, and that'll hurt you. That* does *hurt you.*

He had disagreed, of course. He didn't get hurt, that was what he told her. And even though they had been on the phone at the time, he still knew what kind of expression had crossed her face. She had turned her big brown eyes—so similar to his own—heavenward, as if the Lord Almighty would help her get her point across. Then she had sighed heavily (and he had heard that), and those big brown eyes filled with pity.

He hated it when she looked at him with pity, and she had done it enough over the years to make him feel uncomfortable.

Latisha was the only one of his siblings who could get to him, maybe because she had his number before he even knew he *had* a number. Or maybe because she had mostly raised him because their parents worked two shifts each to pay for the growing family.

After he'd hung up from that conversation with Latisha, he'd found he couldn't get her words out of his head. *That* was when he decided to go to the bar.

Not when Amber broke up with him, two days before that conversation. She had taken all of her stuff and half of his, and moved out in the middle of the afternoon without even a by-your-leave or whatever the hell people called that. Then she'd called him on his cell as he drove his 4x4 into the driveway of their house—*his* house—and told him she was done. Done.

He'd gotten out of the truck, looked around, but didn't see her, even though he had known she was nearby, because how else could she have timed the call? He never got home at the same time of day—his work wasn't regular, one of her complaints. The woman was made of complaints, and all of them had been focused at him.

He'd been relieved that she left; at least, that was what he'd thought until he had called Latisha to see if she'd help him shop for furniture to replace the items Amber had taken in her sudden move.

To his surprise, Tish had said no, and then she had given him that lecture about soft, squishy emotions, and then she had hung up.

He had no idea what her play had been—if she even had a play. He had just known that his sister—the one person he could rely on—had told him he couldn't bluster through his life anymore.

He had never thought of it as bluster. He had thought of it as living.

Which he had said to the bartender that night.

Lashon had gone to his favorite bar, which was a few miles from his house. There were closer bars than Overtime, but none of them had the right vibe. Most were pick-up joints, not hard-core sports bars. Overtime had everything: the big screens, the lights, the best beer, pool, foosball, air hockey, and ancient pinball games lining the back wall. If there was no game that night, the regulars made their own.

There was also an informal book for regulars—not online, but run the way ancient speakeasies worked, with a wink and a promise, and a lot of work in a back room no newbie ever got to see.

Lashon had been going to Overtime for two years before he got invited to participate in the book. By then, he'd discovered that the owner had run Lashon's credit, and figured out Lashon's limit, if Lashon even chose to play.

Which he usually did.

But not on that night.

That night, in that golden period of late fall, when the baseball was heading into final innings, football (both college and professional) was in midseason, hockey had just started, and basketball was just getting its feet underneath itself.

If no one was playing, it didn't matter, because there was always something to talk about.

Overtime had a different sport on each television set, and actually had talking corners set up for guys who wanted to focus on their main sport. The center of the bar had tables for groups, and each table now had a tiny—attached—screen where the group could watch their favorite up close and personal if so inclined.

Lashon usually joined a group when he showed up, but that night he sat at the bar, ordered buffalo wings and a Heineken as dinner, and wished to hell the Pistons were playing. Because basketball always took his mind off things in a way the other sports didn't.

Instead, he was served up one of the final baseball playoff games, which he usually would have cared about, even though the Tigers hadn't been involved in a long time, and an early season hockey game, which he really didn't care about at all.

He chomped on goldfish crackers and peanuts while he waited for his wings, and thought maybe, just maybe, he'd change that order to the appetizer platter and eat the whole damn thing himself.

The bartender, a burly white dude named Greg, who managed to turn one dismal season with the Detroit Lions into enough money to buy his own bar (*Visions of Cheers*, he once said to Lashon, *although owning a bar really isn't like that*), set another beer in front of Lashon, even though Lashon hadn't asked for it.

He hadn't even realized he'd finished the first beer until he looked down in surprise.

"Your cat die?" Greg asked.

"Huh?" Lashon looked up, frowned, not sure where the non sequitur even came from. "I don't have a cat."

"Yeah," Greg said drily. "Not really what I was asking."

That's when Lashon realized Greg was asking if he was okay. No one asked Lashon if he was okay. He was *always* okay, at least as far as the world was concerned.

"I'm fine," Lashon said.

"If you say so," Greg said, and walked away.

Five minutes later, he brought wings. Then a half an hour after that, the appetizer platter, which had more wings and some nachos and stuffed mushrooms and deep-fried mozzarella.

With each appetizer that Lashon tried, he ordered a different beer to go with it.

Somewhere during the evening, Greg asked if Lashon was walking home or if he was planning to drive. Took a while for Lashon to understand that one too. Greg wanted to know if he needed to cut Lashon off or not.

Lashon never lied about things like that. Fortunately, he had walked.

And that decision—not to lie—was Lashon's last clear memory of the evening, at least in chronological order.

His last memory of the evening involved a bottle blonde with breasts the size of zeppelins, and a smile that left lipstick on her teeth, lipstick he (in his drunken state) found appealing.

In between, though, in between, he had spouted wisdom that became Bar Legend.

They actually labeled it, and at some point, Greg made a poster out of it.

Lashon's Theory of Relationships:

To get over a relationship, look at this chart. (Recovery times are the maximum.)

Relationship lasting one year—one month recovery time.

Two years—two months, and so on.

Recovery enhanced and sped up by alcohol, availability of attractive partners, and the willingness to move forward. Properly applied, such things will cut recovery times dramatically.

WARNING: Never expect recovery times of one hour or less. That way lies trouble.

When Lashon looked at the poster weeks later, when he was completely sober and thinking clearly, he regretted not the words, but the lack of pithiness. The inability to say things in a way that caught everyone's attention the first time out.

As he said to Greg, when Greg asked him what he thought of the poster, *I'm no Don Draper.*

Not that Lashon could ever be an ad man. He didn't have a way with words. He wasn't the talking type. Never had been, never would be.

The strong silent type was how his first serious girlfriend, Nita, had described him in college. Admiringly at first, with more and more frustration as time went on.

An uncommunicative asshole had been his fifth serious girlfriend Chloe's parting shot.

Did you even learn English? His second live-in girlfriend, Diane, had asked jokingly on their first date, and then, later, had used as a refrain for every single major fight they had ever had.

Talking would be nice, said Felicity, one of the possibles last year.

What, do you think I'm psychic? asked Irene, who managed six dates with him before walking away.

His response to all of the women was some variation on the same thing: *Talking is overrated.* All that seemed to do was frustrate them more. He had learned, back in high school, not to tell a girl that he wasn't in a relationship to talk to her. That sentence had actually gotten him his one and only slap.

It wasn't that he didn't like women or that he didn't respect them. He had dozens of female friends and several good female friends. He talked to them, but they knew what to talk about. They had *interests*. They liked sports and read books and saw movies. They argued about politics and called him a *fucking asshole* early on in the relationship, not after it became plain he wasn't going to worship at their feet.

His co-worker at Santore Security, Jade LaPiere, laughed at his women troubles.

The problem you have with women, she said, *is that you pick the wrong ones.*

He knew that. It was obvious. He'd had dozens of relationships in his thirty-four years, and not a one made it past the two-year point. Although, truth be told, the one that did make it two years probably should have ended two months in. He had stuck that one out to prove he could stick out a relationship.

He hated that, among his male friends, he had become more famous for his theory of relationships than for the relationships themselves. No one could remember his girlfriends. Everyone could remember how long it took him to recover from them.

Even him.

It wasn't that he didn't want a relationship. He did. He was just beginning to think relationships weren't in the cards for him. He was doing something wrong—clearly, or he would have found Ms. Right by now. He just wasn't willing to change who he was to make sure he lived with someone else.

At least, that was what he told his friends.

What he told himself was that he could get by without a permanent relationship. Lots of other people did. Relationships were overrated.

At least, he hoped they were.

Not that it mattered. He stopped looking for Ms. Right shortly after articulating his Theory of Relationships. He stopped frequenting singles bars. He stopped going on dates. He stopped having his friends hook him up.

He stopped seeing anyone special, which meant he saw no one at all.

Which was why, during the worst month of his life, he was surprised to meet the one woman who could change his future forever.

If he could only bring himself to give her a chance.

ABOUT THE AUTHOR

Since she read her first romance novel at age twelve, Katie Pressa wanted to write a romance. A recovering journalist, she finally decided to chase her fiction dream. The Santore Security Romance series, published by Three Fires Press, comprises her first three novels. Book one, *A Gentleman of the Old School,* appears in January of 2018, with the second and third books in the series, *Lashon's Theory of Relationships* and *America's Sweetheart*, following right behind. Her next novel, *Shotgun Wedding*, will also appear in 2018.

Sign up for the latest from Katie and join her readers' group by visiting her website.

www.katiepressa.com
threefirespress@gmail.com

CPSIA information can be obtained
at www.ICGtesting.com
Printed in the USA
LVHW042136210319
611497LV00001B/334/P

9 781983 401930